Published by:
Grand Mal Press
Forestdale, MA
www.grandmalpress.com

copyright 2011 Robert White

ISBN 13 digit: 9780982945971
ISBN 10 digit: 0982945973

Library of Congress Cataloging-in-Publication Data
Grand Mal Press/ White, Robert

p. cm

Cover art by Grand Mal Press

FIRST EDITION

HAFTMANN'S

RULES

by Robert White

GRAND MAL

PRESS

To Dick Blum in California—scholar, gentleman, and humanist, and the best friend I've never met

PART 1

Suffering is a fact of life; suffering is caused by attachment.
—*The First and Second Noble Truths of Buddhism*

CHAPTER 1

I felt the father's eyes watching me as I read. He said his name was John O'Reilly.

It was hard to concentrate. Twenty minutes earlier I was staring at the hand-drawn lettering of my name, Thomas Haftmann, Private Investigator, across the plate glass of my office window and trying hard not to reach for the gun in my drawer. The man I hired to paint it was one of the Strip's local characters. He always gave the impression of having a mild buzz on. We were sitting at the bar in Tico's Place reminiscing about last year's riot, the one when two motorcycle gangs had decided to fight for ownership of our crappy little resort town. Downing the last of however many boilermakers before I got there, he drew my name in handsome letters with a few lavish strokes across a bar napkin. I was so impressed I hired him on the spot. Now I wondered what happened to those impressive curlicues and bold dagger-like stems of letters in the smeared scrawl I was literally faced with every time I looked up from my desk. He had smudged the last two *n*'s of my surname so that it looked like a child's attempt with a fat crayon.

I didn't know what to make of the clipping Mr. O'Reilly handed me after introducing himself so I read it again. Below the photo of a dark-eyed, attractive girl I read this:

> Cruel Court, you are the enemy of truth, justice, of innocent life.
> You are the enemy of God. Cruel Court, your morality is that of the abortion provider who rips and tears head and heart from the innocent to comfort the powerful and selfish.
> Cruel Court, for years you have inched us, child and father, toward the precipice as you worked to guarantee our slavery.
> Cruel Court, you have killed . . .

I could hear the rumbling of suppressed sobs in his throat, waiting for me to finish so that he could talk, but I kept my eyes fixed to the clipping.

. . . Annaliese, already, haven't you? To protect your dishonestly contrived,

official evidence from truth; to protect your paper excuse
for your slaving operation.

I heard him blowing his nose loudly into a Kleenex. There was
even more maudlin whining in bad prose after this, so I cut my eyes
to the end to see if it was going to make any sense.

> . . . the daughter who knew too much and was too honest and unselfish
> had to disappear, didn't she? You sent Annaliese reeling toward the
> precipice. She fell over the edge, didn't she? Or was she pushed?
> Her sad and lonely grave is another one of your client's dark secrets,
> isn't it? Annaliese—the infant with haunting eyes, knowing eyes; the
> child with quick hand and mind and kind and generous spirit; the young
> woman full of promise. The Human Sacrificeto Corruption. Loved, and
> at last, mourned by her father.

The paper had appended his name, John O'Reilly, in italic script at
the bottom.

Fuckola, I thought, *just another kiddie hunt.*

I looked across my desk and tried to appear sympathetic. His eyes,
brown and moist with sorrow, looked into mine—at least, the only
one that's capable of reflecting much light to a damaged optic nerve
in my left eye. He reminded me of a whippet I used to own. I scolded
him once for wetting the couch and it took six months for me to get
him to stop looking at me that way. The daughter's eyes in the photo
were standard newspaper eyes: flat and black. Micah, my ex-wife, had
those eyes too. *Haunting eyes, knowing eyes.*

I asked questions about the newspaper item he had taken back
from me and refolded carefully like a valuable medieval manuscript.

He spoke slowly, each word dropping like acid as I pried the facts
loose from the scrambled text of his pain. What smoldered beneath
the rant of a simple man's appeal to an unjust earthly tribunal was simple, if not exactly eloquent. My cop years had taught me that real grief
is always numbingly simple. In the pauses of his narrative, the skin
around his moist eyes would tighten or he would suddenly turn his
head to look out my window at the passersby and the cars trolling the
Strip. I watched him blink away tears. When I was a boy, I had come
upon a snake sunning itself along the roadway. It was irresistible. I

had to touch its tail. It whipped off into the tall grass. For a long time my finger held the electricity where the reptile had been touched. O'Reilly was filling up my office with that kind of unease. But there was nothing to put my finger to—just a father lamenting grief for his missing child.

The next part was obvious, so I asked: "What do you want me to do?"

"I want you to find her and bring her home."

"I have to ask this, you understand. What if she's dead?"

"Then tell me where she's buried so I can bring her home."

I asked him several more questions about the Cruel Court's "client"— his ex-wife, not surprisingly, and the "slaving operation," simply his own poetic coinage for the judgment that went against him. He wasn't the first man to come through my office door shaking his fist at the system. Being in Cleveland homicide for as many years as I'd been, I had acquired the cop's distaste for the law's minions very easily, especially trial lawyers. Either they're too chickenshit to go after the bad guys for fear of damaging that all-important win record or they want to plea bargain it right out from under you. And always the incessant clamoring for more evidence, more witnesses, despite the fact that you've spent every moment of your fifteen-hour working day putting together a brilliant circumstantial case against a suspect. They'll give you all the reasons in the world too, lawyers. Sometimes I wish I had gone to law school like my buddy Reggie, now the judge of the Western Court district. That way, life is simpler: Everybody who walks through your door wants only one of two things: either that person wants you to help them keep their money or they want you to take it away from somebody else.

I said, "Let me explain my business to you, Mister O'Reilly."

What followed was my tried and true pitch for services to be rendered and costs thereof. I had heard myself say the same thing to dozens of people over the years—bland and dry as rice cake—and I was never good enough a forecaster to tell whether this client would be better or worse for the answers I might find. He listened, nodding his head several times as I mentioned *per diem* costs, extra expenses the client must reimburse me for. I told him I expected a bonus if I found her. He let that hang in the air and then we talked about him. He was self-employed, had a small furniture business in town, a small inheritance from an older brother. We agreed on a payment schedule; he signed, and left my office. The sob rose once again in his throat, and he couldn't speak, but he nodded his head vigorously once as if I understood what he meant. Then he was gone, back into the daylight world of his own grief. I envied him. It takes a life worth living to feel that much pain. Even suicides have to muster some commitment. I read the news article on the disappearance of Annaliese O'Reilly one more time, but it told me nothing more.

I looked down at my notes and stared at the plain block letters of my handwriting; it looked eerily similar to the nondescript style across my window. One thing I did know: nothing told me why Annaliese O'Reilly had disappeared from her own life.

My cell phone trilled its familiar ring tones. Micah had chosen it for me. I forget what she said it was because it reminded me of a track on an old Black Sabbath album I found when we were dividing up our earthly goods after the split. The caller was Judge Reginald Stevens. He said his hit-and-run trial was going to last another day so he couldn't meet me for drinks at Buster's.

I checked the messages. Very promising. I knew I had no time to kill for this now, and I needed every client's fee now that I was mired in—but I did it anyway. I went online and checked my usual website for cheating wives to confirm that my hook had been nibbled by a lurking fish. The particular fish in this case was Sandra. No last name because there never is. I had been in several chats with another woman—this one a "Mary"—who was trying to embolden herself for the dive off the deep end. But Sandra seemed ready for the jump. She said she was late thirties, "voluptuous," which could mean full-figured or obese, depending. I was sure in a couple days we'd be meeting in some no-tell motel along the Strip. Her husband, she added, "doesn't know," and wouldn't "approve." It sounded like swingers' code from the last decade. My life didn't bear much scrutiny. My phone service was on the verge of being shut off for failure to make payment and my cell phone was abuzz with the prospects of sordid rendezvous with various bored wives. Micah used to say I was "morally confused." But it was straight-arrow Micah who had the messy affair that scuttled our marriage.

I went online to check an Ohio swingers' website. I scrolled through the ads to an attractive, forties-something couple down in

Warren, an hour's ride south of my office. I sent a message asking for a safe motel meeting for a first-time, get-acquainted session, and if all seemed "compatible," we could go from there.

Meeting at a motel is a pretty sure sign that we were ninety-percent there already. Her photos showed a woman with a sleek, tight body from tennis and aerobics. Hubby had a bit of a paunch. She was the more assertive of the two clearly, and proud of her sexuality. One photo faxed two days back showed her looking over her shoulder at the camera, one dark-tipped breast exposed. The crease of her firm buttocks led down to the unshaved cleft, and I found myself aroused looking at it. They say you shouldn't write a letter in anger and something similar goes for online correspondence in a state of arousal. It affects diction and dick both. Maybe there's an art to everything.

Some switch had already been flipped in my head, though, and I was going to begin the investigation for the missing Annaliese O'Reilly, whose birthday on December 22 coincided with the end of Sagittarius and the beginning of Capricorn. There was no other reason except that I was bored with my life and the only means of enlivening it had been to run up my tab at Tico's Place across the street—or else put a Federal Special in the chamber for an interesting game of Russian roulette.

A major city's worth of people disappears every day in this country. Go missing but don't expect some tumult in the heavens to signify anything important happened. We're just cosmic dust. I make most of my living catching runaways. All I had for Annaliese's young life was that on a specific day in June three years ago she disappeared from the face of the earth. If she were still alive, a possibility not belied by the badly written declamation to the Cruel Court, she was an adult who, by all legal definitions, should be making her own way in the world somewhere. Even if I had never been a cop, or seen what people can do to one another even in this two-bit resort town, I still knew better than to believe that.

My first rule is an obvious one: brainwork precedes footwork. Probate Court is six miles away in the city of Jefferson, right off the main drag. I found Common Pleas upstairs and then I found a deputy clerk. I had no case number for her, but she knew me and took a vicarious pleasure in helping me on my cases. In jest I had once given her a Junior P.I. badge I had picked up somewhere, and she thanked me with genuine pleasure.

Annaliese Marie O'Reilly, albeit 17 years old and almost an adult, had been awarded to her mother Ingrid (the father told me that much) but I wanted to see what conditions applied to the divorce and whether Mr. O'Reilly's overwrought keening in print had been stipulated in the Probate Court in Jefferson in traditional lawyer's English.

It wasn't. It took less than an hour to confirm that and the fact that it was a simple divorce. She got the house; he kept the business but had to make token payments of $350 per month until Annaliese turned 18, thereby reducing the payments to $300..I knew the judge vaguely, a tedious curmudgeon with mediocre credentials and intellect. I knew Annaliese's mother's lawyer, though, because he had represented me in my own divorce. Reggie Stevens, in the days before he was elected to the Western Circuit, was an occasional imbiber of spirits at Tico's like me. We met the year Micah and I moved from Cleveland. Our marriage was already headed for collapse, even though I quit my job as a homicide detective and relocated to this godforsaken resort town in the foolish hope I could salvage it. Stupid me: you take your troubles with you. This place might be named for one of the few great presidents in that long history of mediocrity but it's been a long time since Tommy Dorsey and his swing band were booked at the Majestic Lounge. Today it's outlaw bikers, meth cooks, and runaways. I have a bird's-eye view of the action on Little Minnesota, the intersection where teen whores ply their trade in high summer while their pimps and boyfriends lurk in the shadows.

Before he assumed the moniker of Judge, Reg liked to put on cowboy boots and hat and knock back his Bailey's neat at a gin mill on cement blocks just off the Strip known in paint-flecked letters as Buster's Tavern. We used to shoot pool and rub elbows with the same class of clients, the only difference being Reg no longer represents them; now he mostly puts them away. My slide from a cop to gumshoe was all but complete by then. Micah was lost to me. She was having an affair with another lawyer, a local sharpie with a Mercedes Benz and a taste for married women. He also handled her divorce. They were living in one of those suburban estates where your house is picked from a catalog in one of three styles. I last heard she was organizing a tennis club set. I drank hard for a long time, lost clients, friends, and everybody's respect. At my lowest point, I put the barrel of a Charter Arms Bulldog to my head and dry-fired it. I got as far as composing a letter to Micah and putting in a cartridge and putting a little more pressure on the trigger each time until I knew I was a hair from oblivion. Call me old-fashioned. I find the idea of a suicide tweet offensive to my esthetic tastes. I set the gun down on the scarred coffee table and decided to become the sole existentialist private investigator in Northern Ohio. I vowed I would try to be a good one.

The judge who divorced the O'Reillys ruled in favor of Ingrid *née* Pokriefke in granting custody rights of the daughter Annaliese. It was clear that the judge was merely following Annaliese's own preference "until she reaches majority." *What precipice had she been inched toward?* It made no sense, but all cops know everyone lies, which cynical observation has not troubled me since I rode patrol as a rookie with an old veteran in Cleveland PD. Jack used to quote Latin poets, believe it or not. *Homo homini lupus est* was one of his favorite lines. He loved to spout the line as we rolled up on crime scenes. "Man is a wolf to man."

So it was back to the office and time for more phone calls from the usual investigator's directories. Then I was speeding through spring countryside shabby with daffodils poking their heads through lawns seared by the coldest winter I can recall in a life that had seen forty-four of them.

I reached Annaliese's mother in Pittsburgh on the fourth attempt. She told me about Annaliese in five minutes and seemed disinclined to talk.

"She was eighteen. What was I supposed to do? Tie her up in the backyard like a dog?"

I asked her if I could visit her as I had other business in the area, a fat lie she dismissed with a snort of contempt down the wire. After some stalling, she agreed and gave me directions from the airport. I made an appointment for the day after tomorrow, and we agreed on a time.

I reached into my drawer for the letter from the Warren couple I met online two weeks ago. I tore it up and then I ripped the photo they had sent with it in quarters and tossed the scraps into the wastebasket next to my desk. An upturned fragment of the snapshot showed where I had bisected the wife across the torso; near it lay another piece of the photograph: she had her head buried in a man's lap (his face was out of range of the camera) and there was a starburst of light from the camera's flash in the mirror. She must have sensed her husband withdrawing from her to take the photo because she stopped what she was doing and opened her eyes and smiled.

Brown eyes with tawny flecks like Micah's.

• • •

I don't like airplanes, and I don't particularly like the puddle jumpers I board in Erie for the occasional short hop. There's something about aerodynamics I distrust: it ought not to be possible for tons of metal to be sucked upwards on a principle so simple as a discrepancy in airflow over wings. Fortunately, my job doesn't entail much brooding about the intricacies of the design of the cosmos. It's that other part of nature's flux that keeps me up on long winter nights—the hairless biped that talks too much and acts out its impulses received from the limbic brain—a part that, like pigeon shit covering verdigris on a statue, sits atop the brainstem and has created most of the havoc in the world including every jackbooted stomp and eye-gouging horror that's ever been recorded on the long, snarling climb to the top of the food chain. I have seen that same three pounds of pulp turned the consistency of soup after a slug from a .38 passed through it. But as someone long ago concluded about our darkest dreaming, nature made the human head a deficient organ. It's at the very limit of being too big to pass through the birth canal and way too small to solve the crises it insists on creating.

The western slope of Pennsylvania was crosshatched in brown and sienna as far down as Pittsburgh. The Saab/Fairchild 340 followed I-79 all the way down and banked from the sunset in a steep dive that took us east of the airport. I saw Brunot Island jutting against the Ohio's current. High above the looping, silver ribbons of the Allegheny and Monongahela, one might even think well of nature and humanity; up close I could see the dingy churning where the rivers converged. There was still the landing.

The screech of tires finally enabled me to unclench my hands from the seat rests but the taste of bile reminded me how little my stomach appreciates flying anything, anywhere. My legs shook a little from the adrenalin finally beginning to dissipate, and I wondered for the thousandth time what Neanderthal ancestor preferred tall grass to the safety of high trees.

I found her in a rundown neighborhood across the Smithfield Street Bridge. Clusters of young black males sat on porches or stood between houses drinking Colt 45s. More homeless pushed wire shopping carts down street corners and lurked in vacant lots. Children on tricycles were dodging around a group of males who cut their eyes to my taxi and then went on with their business.

Business was obviously crack cocaine. One of the Big Wheel riders, a skinny boy riding in lazy figure eights about the older teens, was probably holding for them; another, about seven years old, on the perimeter of the action, seemingly sniffing the cold spring air, was acting lookout. Easy to spot who was running the show: one male in the center trailed by an orbit of kids with a vast crescent of mocha belly hanging out of his sweat pants, saddles for hips, and three pounds of gold chain around his neck. Wherever he moved, they moved with him. Hard to tell who Fat Boy's bodyguards were because gangs aren't run on bulk and muscle nowadays. Most killers I busted in Cleveland were boys who weighed about 150 pounds. Some of those baby gangbangers would shoot you just to see if the gun works.

The whole place reminded me of East Cleveland with its strawberry girls, drug dealers, and systemic poverty. If anything Cleveland was worse off now: the poorest big city in America two years running, another generation of cold-eyed crack babies all grown up and ready to rock.

I remember one of the worst—one of the King's Men from Atlanta still wearing his colors—a businessman's suit taken from his initiation victim; he had moved up from Atlanta after the Ghost Shadows, an Asian gang, had put too much heat on him for killing five of theirs in two weeks. Another part of being jumped into the King's Men required learning passages from the writings of Martin Luther King—these he quoted before firing into the heads of his victims. His favorite line, he told me in interrogation, was: 'To put it in the terms of St. Thomas Aquinas: An unjust law is a human law that is not rooted in eternal law and natural law.' My driver never bothered to take in the scene but he seemed to know exactly where we were heading. He braked hard, deposited me and my overnight bag in front of a brown and yellow job that looked identical to most of the houses on the street except that no one had boarded its windows and doors with plywood or slapped a red sign with black letters anywhere on the premises. He took my tip, grunted a sound that might have been thanks, and sped off.

A tall black man answered my knock. The italic script on his gray pocket flap said his name was Raymond. I badged him in one practiced move and asked him if Ingrid O'Reilly lived there. He said nothing to me but opened the door and shouted her name in the direction of the kitchen. She walked in, and I was looking at a fortyish attractive blonde. No doubt about it: *Mütti* was a looker—eyes edged with crow's-feet, tousled white-blonde hair and all.

She said hello with a face that was imprinted to exude sensuality from birth. Raymond asked me to sit down and offered me coffee. I declined, and he left us alone to talk.

Her husband, she said, had to get ready for his shift and would be leaving soon. He worked at Three Rivers Stadium. She worried when he left the house and let that drift with a wave of her hand that seemed to encompass the house, the neighborhood, maybe her life. An old Bessie Smith tune was playing softly from the kitchen.

The O'Reillys' divorce was bitter, she explained, but when Ingrid found herself a black man, her ex went ballistic. When he dropped off the copy of the newspaper clipping that afternoon, he didn't exactly wax eloquent in his outrage about Ingrid's progress from "slutty German bar whore" to "coon-fucking bitch." I don't have to like my clients and most of them I don't.

I used a phony cop's smile and let her talk without prompting. In accented English flavored with the hiss of sibilants, she told me how it began.

She had met O'Reilly in Mannheim in the service where he was a radio technician. She was seventeen but passed herself as twenty-one and found work in a bar frequented by US servicemen. He seemed lonely and kept to himself, a quiet drinker who never flirted or dated the waitresses. When he found the courage to seek her out, they began to date and finally, at the end of his tour, she told him she was pregnant. A week later he asked her to marry him and come to America.

She opened her hands in that same casual gesture and shrugged, as if all of it had been inevitable and there was nothing more to say. Annaliese was born six months after their arrival in Boston, where his family was from. He had an uncle in the furniture manufacturing business in Ohio who invited them out and gave him a start in the business, but after things got messy, he went back to Boston and his wife and daughter stayed in Ohio. The marriage was pretty good at first though there wasn't much money, but he began to "make difficulties," she said with a moue of distaste at the memory. Soon, she said, there was nothing more between them; he grew violent, abusive, began to hit her and accuse her of adultery and when she had had enough and could find no reason to save the marriage, she divorced him.

Then I asked my questions:

"Do you know where Annaliese is now?" She didn't. "Did your husband beat you because he thought you were cheating on him or—" I let the question hang in the air. She drilled me with her pretty eyes.

"No."

"Did you file a complaint with the police?"

Yes, when he went from slaps to the side of her head to rolled-up newspapers, then his fists. Sometimes he threatened me with knives, called me *whore, slut* other disgusting names I won't repeat."

"You were pregnant when you came to America, right?"

"Yes, I was. I said I was."

"Was O'Reilly Annaliese's father?"

She looked nervously off toward the kitchen. "What do you mean?"

"I mean, were you made pregnant by your ex-husband?"

"Y-yes, of course. I don't understand what—"

"Let me save us some time. I don't want to be in your life any longer than I have to. But I'm not going to go away with answers that you could have given me on the phone. Let me tell you what I think, OK? You were pregnant with Annaliese, but O'Reilly was not the father. You didn't know what prejudice was until you came to America. You dated black servicemen in Mannheim, right? You had a black lover. You were just a girl, and you wanted to come to America. You told your lover you were pregnant, and he refused to do anything about it—maybe he wanted to give you money for an abortion—but he wasn't going to take you back to America for whatever reasons. You panicked. You picked the quiet guy in the corner who never made a fuss, never groped any of the girls when they passed by. You began to flirt with him—"

"Th-That's not true!"

"How is it not true? Shall I ask Raymond to come in and tell us how it's not true?"

"Leave my husband out of this! He is a good man."

I decided to play the trump card. "What do you mean, 'your husband?'" I pointed a finger in the direction Raymond had gone. "You mean that man in there? Your ex-husband says you have a pattern of doing this. You get into trouble, you find some sucker to pick up the pieces for you and off you go. John says he gave you everything and you cheated on him with every man who looked at you. Says you're still just a serviceman's pick-up, giving horny soldiers all that deep-dish cleavage until their eyes fall out of their heads, a cheap thrill he says, a quickie—"

"How—how dare you speak to me like that! You know nothing at all, you cheap—"

Raymond called from upstairs: "Hey, babe, everything OK down there?"

She answered him without looking at me. "Yes, yes. Everything's fine."

She had that true blonde's pellucid skin that shows color and mapping of blue veins easily, and her face blushed crimson right in front of me—shame, anger, fear, maybe all at once—but I felt her aching, tortured loveliness in that frozen moment, hair a cornsilk halo and eyes like blue lasers boring into me.

Well, here it comes, the truth now . . .

I was wrong. She wrung her hands, muttered something in German and then said something in English but I heard only the words *hate* and *women*. Her hands were reddened and sore-looking. I let her wrestle with her own private demons for a while until she calmed herself, eyes squeezed tight, her blonde head nodding on her swelling chest as if, like a narcoleptic, she had suddenly dropped off to sleep in the middle of a conversation. Her emotions were hers alone; no one feels anything for anybody else's pain, not really. So I waited. Then, as she brushed a strand of hair from her eyes, I asked her to tell me how it really was so that I could find her daughter.

She nodded as if convincing herself of something. She looked me in the face again, reliving the pain and terror of her youth. An old torch song from the forties was playing in the kitchen. I knew she had made a decision. She awoke one day, she said calmly, and knew with-

22

out really knowing that she was pregnant. The baby's father was a black soldier, a missile technician, and she was deeply in love with him. She had been a virgin. He was her first lover. But he didn't want to marry her because he intended to go to college and study engineering at Florida State; she didn't want to get an abortion because she was Catholic. Desperate and alone, she found the drunken hilarity of the soldiers mobbing the bar in their frenzied drinking binges too much to bear. Their own homesickness gave her loneliness and terror a keener edge; apparently, she was marked as an easy lay too because the black soldiers in particular were coming on all the time. There was no going back home to Gdingen with a black soldier's child swelling her womb. When an obnoxious, hirsute staff sergeant from Oklahoma pinched her ass really hard, she burst into tears. (She drew a deep breath here.) Suddenly she found herself being comforted by the quiet soldier. His pidgin-German was hopeless, but soon she learned all about him: he was a second-generation Irish-American from Boston. He was flattered by her attention and soon they were spending time together whenever he could get off-base. She could not hide her pregnancy forever, so soon after they made love for the first time she told him she was pregnant. He said it didn't matter, that he loved her and wanted her to be his wife. She agonized about telling him, but finally decided that there would be time later . . .

Back in America, it all changed after Annaliese's birth. The baby, thank God, took after her except for the tight blonde ringlets and the slightly dusky pallor of her skin. The early years of struggle to make a living kept them both busy and content. He was moody but a good provider and dedicated to their welfare. Then his drinking worsened, and he began calling her the filthiest names in fits of seething rage: *gutterwhore, nigger fuckbitch*. The next day, after the booze fog lifted, he would apologize and beg her to forgive him. Then the beatings—first head slaps, then punches, and finally the all-out fury of fists and kicks—left her marked and swollen for days. Sometimes he forced her to perform fellatio after these outbursts subsided. He began treating Annaliese differently too, colder, shunned her presence and once physically recoiled when she put her hands on his face. Finally, after one beating which caved in the bones of her cheek and left her face a bloody mask, she confirmed his suspicions. She told him the father was black. She never knew the father's last name. O'Reilly wept and

23

sobbed uncontrollably. She knew she had to get out.

Two weeks before she left O'Reilly, she took Annaliese aside and told her the truth about her birth. She showed no reaction, the mother said, but became very quiet around the house. This secret was never discussed again between mother and daughter. Annaliese disappeared a month later.

I asked her if she had any papers, letters, or personal items of her daughter's that might reveal where she went. She had nothing here. Annaliese had moved out when she turned eighteen and was sharing an apartment in Jefferson with another girl she knew from high school. Her mother had given her ten thousand dollars from the sale of her father's house after the divorce. But she had visited her mother only once in Pittsburgh before disappearing.

Was there anything, anything at all, that she might have said then that seemed unusual or unlike her? Did she talk about any plans she had? Nothing. Zero. Zilch point shit. The mother and daughter, now a grown woman burdened by a terrible secret come to light, had turned a corner and neither could express her feelings to the other. It was a bad visit, she said, because things were so unsettled just then. Annaliese had begun working for a law firm in Jefferson and she herself had only just agreed to move from Jefferson to Pittsburgh after Raymond, whom she met at a beer joint on the Strip a month earlier, had convinced her to make a new start.

Her life's destiny was in bars. She said she had not been inside a bar since her marriage to O'Reilly. He wouldn't permit her to go and threatened to kill her if he ever found her in a bar. She was thinking of suicide, she told me, and she wanted one last drink, as much to defy him, as to stiffen her resolve to kill herself. Maybe she wanted to feel human contact one final time too before she stuck her head in the oven. She was composing her farewell note to Annaliese in her head when she must have let out a sob while sitting on the stool inside the darkened Boar Room because the next thing she knew she was being comforted by a tall, soft-spoken man who introduced himself as Raymond and said he was passing through Jefferson-on-the-Lake, visiting friends, on his way home to Pittsburgh and thought he'd stop and have one for the road before the long drive down Interstate 79.

I thanked her, and as I held her hand in mine on the way out the door, I felt its rawness like an open wound. She wished me good luck in finding her daughter and squeezed my hand hard.

"Please don't let anything happen to her, Mister Haftmann."

As if I could do anything about that. I remember sucking down boilermakers in Tico's Place, sitting alongside a local drunk and part-time philosopher, when I heard him blurt for all to hear: "God should never have put love in the mind of an animal . . ." Then he seemed to cave in; his head sunk to his chest, and with a one long suspiration, withdrew into a stupor that lasted until Tico's wife Marta escorted him out the door at two in the morning.

Raymond gave me a ride to the airport on his way to work. We never spoke on the way, but he looked at me with smoldering eyes that said I was not getting another invitation anytime soon. Spring was dirty everywhere this year. I boarded a Fairchild Metro for the ride back to Erie; the pilot, a real air jockey, found all the chop there was to find. I finally threw up on the landing at the airport.

• • •

I had some hunches, and it was time to play them. I called O'Reilly and left a message on his machine requesting him to see me as soon as possible. I left some convenient times and said I'd be in my office.

I drove to Tico's for a chat where I found him mixing Acapulco Screwdrivers. Afterward, I headed for the gym for a workout where I busted muscles for an hour before my ringtones chimed. It was O'Reilly. He said he would meet me at my office at seven. I finished my workout with ten laps, a shower, and drove back to the office.

I considered my strategy on the ride back. The air was cold, a few fat drops of rain hit the windshield, but I was conscious of sweat beads on my forehead. We were in Daylight Savings now and the extra light was welcome. Lake Erie had been iced over most of the winter except during the occasional thaw when a bright blue channel showed through the whiteness. Now ice-free, the lake boats were beginning to churn through the pewter gray murk on their way up the Great Lakes to Duluth and Taconite Harbor and the emerald-green of Superior—too big to ice over. You could see Erie easily from Tico's; he never closed for the off season, and we used to look out over the water as the chunks broke off, reformed in the periods of thaw, and

25

created a shifting horizon of bizarre shapes as the pounding waves chiseled ice sculptures out of the sand and water. I knew Tico, an ex-welterweight from Youngstown, for fifteen years, and I never once saw him outside his bar. Back in my heavy drinking days, we used to bet on the number of floaters the spring thaw would bring. The county nursing home was overstocked with Alzheimer's patients and over the years many had preferred the iron embrace of waves to the misery of their own rotting minds.

I have seen fathers in grief, real bone-breaking sorrow, and my Pittsburgh visit only confirmed my impression of O'Reilly as a weak man—a cruel, self-pitying bully hiding behind that poetic drivel in the newspaper. A bully is the most loathsome of nature's creatures.

He walked into my office carrying a London Fog trench coat over his arm five minutes after I arrived. I turned on the banker's lamp behind the desk so that my face would be in partial shadow. I had a turquoise worry stone in my left hand and I worked at it while he positioned himself. The greetings were disposed of without much pretense at sincerity, and in that way that knowledge instinctively imparts, I knew he did not like me much either.

"Let's not waste any more of my time or your money, Mister O'Reilly, shall we?"

Blood pumped through a vein in his neck. "What do you mean?"

"I mean, don't ever tell me another thing that isn't true. If you do, I'll quit now and you can have my bill for services rendered."

"I don't know what you're talking about, Haftmann."

Well, fuck it, I thought. *No more Mr. Nice Guy.*

"You goddam well know what I mean," I said. "I saw your ex-wife, remember? Your daughter didn't disappear. She left. She got the hell out of an intolerable situation. You have any idea how much of my business is finding kids who don't want to be found?"

He tried to interject but I bored on. "You were beating her mother to a pulp and you treated Annaliese like a leper because of something she was completely innocent of. Don't tell me any more shit about cruel courts, O'Reilly."

Long, baleful stare. He drew a checkbook from his inside coat pocket. Then: "How much do I owe you?"

I shrugged and reached for my calculator. So be it.

"Wait. Wait, Haftmann. Let me explain." He wiped his hand

around his mouth as if there were some kind of stain he had to remove.

I laced my fingers together before me and waited. "Yes?"

"It's—It's hard to explain how it was. Years of it, the *knowledge* that
the woman you loved, slept with, provided for—everything, everything! Do you know what it's like to suddenly realize that your wife is
a whore?'

Micah's name roared in my ears, but I gave him the cop's blank
look. Another rule of mine is to let them talk once they start. He broke
down into sobs, but I wasn't going to let a bout of self-pity distract
him.

"Don't sit there whining and puling at me, O'Reilly. If we still have
business, let's get on with it." A little goad to the hindquarters was all
he needed to transmogrify back into bully.

"I'm paying *you*, Haftmann. I mean, I'm the one putting money in
your pocket, right?"

"Yes, Mister O'Reilly, you are paying me, but I can't help you find
Annaliese if you aren't straight with me. Just tell me about it. Please
continue."

I've grown so used to the dreary phoniness of my own voice I believe that one of these days I will have to forfeit my card in the Existentialists Union.

"She-she was *screwing* a nig—a black man!"

"I've had enough of your racist claptrap," I said. "This isn't nine-
teen-fifty—"

"You ever been in the service, Haftmann? The barracks are no
place for secrets. You got a weakness, a stutter, any kind of handicap,
whatever, and they'll torture you with it. I never had any real friends
over there. To this day I can't stand to hear that language. Everybody
sounds like Adolf Hitler. I hate Germans. I hate every one of them."

"Except her," I said. "Your wife."

He looked broken.

"She was so unbelievably pretty . . . and for a long time," he said,
"there were guys betting on who'd be the first to—to, you know. She
was young and pretty. I never even spoke to her much—that is, besides
ordering beer or food. She treated me like everyone else but the ones
who used to flirt with her, put their arms around her, well, they got the
smiles, she was all white teeth and blonde legs and that get-up she

wore—you know? Big milkfed tits tumbling out every time one of them bends over." His mouth wrinkled in distaste.

"Your wife said the marriage was good at first—"

He ignored that. I could see him getting worked up.

"Christ, they were so eager to get to America they'd suck off men behind the chalet, right on their knees. You could catch them in the headlights. Blacks standing there with their hands on these blonde heads. Christ, I could puke! It used to make me crazy thinking of it, that she might have been one of them. You see, she was so lovely then, so—so innocent. Sweet! Then she started to talk to me. I thought I was the luckiest man in the world. I thought the guys were all jealous of me. I never understood until years later what all those winks and sneers were all about. I still hear them laughing at me every night in my sleep."

It was time to get down to business. "You knew your wife had been sleeping with another man. A black man, at that. You couldn't take it, so you started to beat her a little. Not much at first, but then it got easier and the anger just wouldn't go away. You had to make her pay for all that ridicule. Finally, you couldn't bear to look at Annaliese without your stomach turning into knots. She was beautiful, too, fair like her mother, but she had black blood in her veins—never enough that anyone wouldn't think she was Caucasian, but it must have rubbed you raw."

"I just could . . . not . . . *tolerate* it," he said with a grimace of pain and maybe disgust. "She was just like her mother, and the older she got, the more she brought it all back to me."

"So you threw her out of your home," I said.

"No! I never threw her out. I never wanted her to leave. Ingrid turned her against me. When Annaliese came home from Pittsburgh, she had a wild look in her eyes. I knew her mother had told her the truth."

"Did you hit her too?"

His hands covered his face. "God help me, yes. Yes, yes. I hit her. Once. Hard. Across the face. She smirked at me and I could see her mother in her face, defying me, lying to me."

Micah never had much respect for my intellect. I think "simian" was a typical description of my mental prowess in her estimation, but she said I used to creep her out with these flashes of insight I used to come up with at times. I had one now.

"You had sex with your daughter."

His face went as gray as putty. I waited for the spluttering, the outrage, the denial. It was all there in his face. But he said nothing and that said everything. Before he had time to muster some kind of self-justification that would have had me out from behind my desk with my fist balled, he said the words, none of them cathartic or ones that would seek forgiveness, if even from a hostile stranger like me.

"I wanted them to suffer like me."

A volcano of bile churned in my stomach. *Some men cross Rubicons you can't return from,* I thought.

My instincts aren't as good anymore. He stood up and extended his hand to me. I thought about refusing to shake it, but before I had made a decision, he curled his hand into a fist and hit me under the jaw with it.

It wasn't much of a blow. I wasn't even stunned—just surprised I hadn't seen it coming. I had the distance measured and so I hit him, just once, squarely in the chin—the way Tico had shown me years ago, two knuckles hard and straight right to the point of the chin.

Lights out. I didn't hit him hard enough to hurt him, but he slumped back in his seat and his head lolled back. His eyes had a sheen to them. I got up, fetched some water, and thought about giving Reg a call before the cops and lawyers were summoned. I saw my p.i.'s license sprout wings and fly magically through my plate glass window.

I opened my bottom drawer for the Johnny Walker Red. He came around, sucked in some air, wheezed, shook his head and moaned. I poured him the drink and held it out to him. He tried to bat it away and then he tried to stand but his legs wouldn't work.

"Sit, sit, Mister O'Reilly. You'll be OK in a minute."

"*Mister* O'Reilly, huh? After you just tried to take my head off . . . "

"Nothing's happened. You overreacted a little bit. I responded. Here, drink."

Calmer but still dazed, he took the drink and wrapped a hand around it. He sipped and coughed. It took about ten minutes of silence and then he opened up like a pustule and all the filth came oozing out. Blubbering his way through the sordid tale, he told me what I had guessed. Panicking after slapping her, which knocked her to the floor, he tried to get her up. She was limp in his arms. He dragged her under the arms to her bedroom. Here, he paused to recollect how each of her shoes had slipped off, one after the other.

Inside her bedroom, he gently slapped her face to revive her. Then he began caressing her face. She came to and began to cry. He cried with her. He lay next to her holding her in his arms and soon he was stroking her. Her moans aroused him. He didn't know why, he said. Though he had been impotent with Ingrid for months (discount the forced blow jobs she had told me about), he experienced the most incredible erection, and it was as if every tongue-lolling, hate-filled erotic impulse thrummed through his body at once. Annaliese was doe-eyed with fear, her silence became acquiescence—even participation. When he shoved it inside her, he thought he had kicked himself loose from the universe and his heart would burst from emotion.

He looked at me a long time. His face held an expression for a moment that made me think of Satan wearing a human mask and allowing it to slip a little. *See, everyone, it's me, Father of Lies.* When he awoke, he said, Annaliese was gone. He never saw her again.

He snuffled into a Kleenex he brought out of his pocket, a ragged dirty-white ball. I watched, waited for the rest of it. There wasn't much left to tell as he choked out the last part in the catastrophe that was the life of Annaliese Marie O'Reilly.

"It wasn't actually incest, I think because she wasn't—"

"Shut up," I said. "Don't say another word."

"Help me find her, Haftmann. Please, I beg you. I must make her see how sorry I am. I must have her forgiveness. I'll go to jail if I have to, but I'll kill myself if I don't get this chance to see her once more. It's all I have to live for now. Help me, help, help me . . ."

He wept like a man whose suffering had no bottom to it.

• • •

At the end of my alcoholic tether, when I was plummeting into the abyss of my fullest self-loathing, I used to have the craziest dreams. Intense, eclectic, and erotic, I wallowed like a demented satyr in nightly romps with mature women, willowy girls neither innocent nor debauched. These Lolitas were my sole joy, the end of my psychic tether and my last connection to humanity in any way. I had plumbed depths in my crusade to find the most notorious serial killer in the state's history—the one the tabloids called the Jack-in-the-Box killer because of his ghastly propensity for leaving severed heads in boxes in his wake; my dream life upped itself a notch as it must have fed on this grisly matter stewing inside my psyche. In these fever dreams of blood and sex, I had varied carnal relations with women and girls in a tangled heap of sweaty flesh, pumping at any and every hole offered. Sometimes my exhausted but liberated libido made me a fish in strange waters for my nightly fare, but I awoke from them all the same way: sheets clammy with nightsweats and a terror in my heart that I was losing my sanity in my sleep. I am no repressed product of the fifties, but I am no unreconstructed flower child of Haight-Ashbury either. I had absolutely no control over what my dreams did to me; in fact, I awoke every day or afternoon or whenever I opened my eyes to the light with self-loathing and a terror about my latest night romp.

I have never considered myself, my real self, to be the dreaming partner; it was that vile essence of my hidden self that dreamed *to me*. One, above all, sent me retching to the toilet. My despair over the loss of Micah was keenest at that time, and I indulged myself with sport-fucking wherever available. Here on the Strip, where teenaged misfits and blonde farm girls from Minnesota sometimes take a wrong turn on their way to LA, the available flesh is out of proportion to the local population—that is, until I met Sheila, the dispatcher at the station house. No sooner had I felt myself becoming a human being again than I became impotent with the one woman I cared deeply for.

But the dreams did not last and as my body readjusted to a metabolism that for the first time in twenty years was not being driven by alcohol, I had found an interlude of nondreaming—the sweet blankness of oblivion. That too in time became a terrible thing to anticipate nightly. I felt as if I were dragging myself by inches across a wasteland deserted of life except for rattlesnakes and scorpions.

The night after my last interview with O'Reilly brought back the dreams of my serial killer-hunting days. I was staggering up an impossibly high hill with others, all of us in drab colors. It was a road that seemed to lead straight up, but there were unpainted shanties along the side from the windows of which distrustful and suspicious eyes would peer out. Queen Anne's lace fringed the roadside, but there was nothing to be seen beyond these few shacks. At last, as I scaled the top and was about to seek whatever freedom lay beyond, I turned back to see a young woman, isolated from a pocket of travelers, cry out in fear. There was a baby-faced youth in olive green colors clutching her arm and leading her off to the edge of the road; he was holding a Mac 10 machine pistol with a barrel silencer.

I knew them well, and like every street cop at that time, dreaded with a bowel-twisting fear the very thought of confronting one some lonely night in the hands of a gangbanger on angel dust. Six slugs per second, 158-gram round nose—*Jesus Christ*, it didn't bear thinking about too long, and no one who's ever been shot wants to see one of those ugly guns on the street.

I once worked a case with the feds and ATF on a Mafia contract killer who manufactured those silencers in his garage. In the crazy logic of dreams, the boy with the MAC 10 had one, and as he stepped away from the young woman, I knew she was going to get blasted from that awful weapon. I froze near the top, not knowing what to do. There was nothing before me, but I was sure there was horror and death where I had been. On impulse I ran back to the girl—stupid, really, because *he* ought to have been the one I threw myself at—but I got there in time to see her body explode from a burst of .9 mm rounds. She dropped into the road like a puppet whose strings had just been scissored.

It was Annaliese and she opened her haunted eyes just once to take me in, and then she started to say something but a gout of blood stopped her words. As I lay her in the roadway, I felt my hand sticky with her blood. An oily puddle was oozing behind her black hair in the dust and pooling in a viscous red halo. Some killshots don't bleed and some head wounds look worse than they are despite profuse bleeding, but the very worst are the distortions and bulbous eyes from the skull's ballooning under great pressure caused by a slug to the brain. I had my fingers working her the way I used to do victims at crime scenes. Desperately wanting to save her, and all the while I'm kneading her flesh looking for the bullets under the skin, as if locating them would save her life. None of the others streaming past like the marching dead even looked at her—no one even stopped walking in that gait of town locals participating in one of those zombie movies. The killer was nowhere in sight but I ran down to one of the shacks and banged on the door for help. No one came. Then I ran back, crazed with fear that the killer should return for me, and I scooped her up from the road despite the fact of her staring eyes and matted hair and ran right for the top of the hill. It was one of those dreams where your legs are cement as you try to flee danger, so of course, I never reached help: at the very moment of cresting the hill, I beheld a massive slave labor camp below, teeming with the naked and the walking dead, soldiers, barking dogs, barracks, and coils of barbed wire. I knew my fate was beyond hope.

Every existentialist in good standing must own a gun, and every week the existentialist rulebook says that gun ought to be inserted barrel first into the mouth. Then you make a choice. Is life worth the trouble it takes to live it? I have used Sundays as my day of choice for the last several years because it is fitting to make this choice on the Sabbath. The world begins anew or one takes it into oblivion, demolishes it all in a flurry of exploding brain matter. I have had one emotion left to me since my career and my marriage ended: jealousy. I cannot erase the image of Micah from my mind. I see her locked in coitus, sweat-coiled in lustful exertion, fat drops trickling down her backside to the crack of her ass. I know that I perversely cling to this, embittered, as I wade through the cesspit of human misery that washes up to my office door. Maybe I like to suffer rather than to think. Except for serial killers and saints who imitate human emotion, it seems to me that suffering is all there really is to know of life.

On the morning after my dream, I knew I had been condemned to find this missing girl. For what good or purpose, I didn't know. It wasn't as if I had the leisure or the money to waste either. Much as I hate them, I'll take a messy divorce case for the money; but mostly nowadays I just find people and try to bring them back to the people who want them found.

There's an axiom in cop work that goes: if you don't have a suspect in the first 10 to 12 hours after the crime, the trail grows cold fast. Too much time for people to hide evidence, get their stories straight, flatten out the corners of tales that don't mesh. It's similar in my line: if you can't get a lead on someone via the telephone in the first 24 hours, that person is almost certain not to be found. I feared a stranger crime because it opens up chaos in any investigation. You walk into any Crimes Against Persons bureau in America and eyeball what cops call the board, you'll see the "dunkers" are all cleared in black because the husband is standing right with a smoking gun in his fist still spitting curses at the bitch he just aired out. But a whodunit is always in red until cleared and that's an investigation that may never be solved. Three out of ten murders in every big city never get cleared year after year. If you happen to be a citizen of Oakland, California these days, that figure is thirty-five percent.

Annaliese had been missing for three years. I felt like a man standing behind a large rock at the bottom of a very steep hill about to commit his strength and sinews to the first inertia-breaking shove.

CHAPTER 2

Every investigator I know has a special case: one that keeps you up when you need to be sleeping, one that obsesses you through the years and does not let you ever forget it. You'll track every lead and follow a trail to the ends of the Earth to solve it. It's called being on a mission, and like zealots talking about God, there's something sacred in it. Other cops understand this obsession, and they'll leave you alone when you're wasting your time, missing your rotation, doing halfassed investigations and irritating superiors. You'll review the case file dozens of times until every lead or clue is a shifting mirage in your imagination because nothing must be overlooked; you'll drive 300 miles to the state pen to interview some deadass just because scuttlebutt has it that a cell mate overheard him say something about the case to someone who told it to some cop up there, and this cop passes it along to you, knowing full well you'll do anything to keep the investigation alive, read chicken entrails, grasp at any straw, however flimsy—and thank him for it because you just can't let it go. So you drive the 300 miles the next day to waste your time talking to the con, a liar and probably a snitch looking for good time, knowing in your guts that it isn't going to pan out, but there's nowhere else to go, no explaining your mission to anyone else. It's your sanity and it's what makes you crazy until you solve it or you walk away from it, burned and scarred for life. One red ball case like that, one mission, and you go from rookie to veteran overnight. I've seen it happen. It happened to me.

Annaliese O'Reilly wasn't under my skin. I didn't even know if she was a victim yet. That matters. A few years ago, I'd have gone to Tico's or some darkened watering hole on the Strip and drunk with the locals until I felt reasonably sane again. Instead, I made a few quick calls to some friends left over from my detective days at the Jefferson-on-the-Lake station house and played mah jongg on my computer for four hours straight. It's not like solitaire; it's about freedom and confinement.

I asked another drinking comrade filling out time in the weapons room until retirement to check her out. Annaliese O'Reilly had been arrested for DUI in the summer before she disappeared. She'd been weaving a mile west of Route 45—right at the curve near the Billow Beach Lounge—and the arresting officer radared her. I knew him: an OK cop working plainclothes out of the Jefferson PD.

The report says he smelled alcohol on her breath and he found her to be intoxicated when she flunked the field test. She herself wanted a breathalyzer at the station house, but she flunked that too with a 0.21. It was her only violation. That didn't say much, however, because the chief of police had to play ball with the Chamber of Commerce, and there's nothing like a buzzkill for a resort town when ticket-happy cops start bagging motorists up and down the Strip. It can spoil a summer's revenue mighty fast. Even the staties in their basic black observe the custom of staying clear in high summer and wait for motorists at a respectable distance. One gung-ho cop named "Red Dog" from his academy days in Columbus learned his lesson the hard way when he mistranslated the daywatch commander's pep talk about reducing drunk drivers and filled his monthly quota in a week. Typical of police logic, he was given a commendation and then transferred to community service where he spent the next year visiting elementary schools in various seasonal costumes talking to kids about D.A.R.E. When he refused a direct order from Chief Millimaki to don an Easter rabbit costume, he wound up on suspension for six weeks. Not one of my rules necessarily, but it's the old golden rule at work: He who has the gold rules.

Something else I learned from another contact in Children's Services: Annaliese had an abortion when she was seventeen years old. By law, she was required to notify at least one parent that she intended to abort a fetus and that she had to observe the 24-hour, state-mandated waiting period and listen to alternatives to abortion. One of my best contacts in county welfare faxed me a copy of the parental consent form. Annaliese had forged her father's signature. I knew that much because the signature on his retainer check was not even remotely like the one I saw beneath Annaliese's own signature on the form. Was it her father's child she aborted? Either he knew and was too ashamed to tell me or he didn't know because she didn't tell him. There is no corollary to the universal cop rule that everybody lies. This admits of no exceptions because everyone lies, principals and witnesses alike, some people for the sheer fun of lying to a cop. You want truth, find it out for yourself.

There is a word I learned from Jack, my former partner in Cleveland PD, who never missed a chance to smirk at my rookie zeal. I have a photo of us at a crime scene: he's resting against the black-and-white, one of his stinking cigars sold at fine Dairy Marts everywhere clamped in his mouth while I'm scouring the grass in the foreground—presumably for evidence but I can't remember now. There's a look of patience fighting exasperation on his face that I used to dread because it precipitated a long lecture at some perceived incompetence of mine. He used to talk about achieving a higher state of being, *ataraxia*, he called it, a serenity borne of tender indifference to the human avalanche of misery that threatened to wash over any cop dumb enough to take his job seriously. We weren't fighting crime, he used to say: we were stirring up the shit in the swill bucket and watching it resettle to the bottom. Cop wisdom.

I look at that photo now and then, and I see in my furrowed rookie brow the light of initiation and beatitude. I see Jack looking at me and I recall his amusement at my blundering efforts to control a crime scene. Jack never saw me make it to the elite ranks of homicide because he ate his gun a year into his retirement, a year before I earned my detective shield.

My cell phone rang. My ex-wife's voice told me she was expecting a child. I asked her what she was going to name it. I don't know why I asked because it is a matter of indifference to me what name it has. Everyone is condemned to live out the destiny of the name we get at birth, and it is never one we choose for ourselves. I heard myself congratulating her. She always wanted a child but we could never have had one together because I am sterile. A man I fought with in an alley had a knife and he cut my scrotum; the infection left me unable to have children. That was shortly before I joined the cops when I had just quit the ore boats and a life on the Great Lakes to come home to bury my grandmother and marry Micah. Sometimes I slip my existentialist leash and revert to my boyhood faith—all the years of bending the knee has done its psychic damage and I am unable to rid myself entirely of superstition. When Micah said goodbye, I thought: *We're just mud pies God likes to play with.* I can forgive her for her treachery and her lying while our marriage was collapsing; I was a useless drunk wallowing in my own unhappiness. She found a way out, and though I loathe her choice regarding my replacement—a man whose morals are lower than a gangbanger's pants—I don't begrudge her that right to choose her form of happiness. Happiness, as Reggie used to say on his way to sinking the 8 ball, was the maximum agreement between reality and desire. The day I signed my divorce papers in his office, I snarled at him from under a murderous hangover and asked him *who the fuck said that.* "Stalin," he grinned. He showed his scratch pad to me; he was doodling wolves. Right there and then, in my office in a boxy room full of nothing but stale Ohio air and the white noise from my computer, I decided that my happiness depended on finding Annaliese. When it's a mission, you just have to go. That is all there is left to do.

• • •

On Monday I found my first lead to Annaliese—just a tickle but a palpable one nonetheless. I reached her Jefferson landlady and from her I obtained the phone number of a high-school classmate. She agreed to meet me at the diner opposite the Courthouse that afternoon. She said she'd bring photos of Annaliese.

There was a thunderstorm moving up from the south and temperatures were dropping fast; someone spoke of a last gasp of winter, and the farmers in the diner where I was waiting for Brenda Holbacher were bemoaning another killer frost just as the shoots were clearing the ground.

She came in, hair in spiky bangs all streaked and moussed, and gold earrings the size of dog collars. A stud in her lip. I was too out of touch to know whether gothic or grunge were still the fashion. She smiled at me, popped her chewing gum, and then sat in a single swift motion.

"I appreciate your coming, Brenda," I started.

Her eyes darkened. "Yeah, whatever."

She smiled big. I detected prettiness the frumpy clothes couldn't belie but the eye make-up must have been ladled on with a spatula. She chewed her gum while I spoke, interrupting me once to shout an order for a cheeseburger at a passing waitress, who was someone she knew well enough to tease about her "muffin tops."

"What's that?" I asked.

"Love handles, man," she said. She needed no warm-up, and I

doubted that there was anything she wanted to hide. Her mannerisms were the fidgety ones of youth rather than deception.

"Brenda, Annaliese's father has hired me to find her and bring her back. If you know where she is, you can save me a lot of trouble and him a lot of expense if you can tell me where she is right now."

"Her old man," she began thoughtfully. "Did Annaliese—did she tell you about him?"

"I know all about it."

"Yeah, uh-huh. Why should I wanna help you find her?"

"Look, Brenda. I could lie to you and tell you that her father is sorry for what happened. But I know that doesn't cut anything. I could say he's dying and wants to leave her all his money and there's a finder's fee in it for you. But the fact is I just want her found. She may be in trouble. Maybe she's OK and wants to be left alone. If that is the case, I'll just verify it and go away without her ever seeing me and then I'll tell her father that she doesn't want to be found."

"Why should I believe you?"

"Because I haven't any reason to hurt her. We both know she's been hurt enough."

"You don't know the half of it."

"Tell me then."

She had told the detective who came to see her three years ago when her father first filed a missing person report on his daughter that Annaliese never returned to the apartment she shared. This was late in May, she said. She herself had been out of town with a boyfriend, a married man who took her to Chautauqua Lake region in western New York. When she returned, there was no Annaliese, no message from her stating where she had gone or anything unusual about her disappearance. As far as Brenda remembered, all Annaliese's clothes were still in the closet. It looked as though she had disappeared with the clothes on her back and nothing else. She turned over to the police all of Annaliese's papers—pay stubs, one letter from her mother, bills, bank statement—the whole kit and caboodle. There was nothing left of Annaliese O'Reilly except three photos she had held back from the police as keepsakes of their friendship.

I asked to see them.

Annaliese was alone in the first two of them. In one she had been caught stepping from the shower. There was the expression of surprise and shock as she inadvertently mimed the classic pose of modesty, one hand to her crotch and the other across her chest. One shell-pink aureole peeked through her fingers and her caramel thatch was evident despite the splayed fingers. In the other photo, she was dressed for work across the street in sedate gray tones—a navy blue ensemble of pleated skirt and white blouse. Her eyes were a warm liquid brown. She smiled with the same smile of the newspaper clipping her father brought to my office.

The third photo was graphic, electric, and pornographic.

She was on her knees performing fellatio; the man's torso disappeared above his belly button; his penis was thick and fully extended—about half of it was in her mouth.

"Well," she said, watching me to see what my reaction would be.

"Well, what?" I asked.

"Thought, like, you'd have something more to say."

"Why, Brenda?"

"Well, you know. Like I thought you'd at least show some curiosity."

"I was a cop in Cleveland before I got into the private investigations. I've had a lot of experience looking behind door number three. That's the one everybody's interested in, right? So tell me about this one."

"You know, I thought that, like, since you were looking for her for that fucking scumbag, that you might reconsider."

"Why?"

"Well, you know. Daddy's little darling on her knees with a big dick in her mouth. Maybe he won't be so eager to have her back now and he'll leave her alone."

"Was the photo taken at the same time as the others?"

"No. The first two are old ones. We were just out of high school. That last one came in the mail, no letter, nothing. Just the photo."

"What did you think?"

"If she meant to shock me, well . . . I had walked in on her once with Marcus. I saw the two of them before. Like that. You know, *engaged.*"

"So you weren't shocked?"

Her face wrinkled a bit. "You mean because she lets her photo be taken? Why should that surprise me? You never heard of sexting?"

The insouciance of youth, I supposed. I was getting too old to relate to anyone who didn't know who Squeaky Fromme was.

"Did Annaliese date any African-Americans?"

"What makes you ask that?"

I knew many cops who saw things on the street that sent them reeling off into blind racism, an easy psychological niche to carve under the compelling circumstances of the street's mindless violence, and it was all *nigger this, nigger that.* It wasn't just a Crip or Blood thing anymore to find a strawberry girl, usually some ADC type with a kid or two, take over her apartment and steal her welfare check. Hatred for another human being nearly destroyed me once. Instead of telling her this, I said: "I had a partner once, a self-educated man and a first-rate cop. When he was teaching me how to be a real cop, he used to quote a philosopher named Spencer who said, 'There is a principle which is a bar against all information, which is proof against all arguments and which cannot fail to keep a person in everlasting ignorance—that principle is contempt prior to investigation.'"

"You are weird, man."

I flipped the photo over and tapped at some writing in block letters. "What's this mean?" BEST FRIENDS. The *e*, however, was drawn like the schwa, a tipped arrow.

She squinted at me, arched eyebrows and bangs. "What's it supposed to mean? I dunno. They're, like, best friends, I guess. Sorta looks like it, eh?"

"Do you still have the envelope the photo came in?"

"Hell no, I tore it up long ago. When she got back from seeing her mother that summer in Philadelphia—"

"Pittsburgh?"

"Whatever. She told me everything about how her mom had an affair with a black guy in Germany and how her father beat the shit out of her when he found out."

"Think hard, Brenda. Where was the postmark on the envelope from?"

"I don't remember."

"You do too. You had to be curious after her skipping off—"

"All right, all right. No—wait, Boston, I think. Yeah, Boston."

"Do you remember the address? Anything at all about the postmark?"

"No, man. It was too long ago, like."

"Do you have any idea where Annaliese might be now?"

"I'm not sure I'd tell you even if I did know."

"Fair enough."

"Listen, you said you don't want to bother her. Well, how do you know she won't be bothered when you show up and tell her that her goddamned father who messed her up wants her to come home, all's forgiven and all that shit?"

"I don't know what she'll think or say until I have a chance to ask her. If she's happy wherever she is, I won't bother her, and all her father will get from me is my word she's safe. I can't promise more than that. I owe her father something too. He is my client."

"He's a piece of shit," Brenda said.

"I don't have to like him," I said.

She stayed silent, looking at me through those raccoon eyes, her thumb and forefinger stretching out a stray spit curl. I thought how much harder it is to have a girl nowadays. We've abandoned them in this hook-up culture.

"If you still have doubts about my intentions," I said, "we'll go our separate ways and no one has to be told anything. You don't know me and you have no reason to trust me, but maybe I can give you proof that I don't intend any harm to her. Is that fair?"

"All right," Brenda said, "but let me warn you. See this purse? I'll keep one hand on my gun, so don't get any stupid ideas."

My hands flew up in mock surrender. "I'm your prisoner until you say I can go."

Damn. Ask any cop: a civilian with a gun is one of the scarier things around, but a girl just out of her teens? I knew many professional women in Cleveland who used to pay their parking fee with one hand and keep their other tightly around the butt of the .25 in their purse. I could see Jack smirking at me from beyond the grave: "*O tempora, O mores . . .*

"Where's your whip at?"

"My what?"

"Your ride, man. Wheels. You know, C-A-R."

"Over there," I said, pointing to my trusty gray steed sandwiched humbly between some lawyer's Escalade and some circuit court judge's Benz.

"That piece of shit? Oh hell."

42

● ● ●

I drove to a place I sometimes visit along the lake shore when I need to clear my head; sometimes the ducks and Canada geese come in to roost and there's a lot to see that has nothing whatsoever to do with the affairs of humankind. I brought a thermos of coffee and two paper cups, but Brenda refused the coffee with a yuck. "I never drink that shit," she said.

"To each his own."

Curlicues of steam in widening gyres drifted above the cup in the chilly air, then dissipated into nothingness.

"What the hell's that supposed to mean?"

"It's just a saying," I said. "It means we pick our own poison."

"I dunno about that," Brenda said. "Know that Annaliese never asked to be raped by her old man. But that wasn't all she *didn't* ask for either."

"What do you mean?"

"I mean her whole life was fucked up. When she was at the Vo-Ed, she used to talk about this older guy she was dating, used to drop big hints about his being a married man, so it wasn't going anywhere."

"Who was the guy?"

"I don't know. She was real secret about him on account of his being married. This was before Marcus. I think she picked Marcus up on the rebound."

"Marcus still around?"

"Jesus, how should I know?"

"What was her relationship with Marcus like?"

"Good enough at first. You know, like most relationships. Then it got crazy with his drugs."

"Marcus, is he a dealer?"

"Why? You think because he's black he's all about the drugs?"

"No, I didn't know he was black till now, I just asked a simple question."

She frowned, remembering. "That whole damned summer before she disappeared was getting crazier by the minute. At first it was just G-Money, I mean Marcus. She brought him home one night from the Down Under. Then it was drugs. Using, I mean. Him and her—well, me too, sometimes, but not like those two. He really had her hooked.

They were doing speedballs, ya know?"

A dangerous roller coaster, that. "What else?"

"He was really possessive. She had to do everything he said. He took her on buys. He used to run with a gang somewhere in LA. He was always talking about the Rolling 20's. He said he quit gangbanging, but who knows? Marcus liked to talk big. Annaliese told me he was just a wannabee."

Just to be sure, I interrupted. "You said he quit the Crips?"

"That's what he said. The drug deals were all his."

Gangs, the modern plague. I had shoveled enough bodies from both sides off the west side of Cleveland streets, but gangbangers rarely quit. *We don't die, we multiply* was familiar graffiti spray-painted on home turf after a gang killing.

"So what happened?"

"Well, she got scared. I mean, we both did. They—"

"Who?"

"Friends of Marcus. They used to come around and take over the apartment. Some of them must have spent all their time in prison if you ever saw them eat, all hunched over their food like snarling dogs. Every time I got up to leave they'd ask me 'where was I going?' 'Why was I dissing them like that?' I mean, it was like I had no right to be there, like they were paying the rent. I said to Tyshawn, that's one of Marcus' homies, 'Man, I ain't seen the color of your money for rent.'"

"What are their names—Marcus' friends?" I brought out my notepad and hoped she wouldn't spook.

She looked blank.

"Brenda, what did Annaliese say about all this? These friends moving in, taking over the place?"

"Oh, at first she was on my side and then—well, it was just Marcus dropping by. Then it was like his friends just followed, took over and we couldn't do nothing about it, ya know."

"Did she have sex with just Marcus or the others too?"

"I don't know for sure, but before she split, I asked her once. She just looked at me funny and, like, sad. There was one called Butt because his ass used to stick out behind him like a shelf. He once made a move on me but I told him I'd rather screw a dog. He had these really cold eyes, and he said *that could be arranged.*"

She shivered. "He was a really, really creepy."

"Why did Annaliese run off?"

"Oh God damn, I don't know. Things were just getting out of hand—the drugs, the whole mess." She smothered her face in her hands for a long moment. "She used to make me so mad for letting people use her all the time. She had no backbone."

"Did Marcus say anything that might lead you to guess where she might have gone?"

"He was furious. Tore the apartment up and called her a no-good bitch."

"How long before Marcus took off?"

"What do you mean?"

"How long after Annaliese disappeared? When did Marcus and his friends stop coming and going—"

"That's the *point*. I told him the cops were gonna come hammering down the door any day. Marcus was constantly at me to get in on his little drug business, always trying to set me up in something he had going on."

"Making buys for him?"

"No, not that. He didn't trust anyone for that. He used to take Annaliese along for—uh, what he used to call 'protective coloring,' she being white and all. I guess he wanted me to try to score illegal drugs over the counter, phony prescriptions or something. He was always talking about big scores. Funny thing is, we never saw any of his money either when it came time to buy food or pay bills. One time he smacked Annaliese across the face when she suggested he spend some of his cash on the food he and his friends used to gobble down—"

"Did he beat her?"

"No, not, like, every day or anything. Except when he was really stoned on something. The pipe would make him crazy, paranoid. Mostly he did it to impress the others. Once he dragged her around the kitchen by her hair. She hadn't said nothing that deserved it either. That bastard Demetrius just about split a gut laughing. Sometimes I actually hated her for letting him beat on her like that."

"Did Marcus do a lot of crack?"

"He used to peddle crack on the Strip. Some bartenders at the Lake used to buy from him."

Heroin and crack were easy to get on the Strip, and any teen could score weed, but last summer meth started to make headway in the shitkicker bars. I knew some of the narco squad, Millimaki's handpicked men, and they were a close-knit group, kept to themselves, drank together. A desk sergeant told me that Millimaki kept them on a leash for selective hits. I had heard the payoff rumors. The drug busts in recent years were all cosmetic raids, something for the paper accompanied by two or three columns of "war against drugs" yak by the publicity team from the station house. Not a serious takedown in years, as far as I could recall.

"Was Annaliese using?"

She hesitated and shivered but whether from the cold wind crossing the lake or the recollection I could not tell.

"I think so. I never saw her shoot heroin, but Marcus turned her on to all kinds of crazy shit. I came home one time and the turpentine fumes were enough to gag a maggot. I even accused her of huffing, but she denied it. God, did I swear at her."

She looked at me then, her eyes assessing me or something deeper.

"Maybe she sent me that photo—"

"What?"

"Maybe it was like her way of saying, see, 'I'm no good. I'm just like you said.'"

Brenda finally took her hand from her purse. She wiped her eyes.

"If you do find her, tell her I'm sorry and I miss her like hell," she said.

I turned the heater on. I could see from the windshield the spot I had walked down a path to the lake's edge with Micah just before the divorce. The sun's dying rays had lit splinters of reddish gold in her hair. I was talking about a dispatcher at the station house whose husband killed her. I had met the guy once in Tico's Place. He seemed like an ordinary guy, and he liked to talk about cars. *A candyapple-red Corvette. You musta seen it cruising the Strip? I built that car from nothing, man. Twenty-four coats of paint alternating with lacquer. You put it under black light, you can see a rose tattoo on the hood . . .*

"I'm beginning to fuckin' freeze here."

"You've been a great help. One more question: Do you have any idea where Annaliese might have gone to from here—let's say, she was desperate to get away from Marcus . . . ?"

"No, I don't. She never spoke of any family except her father's people in Boston. Just the one time."

"You remember why she spoke of them?"

"Damn it, man, does *one* mean the same thing in your language?" I tried on a pout.

"Jesus, stop making that ugly face. What's—why does your eye look funny?"

"I had an accident a few years ago."

"No wonder those drivers were honking at you back there."

Her left hand suddenly reached out to touch the pale starburst of scar tissue on my cheek. I let her.

"You've been around the block, haven't you?"

"Occupational hazards," I said.

My memory is pathetic now, and so I have to write everything down. Years ago some Cleveland attorneys looked shocked when they asked me for my notes on the witness stand and I told them to go ahead and ask their questions because I remembered it all. I have a cloudy recollection of a lot of booze and one particularly bad beating that left my head a damaged box of memories.

"Listen, Brenda, you said a moment ago that Annaliese spoke of her father's family. What about it?"

She sighed. "One more last question? She was talking about her mom and said that her mother and father had lived in Boston when they came from Germany and she said her grandmother had a beautiful porcelain doll collection that her mother raved about for years. Annaliese was drying her hair. We were on our way out to a club and she was toweling her head." She touched her own ginger hair with the spiky black tips.

"Let me buy you a drink and take you home."

"Just home." She looked at me in a hard stare. "When I start dating one-eyed weirdos, I'll be sure to give you a buzz."

I gave her my business card when I dropped her off. What had been a rosy spring mackerel sky a moment ago had changed to pewter masses of scud in shapes of torn, dirty rags. I whipped down Ninevah and turned right on Erieview and almost fishtailed an oncoming Tundra. The driver's eyes were big as we passed. Why name a car for a fiercely cold and treeless biome, I wondered.

I glimpsed the lake between the trees just now filling out in frozen meringue light. *An omen*, I thought. What I couldn't fathom was whether it was for good or ill. Sometimes I'll even check out the loopy scrawl of gull shit on the side of my car for secret messages.

One thing was writ large on my future itinerary: Boston.

I called Phil at the station house and jerked his chain to see what the computer had on this Marcus ("G-Money") Gordon and his friends. I read Phil the names and gave him two of the street aliases Brenda had mentioned in case the department cross-referenced. I told Phil to leave me a message with my answering service. I could use Phil to check out what NCIC had, if any of these characters had a rap sheet. Phil owed me for a big favor years back, and being the wily veteran of station house politics he was, I knew he could cover himself in case Millimaki got wind of anything. Cops are a fraternity like the priesthood, but once you leave it, you're just a civilian. A private eye, ex-cop or no, is maybe higher than a civvie but not so high they'll take a bullet for you.

I still had a lot of phone calls to make to people I didn't know. I needed to see O'Reilly to get some things cleared up in Annaliese's messy past. In homicide you have two methods of investigation, a I knew some good detectives who liked to run full steam down one trail and hope it brought them to the perp; the reasoning is a *blitzkrieg* can get you from A to Z very fast while the trail is hot. It's like hollering at three suspects in three different interrogation rooms and hoping one cracks. You can always apologize to the other two. Without a detective's caseload to pressure me, I can take my time and finesse things a little.

I had one more loose thread to tie off. I was casting as wide a net as possible using Annaliese's social security number, and one more odd fact of her young life emerged: she had been a uniformly indifferent student all through elementary and high school—straight B's and C's. With one exception: she received two A's from the same social sciences teacher in her senior year at the high school. What made the grades stand out even more was that she was completing her Vo-Ed training and was never destined for college. Her social science courses were strictly electives. I called the high school and spoke to the principal, an ex-jock who, like so many in the profession, found in education a warm wing to crawl under and the right social clubs to join. He told me what he knew and then he gave me the name of his predecessor, a man whose contract had not been renewed by the school board. He was reluctant to speak about Lawrence Gallatine, but he mentioned that the firing was over a "private confrontation" that wound up embarrassing the school when it became public.

• • •

Lawrence Gallatine lived two miles south of Andover on Route 7 in a two-storey ranch house surrounded by what looked to be fruit orchards, maybe grapes and raspberries.

When I left a message earlier about meeting him, he came on the line in the middle of it, and agreed with some reluctance to meet at his house that evening.

A tall man with sable chin whiskers in a charcoal suit greeted me at the door. He wore leather sandals and held a copy of the *London Times* in his hand. I was introduced to his wife and three of his children; two more were away at college and two more were at a Christian camp, he told me. The rooms had religious pictures and sacred statuary on every table and wall. I saw the flaxen-haired, blue-eyed Jesus staring at me from the dining room. Another one of Jesus on his knees, praying in the Garden of Gethsemane. Bullets of blood dotting his forehead as the hour draws nigh and the soldiers are about to come.

He was in his mid-forties. His hair had gone salt and pepper. He looked fit. He had a way of clipping off his words sharply that implied a businessman's sense of time's value. He had expressed a concern for assisting my investigation over the phone, but now I sensed my presence was an intrusion.

"Mister Gallatine, can you tell me why Annaliese received A's from your classes?"

"She was an excellent student."

"It's a long time ago. Do you recall all your students' grades that fast?"

"The good ones, yes."

"Did you know that you are the only instructor she's ever had that gave her a grade higher than a B?"

"She received A's from me because she deserved them. Simply put, she was an excellent student. Wrote one of the finest amateur papers I've ever had from a student her age."

"Do you remember what the subject was?"

49

"The psychology of incest, I believe."

"Mister Gallatine, they told me at the high school that you filed a suit against them with the American Civil Liberties Union for—" (I had my thumb on the page in my notebook for reference) "—uh, yes, here it is. For discrimination against you and denial of due process. Why 'discrimination?'"

"Someone attacked my ethnic background. I was born in Germany and came to the United States at the age of seven. My father was a distinguished professor at Goethe University." His facial muscles moved with what I took to be repugnance or irritation. "I thought you were here to ask about Annaliese O'Reilly, Mister Haftmann? I see no reason why this matter has anything to do with your investigation." His wife and children had discreetly disappeared. I heard a television going in the den.

"Humor me, Mister Gallatine. Old cop habit. Is there something about that lawsuit that you can tell me?"

"It's public record. I can tell you that I won that lawsuit and there was an out-of-court settlement. The school failed to prove there was a single witness with first-hand knowledge of misconduct and that they had unfairly tried to dismiss me."

If I'd had the advantage of an interrogation room and plenty of time, I could crack that smug demeanor, but not in his home.

"Wait," he said. "I'll show you something."

He left and returned a minute later with an accordion file folder; he handed it to me; inside were documents—legal papers, mostly, and newspaper clippings.

I skimmed through the pile. At the end there was an agreement and release form containing itemized statements, the result of which was that both parties agreed to drop their suits. The clipping from the *Plain Dealer* quoted Gallatine as victor in the arbitration dispute: "'No employee anywhere should ever be subjected to the gross violations of due process as I have been. They have an essentially bone-chilling effect at an educational institution.'"

I wanted to slap the sanctimonious look off his face; instead, I stuffed the papers back into the file and handed it to him with a smile.

"I hope that this modest victory will help protect area educators and other employees from abuse, intimidation and rumors designed to silence or destroy them," Gallatine said. It was a line he must have repeated often since his case.

"What happened, Mister Gallatine? Were you threatened?"

"Yes. I had the evidence and gave it to the police who turned over three notes—clearly actionable in their tone and language—that I had received from this disturbed individual but the city solicitor's office refused to prosecute. Instead, *they* attempted to dismiss me from my job."

"May I see the notes?"

"I don't see what this has to do with Annaliese's disappearance, but all right."

He left once more. I looked around the room. It was as middle class and bourgeois as any other. I stared out the front picture window. A chickadee landed on the porch rail and cocked its head from side to side. The black-and-white swirl pattern of its head made me think of a story about a sailor on an expedition in the North Pole. He was out on the ice peering down between his legs at a black speck. The speck grew larger. Before anyone else got there, the ice exploded where he was standing. A killer whale had mistaken him for a seal.

Gallatine returned with his notes and handed them to me. They weren't much. Handwritten penciled notes requested a private meeting with Gallatine at a time and specific place. Gallatine was saluted by various obscene names. In the third note, the writer had apparently lost control and demanded a private meeting where they wouldn't be "disturbed." I had to laugh: academics in fisticuffs—isn't that an oxymoron, or whatever they call it? A puff of air would knock most of them down. It smelled like an academic teapot tempest to me, which is about as violent as a stoning by popcorn.

"Before you decided to make the notes public, did you go see this person?"

He looked at me as if I had just arrived from Mars with a balloon-blowing goat. "I faxed the police, the school board, the newspapers, and the state board of regents. I was given an unsatisfactory apology. I hired a bodyguard for the remainder of the semester."

"So you sued. Did this individual threaten you?"

"He accosted me in the hallway after my class one afternoon and demanded a private meeting with me. I told him to get a grip on it."

"He lost his job, didn't he? So did the principal. They told me that you—"

"Who is this 'they, you keep referring to?"

"The principal."

"A liar and a fool."

"Also the individual you took to court. He said he only wanted to meet with you privately to straighten out a few things about your actions toward the rest of the faculty."

"A time bomb waiting to go off," Gallatine sniffed.

"He said you created . . . 'an intimidating and menacing atmosphere' that had people frightened of you."

He stood up. "Are you here to accuse me of something? I thought you were here to seek my aid?"

I played another long shot: "He said Annaliese O'Reilly was one of those things he intended to straighten you out on."

"You're a liar, and not a good one. Is that what they teach you in private-eye school?"

"Who's 'they,' Mister Gallatine?" He favored me with a thin-lipped smile that would look well on a cobra.

"My concern with him had nothing to do with Annaliese."

"Then what *did* have to do with Annaliese, Mister Gallatine?"

"Nothing, as I told you. I was her teacher. She was an excellent student, as I said, and that's the end of it."

Brenda told me Annaliese had picked Marcus up on the rebound. What did I have to lose?

"Did you sleep with her?"

"You—Get out of my house!"

"One more question. You were dismissed from a high school in Pennsylvania before you came to Ohio. You sued them too. They settled. You seem to have a pattern of suing and collecting, don't you, Mister Gallatine?"

No disguising those little facial tics and muscle movements in the human face. Better than a trio of polygraph experts. The skin around his eyes and his jaws tightened, and his dark eyebrow humped over the bridge of his nose.

"Get out! Get out of my house!"

He didn't move from the sofa. "Get out or I'll call the police!"

I folded up my notepad and tucked it inside my sport coat. "I know a guy like you. A little con named Artiss Clay. Could sweet-talk the birds from the trees. Knew how to use the system. It's almost socially acceptable to steal money with a lawyer. Some jamoke tries it with a gun and we give him eight years in a hellhole like Lucasville. Unless he's big enough to keep the predators from reaming his ass inside out or putting a shiv in his guts, he might live to do his sentence. Artiss wasn't big enough. They threw a blanket party for him his first night in the joint."

This time he hissed like a basket of snakes. "Artiss—who is Artiss—? I said—"

"Inground pool, twenty acres from I what I can see, probably a redwood sauna out back, two-and-a-half car garage. Nice digs for a teacher's salary."

"I'll get your investigator's license revoked. You make one statement to anyone and I'll sue you for slander."

He almost scissor-walked across the room to the phone.

I couldn't resist firing off what Micah used to call my Parthian shot. "When I was a kid growing up around here, I went to a Catholic school. My grandmother was from Germany. She'd been raped like every woman in Berlin. In the sixth grade, I was beat up by the Mc-Goneghal twins for having a dumb 'Adolph Hitler face.' The stupid clowns punched me silly on the playground and called me 'a Nazi kike.' Imagine that? I lifted weights and learned to fight back, but the lesson I learned was no one cares. No one ever stopped them, not my classmates, not the teachers. Their old man was a big shot—church donor, social clubs like the Ancient Order of Hibernians, all that kind of thing. Bullies never change."

I was almost out the door when he put his hand on my shoulder. It was what I hoped for.

I placed my hand over his, turned and had his thumb in a come-along.

"Aaaah, get your hands off me, you psychopath!"

"All I want to know, fucker, is why you slept with a child." I said it very close to his face.

"I'll—I'll sue you—"

I drew him a little closer to my face. "If I can prove you had sex with Annaliese O'Reilly, who was a minor at that time, I'll call in every favor I've made in twenty years as a cop and see to it you do a stretch in a real jail."

I was seething spittle in the corners of my mouth, a real sign I was losing it. I realized that his wife was standing close by. I could feel her presence near my bad-eye side.

"Let him go. He slept with her. Let him go."

Gallatine blanched, his eyes like cue balls, staring at his wife, then me, and then her. He was in shock, his world turned upside down like that sailor on the polar ice.

She looked at him and I could see pity and hate in her eyes.

"Did you think I wouldn't find those pathetic love notes from that foolish, love-starved schoolgirl that you were carrying around in your briefcase like trophies?"

Gallatine dropped to his knees. I made my exit, but neither one watched me leave. Their two children had come in from the other room and were standing there looking at their parents in that uncomprehending way children do when confronted with life's terror. The tableau from a TV family sit-com was gone like smoke. I closed the door on the wreckage behind me as gently as I could.

● ● ●

On the ride back, I noticed the fluorescent green of the leaves beginning to take hold in the woods far back from the road; lilac bushes and dogwood were in bloom. The air was redolent of smells in the drizzle, noisy with the chirruping of insects and the scree-caw of red-winged blackbirds among the cattails; starlings roosted on the wires above, perhaps soothed by the hum, utterly oblivious to hundreds of thousands of volts humming beneath their warm bodies. I needed my headlights by the time I arrived back home, and as I pulled into my driveway, I caught my own tulip tree in full bloom. There was a message from Phil on my answering machine. Marcus and his doper friends were clean, no rap sheets or priors, just a couple FI's, Field Interviews, which could mean something or nothing. A gang intelligence cop in Cleveland used to call FIs a semi-legal excuse to get to know who's banging—stopped for "mopery with intention to gawk," although he'd write it in cop jargon in his reports.

I'd have to check them out later. I walked into the kitchen and made a cup of tea. Micah's eyes turned that sienna color whenever she was aroused or angry. In the days leading to the divorce, that tea-color was reflected back at me in angry outbursts over nothing, which I now realized was her own way of deflecting her self-disgust at her betrayal. Blame the victim.

It surprised me that I had not noticed spring's arrival before this. My grass would need cutting in a week. Spring is the season of death, not autumn. Ask any cop: the statistics on suicide jumps exponentially. It's simple. If you reason from the suicide's point of view, the whole world is renewing. It's just you that's not. Whenever I get the urge to stop doing the backstroke in the toilet bowl, I think about the universe—all that emptiness and blackness out there, all the galaxies roaring away or colliding with one another, stars a million times bigger than our sun imploding into black holes. I imagine billions of comets with ice hurtling through space, maybe destined to crash on another planet to bring that precious substance that exists between gas and matter, water that is so rare because its molecules slide over one another. I figure it this way: we're just dust anyway. Why do anybody a favor? Call me a sentimental existentialist.

I did some further checking on Lawrence Gallatine, and I found some strange bedfellows in his past. He had gone to work for one of the most corrupt politicians in Cleveland, a man who might have become Attorney General if a scandal involving mortgage fraud hadn't come to light. Gallatine had, it seemed, political ambitions of his own, and some of his biggest donors were either front men for some very conservative causes—and I mean to the right of Attila the Hun—or they were impossible to winkle out of hiding. I got lost in a maze of front organizations and banal acronyms that hinted at "family values" and other kinds of neoconservative affiliations with various right-wing groups in Ohio. I crosschecked a few of these and found some names in common with shifty organizations Hate Watch liked to keep track of. Behind the political dollars he raked in, he seemed to have a finger in some strange pies that were not exactly off the charts but weren't the sort I would cast him as a spokesperson for. The image he presented didn't fit. In the past he did some propaganda writing for a few of these Second-Amendment rights and Michigan militia groups. Gallatine was a man more than the sum of his parts and none of the parts added up to a profile. Family man, educator, political aspirant, right-wing proselytizer, born-again Christian, and finally, most confusing of all, older lover of a biracial girl. Who was Lawrence Gallatine? I had known men like him who had gone fishing in strange waters; sometimes they came up with a thing best left in the murk.

Chapter 3

Before I left for my redeye flight from Cleveland-Hopkins to Logan, I called on O'Reilly at his office on Bridge Street in Jefferson. Jefferson is the county seat; it's where Micah worked and where she found her lawyer. It's quaint, small-town, mind-numbing, and full of secrets. Most of the professionals work for the government in one capacity or another. Backroom deals and political fixes are made here. A couple years back, a nasty scandal broke out when one of the country club wives and a pediatrician decided to run off together. They belonged to a suburban "key club," wife-swappers, in other words and the resulting divorces were messy. Two of the children from each side, teenagers, were collateral damage. The boy OD'd before his senior year at Jefferson High, and the girl ran all the way to Florida and got herself involved in some big trouble. I remember it well because I extricated her from that mess and I took a beating from a couple hard guys for my trouble. They claimed she was working off a debt for them.

John O'Reilly, middle name Hugh, father of a missing daughter and my client, was dulling his pain in the middle of the afternoon with expensive whiskey when I found him. I drove to his furniture factory located some miles from the Courthouse where my friend the judge presides. It's part-rural, part industrialized in the northeastern section. Many Amish live and farm here. Some of the more liberal sects work in Gallatine's factory. He was one of the lucky ones. He makes blonde wood furniture that has a gimmick to it: everything fits together with pegs rather than nails. Somebody from the Department of Defense thought that was a nifty idea and John O'Reilly woke up one day to a small but tidy fortune in a no-bid contract to sell furniture—including tent poles—to our armed forces in Saudi Arabia. There are a lot of soldiers over there who need chairs and tables to go inside those air-conditioned tents. He still pays minimum wage to his workers.

He was slumped in front of a bottle of Glenlivet, disheveled, yo-yoing between maudlin self-pity and black-humored nastiness. The worst kind of drunk.

It was ten o'clock at night and I had given up waiting for him to return my call. I found him at his business, alone, drunk behind a walnut desk, his face bleached white behind the glare of a banker's lamp. He looked up at me.

"You lousy cockshuck—cocksucker, Haftmann."

"Why do you say that, O'Reilly?"

"You just discovered who's payin' your fuckin' bill, Mister Private Eye? Little more resh-respect is what's needed around here, by God."

He pinched off a smidgeon between thumb and forefinger to show me how much was needed. "Ain't takin' no shit offa you—anybody. Alla you, all you fuckers."

I reached for the bottle and gently put it out of his reach with a sideways motion.

"How's about I ask you a few questions—"

"Questions, questions, questions. How's about you kiss my big wide Irish ass?"

"That's not a nice thing to say," I replied.

"No, no. No more questions! I'm all outa answers for your questions, Mister Big-Shot Detective. You find Annaliese!" Trying to straighten up in his chair, he almost went ass over teacup.

"I'm trying," I said. I looked at my watch.

"Oh, you got an appointment to run off to, huh? Mister Big Spender. On my money no less, you . . ."

"I can return your money to you right now," I said. I reached inside my jacket as if to extract my checkbook, safely tucked in a drawer at my house.

"Wait a minute, you. All I'm sayin' is, I'm not paying you to ask all these goddamned questions."

"I want you to agree to something first."

"Oh fuck me. What is it?"

I pushed a folded sheet of paper over to him and watched him attempt to read it. He was long past the point of no return, however. I watched him scrunch up his face but his neocortex would no more handle English than Martian at that point in his inebriation.

"Whassiss?"

"It's a contract. It says that if I locate her, and if she's willing to return to Ohio, she's to be given a living allowance from you which include rental payment and a monthly stipend regardless of whatever income she makes on her own. There is to be no unsupervised contact between you except at her discretion."

"Fuuuck you, Haftmann. Who do you think—" Whitened spittle collected in the corners of his mouth.

"Sign it, O'Reilly."

"No fucking way, asshole."

"Then our business is finished," I said.

He gathered himself in a parody of an opera star collecting wind for a long heroic passage—in O'Reilly's case, I assumed a rendition of what I had just heard. So I reached over his desk and clamped my hand over his mouth.

His eyes bulged in pure fury, and he attempted to rise. His own hands flew to his face to tear away my hand but I stiffened my arm and squeezed it tighter. Panicked, airless, he attempted to rise from his chair, but I used my leverage to shove him down, not easy because of the damned swivel chair. He thrashed about until I rammed him backwards against the wall and then pinned him with a knee to his chest.

Finally, I eased my grip. I said, "If I take away my hand, will you be reasonable?"

He nodded for yes.

I eased my hand away but balled it in front of his face for emphasis.

"You cocksuck—"

Whap. I backhanded him across the meat of his cheek. The sound was more significant than the blow. I did it again. *Whaaaaap,* a real bell-ringer this time, and it made the impression I hoped for.

He was stunned, jowly flesh aquiver, but unhurt, appalled that he had been hit by an inferior, his own employee, no less. I don't know what got into me. He brought out the Neanderthal in me.

While he rubbed at the red striations on his face, I repeated: "Sign it now, please, or our business is through and you can hire someone else for the job." In truth, I was hoping he would. Any sober man would have and done it while phoning the police to press charges.

He spluttered, his voice rising in tremolo notes to the top of the range. Then he said: "You psychopath! You're damned right I'll get another private investigator, you dime-a-dozen, flatfoot."

I complimented him on his articulateness. It was a relief after so much mushy-voweled drunken bullying.

"You're going to prison for assault and battery, you cheap

shamus . . ."

I said, "You civilians will never learn the difference between simple assault and assault and battery. Oh well. Have it your way, O'Reilly, but I want you to know something. I'm the only one who can help you find her."

"You listen to me, fuckface. I made three and half million dollars last year!"

"Congratulations. You can afford me now," I said.

"How much did you make, gumshoe? Huh? How mush—much?"

He was trying to stand up but only succeeded in knocking over a pile of papers from his desk. "You don't make money, you low-rent nobody. I can buy and sell you twenty times over!"

He started to come at me but he zig-zagged like a man trying to stand up in a bass boat in choppy seas. He cocked his fist and drew it behind his ear telegraphing it all the way from San Francisco. His entire body led by his fist hurtled past me. I barely moved four inches to elude the whole package and he crashed into a small table—one of his factory samples probably—and wound up on the floor.

I watched him try to get up. There was blood coming out his nose and he wiped a smear of it across his face. He looked at his hand and sat crosslegged on the floor and grunted—or laughed. I'm not sure which.

"Are you done, Mister O'Reilly, because I have a flight to Boston to catch, and I need to know whether you're going to authorize me to be on it."

He blinked at me a couple times and I thought he was about to blow up in another rage. Instead, he crooked an index finger and made one of those come-hither gestures. I brought the paper to him and he signed it without reading any of it still sitting on the floor. A couple drops of ruby-red blood hit the paper while he was signing it. His signature was illegible, a drunken flourish, but I guessed it would stand up in court if it ever came to that. O'Reilly wasn't the first rich prick I've dealt with in my career. I brought a sixteen-year-old daughter back to a mansion in Columbus once and waited while the father's lawyer did a line-by-line scrutiny of my listed expenses. I don't pad bills. I got tired of explaining everything in detail and agreed to reduce the bill by a third. I'll never forget the father's smirk as I was leaving.

"Thank you, Mister O'Reilly," I said. "I'll call you from Boston."

"Go to hell," he said.

His secretary came in from the outer office and looked at her boss sitting there with blood leaking out of his nose.

"It's all right, Mary," he said. "Contracts with the devil have to be signed in blood. Cut him a company check for fifteen hundred."

She stood rooted to the spot cutting her eyes between O'Reilly and me. A look of terror on her face.

"Haftmann," he said, weary resignation in his voice, "find her."

I left him sitting there with whatever shred of dignity a man could have under those circumstances.

• • •

My detective years were not misspent. There's something every homicide officer learns fast: how to hustle a sale past an unwary customer. When you get a suspect in an interrogation room, you have to tell him his rights. The big one is Miranda, of course: the right against self-incrimination. The art of interrogation requires you to sell yourself to the suspect despite the fact that everything he says is going to be used against him. Unless a suspect is completely braindead, he shouldn't open his mouth to a detective—ever. Because a detective is selling one thing—jail. Nobody gives a rat's ass about the victim at this point; you show the suspect that you are in total control and he controls nothing. You tell him the vic he knifed or shot or bludgeoned must have had it coming. Did he sodomize that young girl and leave her bleeding on the highway or in some deserted shithole to die? 'Oh well, we all like to go up the old dirt chute once in a while.' You hold your stomach in, but you tell him anything to get him talking, which is to say, confessing. Nothing else matters. Miranda stopped the brutality of the interrogation room. That's all. After the Mirandizing, you just glide right past that old waiving rights and having an attorney present as smoothly as you can. This is the one thing the lawyer in Reg could never understand whenever we got to knocking back a few on the Strip. "I actually have to tell these idiot clients of mine not to open their mouths to you guys." He'd shake his head and mumble something like, "I'll never understand why they do it." I'd bug him by giving him my most soulful father confessor look, which would usually irritate him more: "Haftmann, the day your face inspires anybody to confess is the day the pigs eat my brother."

I was lucky. I'll admit it. A belligerent drunk like O'Reilly could have had me jugged for assault. Jack, an ex-jarhead who did two hitches in the Marines and fought at the Chosin Reservoir in Korea, had another saying he'd apply to dicey situations for a cop in East Cleveland, "If you kick a tiger in the ass, make sure you have a plan for his teeth."

It's a rule of mine never to push all my chips on the table just to see what happens, yet in the span of a single day in one man's house and another man's office, my own client no less, I had risked my license with two men who clearly didn't have much affection for me. Trouble is, I had too many years' experience interrogating street-wise shitbirds, normally incapable of firing two brain cells in sequence unless it concerned their own illegal profit, not to mention the assorted human debris of America's streets today: the homeless, the distressed, the witless, the violent, the doped up and the out-and-out deranged. All this hopeless human scrap vomited up from an urban hellhole blunted, if I may say so, what used to be a fine precision in my interrogation skills. I could play a street thug like a harp, but I lost my touch with regular people. Micah always said I'd go too far someday and I'd be ringing up one of those lawyers I despised. I wondered if Reg would recuse himself if he saw me standing in front of him at an arraignment hearing.

O'Reilly had started me on a snipe hunt with his crappy poem. Too much time had passed. For some reason, maybe I didn't know myself, I wanted this girl found, and I wanted it to be my case. I had myself convinced that I had a really good shot at bringing her home.

Call it luck but I had his signature on my contract now. Binding or not, I wanted to rub his nose in it and make him understand that there was no forgiveness. He made a young girl suffer; she was his responsibility, her flesh his to protect, and he squandered a priceless gift. I had to think about this because I was stuck in traffic on Dead Man's Curve for an hour. The entire Memorial Shoreway back to the MLK turnoff was one long stream of cars. My Tom-Tom informed me there was an eighteen-wheeler that didn't negotiate the 35 m.p.h. curve in the slick drizzle coming off the lake and spilled a cargo of frozen turkeys all over the highway. I thought of O'Reilly as I last saw him on the floor, past the blubbering, teary-eyed whiskey stage I had found him in and locked into some cold place where the truth was staring back at him.

Tough tittie, I thought. Every good existentialist has to learn to shore up a fragment against life's ruins.

With a name and an address in my notepad tucked into a pocket, O'Reilly's deposit converted to some badly needed traveler's checks, to Boston I was going. My case was finally kicked into gear.

Why, then, if I had exactly what I wanted, was there a taste of ashes in my mouth?

● ● ●

I hate Boston in April. Boston can't live up to its promise. Some things I do like: certain piano bars on Fisherman's Wharf, the smell of pizza in the late afternoon off the esplanade near Copley Square. I like the déjà vu feeling from meeting a glut of Kevins or Seans and Bridget Colleens in a city of indomitable Irishry. When it's winter or summer, though, everyone seems hell-bent on ramming ebullience down your throat or ripping all the silver linings out of every cloud. Maybe it's the soggy wind, an Atlantic Santa Ana, off Boston Harbor that causes the compass of my temperament to yaw from serenity toward prickly sensitivity. Changeable people, changeable weather. Too many false springs before the temperature soars and the humidity drowns you in prickly sweat. Apparently my existentialist angst is triggered by fluctuations in barometric pressure in the way some people react to lack of sunlight. Boston is practically an island.

Another reason I don't like Boston is that it's a prevision of the end of America, the cultural sink that, like a black hole, is going to suck down everything east of the Rockies into its hungry maw. LA is that other cultural sinkhole, a noisy smug capital of the Fourth World that'll take care of whatever's left. Boston is a seething rat cage where the rats are never at rest. I add to my catalog of dislikes the cutthroat traffic east and west of the HoneyFitz Expressway all the way to Charlesbank Playground. Toss in Beacon Hill snobbery, Harvard ("I-smell-excrement") elitism, the Kennedys and their toadies and you'll understand why nothing good has ever happened to me in Boston.

Two years ago I was in Boston for a convention to check out the latest in eavesdropping gadgetry and yawn-inspiring lectures at the Westin on Forensic Accounting as an Investigative Tool, when I witnessed two teen males meeting on a street corner. Like rival baboons, they were from different worlds. One was a street punk, all black clothes and unlaced high tops; the other a prep-school type with clean-cut, razor-creased trousers and a gray blazer with some logo that bore a creepy resemblance to the SS's lightning runes. They were enemies, leaders of their gangs, but they shook hands and ended whatever rivalry their two misfit groups had in the middle of a windswept Boston afternoon. The rich kid and the urban punk: friends, allies. The top and bottom of society combining forces at last—and why not? In the language of political correctness, both are equally morally challenged.

Normally in cities on cases I like to take a room in some downtown flophouse. I felt like sticking it to O'Reilly so I drove my rental SUV straight to the Marriott. I was in Boston less than an hour before I learned that Annaliese was somewhere in the city. I phoned the number O'Reilly had given me for his father, and I got the old man on the tenth ring. It took awhile to sell myself to the old man, but he eventually gave me permission to drop by. He and his wife lived in Roxbury which, if the sky weren't shrouded in a pewter drizzle blowing in from the Atlantic, I might have been able to see from my room on the twelfth floor of the Marriott.

The father, like most second-generation Irish-Americans, measured success in smaller increments than his children. He had gotten from East Boston to Roxbury, just ahead of the hordes of blacks and Hispanics, a crosstown trek that took him a lifetime of making furniture for others. The house was a yellow Cape Cod on Kendall.

O'Reilly's secretary told me to look for a park and a high school. The old man had glasses with tape over the bridge, wore red suspenders and a starched white shirt. He had a washed-out look and deep lines at each corner of his mouth that made him look like a giant marionette. The house was too warm and a faint urine smell wafted about. After we settled ourselves a bit, dispensed with the watery coffee, I asked him point blank:

"Mister O'Reilly, your son wants me to find Annaliese. Can you tell me where she is?"

"I don't know where she is. I haven't seen her in a year, maybe a year and a half."

The tone of his voice was emphatic. He wanted to get something said, so I asked him, "Was everything all right between you and your granddaughter?"

"She isn't my granddaughter."

"I understand that."

"My son was betrayed by his wife. There was no marriage. Not a real marriage based on love and trust in the eyes of God."

God's eyes. Oh shit, here we go.

"God can use a pair of glasses then, Mister O'Reilly, because I saw your son's wife not too long ago, and it seems to me she is the one who ought to feel betrayed."

His face darkened. Like father, like son. "That hoor betrayed my son."

"Do you know where Annaliese is right now?"

"No. And I don't care where she is, if you want the truth. She and her *boyfriend.*" He spat out the word.

"Boyfriend?"

"Yes, a darkie sonofabitch. Blacker than Toby's ass, this *moolie*, and she brings him into my own house."

Blacks and whites are the worst at identifying someone from the other race. "What was his name?"

"I dunno. Just a damn nigger."

I could hear the *click-clack* of something approaching from the kitchen. His wife was pushing a walker in front of her, huffing in at a snail's pace, and began giving him hell for his language, but all that did was prompt a vein to throb in the center of his forehead. He sent a volley of obscenity her way that silenced her. I watched her plant the walker in front of her and shift her large body to it and then do it twice more until she was able to walk back in the direction she had come from, a slow-motion parody of a three-corner turn. Neither the old man nor I said anything as she made her slow way stiffly and noisily back to the kitchen.

Then, as if electrocuted, his head snapped back to me on a stick of neck so fast it made a lock of his thin white hair flutter on the top of his head.

"I don't know where she is, and I don't give two fucks."

Micah made me read Dante's *Inferno* in the early years of our marriage when she thought there was hope for my education. I remember laughing at some of the punishments meted out in a few circles like the ones pelted in a burning rain or buried under the ice looking up at the hordes of passing souls overhead. Some with their heads on backwards or buried upside down so their feet stick up. The ones entombed in excrement actually made me laugh out loud in bed and Micah gave me an elbow in my ribs for disrespecting a classic—or some such nonsense. But I always thought Dante might have made a good homicide investigator; after all, he knew the black hearts of people just like me. On my way out the door of the House of O'Reilly, I wondered where the old man would best spend eternity if Dante got to make the call.

• • •

You always hope it's going to be easy. It never is. I gave myself one week before I had to get back to Jefferson-on-the-Lake and salvage what little summer business I could count on. My cell phone rolled over my office calls and so far nothing but a few telemarketers, a bank manager wanting "urgently to meet over my mortgage default" and a couple possible clients. One caller wanted me to find his daughter's missing pooch, which should tell you something about the state of my financial affairs because I actually thought of calling him back.

I spent two days on the phone in my hotel room calling employment bureaus, real estate offices, and clinics, and I must have spoken to dozens of young women with receptionists' voices. I was claiming to be the father of Annaliese O'Reilly and said I was "hoping to pay some of that rascal's overdue bills, ha-ha." Sensing a sympathetic ear now and then, I would spiel on about "my daughter, that girl, ha-ha, being a little bubblehead with money, you know . . . "

Some went into their databases for me but none came up with a single female named Annaliese.

All I did was rack up zeroes; she never checked into Boston State Hospital or any other in the metro area, no ER's anywhere in the last 90 days, or had ever scheduled a pelvic exam, or used a dentist's services. I planned to widen the arc a little tomorrow with the same routine to cover those places in South and East Boston. State detox centers were on my list too, but I had no story good enough to get past HIPPA.

Just then, however, I needed an hour in the weight room to take out the kinks, get a massage, shower, dinner downstairs, before hitting the streets. Between 7:00 p.m. and the early hours of the morning, I planned to check out the nudie bars in the Combat Zone. It would figure Annaliese might be working a job similar to the one she held at the Jefferson Courthouse, but my intuition, and maybe Brenda's photo too, was telling me otherwise: attractive young girls, footloose in the big city, often wind up in places like Detroit's Cass Corridor or Boston's Combat Zone. Two or three years in that steaming sewer is about average; few of them survive the drugs, booze, beatings from their pimps, run-ins with the cops. I've chalked their bodies in rowhouses all over Cleveland's west side. One year in Cleveland we had eleven of them, all strawberry girls, dead in vacant lots, alleys, and crack houses. All between 15- and 35-years-old. Skirts hiked up, most pantyless, no wounds, ligature marks, or petechiae—the pinprick bleeding in the whites of the eyeballs, a sign of manual strangulation. Every one of them posted and coming back with cocaine in the bloodstream, semen in body orifices. The crime beat writer for the *Plain Dealer* speculated a serial killer. A cardiologist was quoted on cocaine-induced heart attacks and the possibility of death from the simple exertion of sex for sale as if their young, worn-out bodies would simply cave in. The death certificates usually said heart attack or "insult to the brain" but nobody ever solved these cases and they're all by now transferred to the Justice Center quietly sitting on shelves and forgotten by everybody.

When I got back from my bar-hopping rounds, swathed in a neon mist of icy drizzle, I returned empty-handed and bloated from a dozen soda waters with twists of lemon or lime, throat-sore from talking to braindead slugs, bouncers, and bartenders—anybody I could get to look at her photo.

I took a shower to wash off the sleaze and stink. I ordered a soft-core porn film and lay on the bed reviewing what few notes I scribbled from these itinerant conversations. Nothing stood out. My mind drifted away from Annaliese and her father and grandfather. What's a dysfunctional family today anyhow? How would life, even a shabby, unproductive one like mine, mean anything? I watched the sexual mimicry on the HD screen with its indifferent coupling, the sound track off by a split-second. They would alternate moans in time to the thrusting. I hit the mute button, tossed my notepad onto the night table, and took out a deck of cards for a game of solitaire. After a while I knew I was going to win, but it didn't mean anything more than the pair simulating sex on the TV. I went into the bathroom to urinate for the third time, wondering if my prostate was swollen or if I ought to switch to something else to drink while I'm showing photos and buying rounds for deadbeats. Liver, kidneys, pancreas—I had hurt them all in some scrap or dustup over the years. Payback time.

The porn film had ended when I returned to the bed, so I flipped to a movie channel and settled on *Schindler's List*. It was at the part where Eamon, the Krakow commandant, had been shooting some Jews from his balcony with a high-powered rifle and scope. His fish-belly-white skin glowed sickly in the dawn light. His stomach sagged over his pants and the rifle was rested across his back with one hand dangling from the butt and the other from the barrel. From behind, he looked like a dissipated Christ. The camera took the scope's eye-view for the next sequence and it followed some inmates at their tasks about the work camp; then it settled on a woman who was hunched on the steps of a barracks. Her brains were blown out of her head and she jerked backward. It bothered me that her head, like Kennedy's, did not snap reflexively in the direction of the shot. The muzzle power of a rifle slug cleaving through the meat of a brain inside a packed skull leaves no room to expand. Spielberg should have spent a few bucks on a technical advisor.

I turned off the set. I opened all the drapes and looked out over as much of the city below as I could see. The wind was trying to pop the rivets out of the Marriott. I stretched out on the bed and felt the ache of all six muscles around my dead eye, phantom pains that reminded me of the worst beating in my life. Before I fell into the black hole sucking me down, I vowed once more that, even though I had been born in a hotel room, I was not going to die in one.

• • •

On my next round of the city's clubs and night spots, I greeted and spoke to dozens of bartenders and their clientele including the lushes, barflies, slumming businessmen, drifters, and college kids. No one remembered ever seeing Annaliese.

I showed them her skirt-blouse photo, but I kept the other two handy. If at any time I had the right feel while working the crowd, I might have to show the bathroom-surprise photo. Brenda reluctantly gave me the third photo, and I promised her I would return it in tiny pieces once I had found Annaliese. Invading people's privacy is a conditioned reflex of every cop and investigator, so my squeamishness irked me.

I ordered pots of coffee to my room every couple hours, made calls all morning and took a break at noon for something to eat. I walked around the mall and let my mind drift. At one o'clock I went back to my room and made more calls. I even called O'Reilly's father and attempted to make peace with him, maybe jog his memory a little, but he hung up on me.

By three o'clock I was incapable of speech, of fashioning one slick story. For lack of a better plan, I was going to include corner markets and neighborhood taverns in working-class districts of East Boston. I had no hunch. It was just to do something as I worked my way toward Logan and the end of the allotted time I had given to the job. There were more bars in the Combat Zone, and a few bartenders had exchanged a little information for the twenty I displayed beneath the wet circumference of a shot glass of Bushmill's or Four Roses. It was not to drink, but to relax the house before I made my switch to club soda. I asked which bars in particular seemed to attract young girls. About six topless bars were mentioned, and I had them written down.

I took a cab to Chinatown and ate in a McDonald's. Then, with a map of downtown Boston and a small roll of twenties, I marked out the route I would take. The first two on my list were close enough to the business district to justify a cover charge. The first one advertised nude dancing in neon letters across the window.

I paid the five-dollar cover and walked in. I stepped away from the door and let my one good eye box the room. A dingy place which once must have had pretensions to being a sports bar before it settled to its current strip-joint status. The girls were young, looked fifteen, both white, and alternated dancing and serving duties. I spoke to each without results, declined a table dance for twenty dollars, and chatted with the bartender, a tough hillbilly woman with a cigarette dangling from her mouth. One of the girls, Traci, mounted the stage and, baby-fat jelloing in a white teddy cum garter and bridal veil, drew modest hoots from the crowd of five black males and six whites. The song was by Lady Gaga, and it was some drivel about love taking you to the edge of glory, hardly wedding song material but there seemed to be no music critics in the house to protest. She pushed the veil aside from time to time, but not as if she were interested in the crowd's reaction.

I thanked her, left her a twenty and headed for the next place with an old Bon Jovi tune booting me in the ass.

My luck was no better at the Queen of Hearts, a dingier place with a more raucous crowd helping out the joint's hi-fi system with some impromptu *basing* in rap time. This time there was no cover and three girls were alternating dances.

The drinks were watered to a pastel shade and my soda cost me as much as a shot and a beer. I asked the bartender, a black man with a bullet head and a gold earring, if I could show my photo to a few of the customers. He grunted, I laid a twenty on the bar, and he walked away with it crumpled in his big fist. When I had the urge to piss, I found a filthy urinal showing encrypted gang graffiti on all the walls and a myriad of crude art depicting organs of both genders. The mindless and obscene chortling below the pictures suggested a primitive form of blogging. None of it helpful. No Annaliese here either.

I headed for the third place on my list of watering holes, a place called Peaches off Utica down by the Fort Point Channel.

Her name was Lorraine and she was the only brunette among the dancers. She had a cage off to the side instead of the ramp where three girls were dancing simultaneously. All were blondes, one genuine if the tawny thatch, shaved to a kind of upswirl cowlick between her meaty thighs was any indication. I took a table and watched the brunette for an hour until she made eye contact. All beverages were seven dollars. They even served food. I was hungry, so I ordered a BLT.

The girls on the ramp were gyrating in an old-fashioned bump-and-grind to the music, whereas the brunette used her long legs to advantage by bending at the waist and feeling along both right to her ankles. It was during one of these caressing moves that I caught her eye and semaphored an invitation to my table. She showed me nothing, and went on with her routine in a practiced manner oblivious to anyone looking, and I wondered if she were used to ignoring all such gestures as the occupational hazard of her trade with loutish males.

She recognized Annaliese. It was like a shot of adrenalin to a fading heart. Unlike the others, she didn't cut her eyes away the instant she saw the photo. According to Lorraine, Annaliese showed up with a black male companion, fitting Marcus's description, who attempted to get her a job in the place. She looked a little spaced, not interested in the conversation between the black dude and Benny, had a cute shape, though. Lorraine recalled it easily because the boyfriend became obnoxious when the manager refused to take her on. She had no experience dancing, and Benny, the lame-o prick, didn't care that she was willing to show her twat.

"That's when Benny made a grab at me, the fucking creep, because I happened to be walking by at the time," she said. "They were sitting right at the table over there." I asked how long ago. "Two, three weeks."

Close now.

"Do you know the black guy's name?"

"He, like, her pimp?"

"I'm just trying to find her. Her family's worried about her."

"They oughta be, man. I've been dancing in joints like this for five years, the owner's keep finding new ways to take your money. Most of the girls doing this start tricking to pay for the nose candy."

"Any idea where they might have gone from here?"

"Fuck no. Try the Gryphon in East Boston. Lots of girls start out and some of them end up there too, come to think of it. Look for a guy named Tyreese Washington. He's always around sniffing out fresh talent."

I gave her my business card and wrote the Marriott's phone and room number on the back. "Call me, please, if you see her around."

"Any money in it?"

"Sure. I'll take care of you. Just call me."

"Hey, man, fuck it, I'll call you if I see her and it won't cost you nothing."

I put the ballpoint away in my jacket. "Thanks, Lorraine," I said and tucked three twenties into her garter belt. A small rivulet of sweat was worming its way between the cleavage of her small breasts. "Fuck, man," she said,this time with a little girl's lilt in her voice. "I had family once too."

• • •

The cab to East Boston cost me $15.05, twenty including tip. My driver spoke enough English to ask me how much I wanted back from the bill.

It was ten o'clock and the Gryphon was doing good business if the figures moving in and out of the place were an indication. There was a 300-pound bouncer in the doorway who took a long time before stepping aside. He wore gold chains, yellow pants and a pullover shirt. The clientele looked all-black. Half the girls were white.

One was dancing in an orange thong bikini at the end of the bar; one girl, a leggy black about twenty, was chatting with the bartender at my end. I took a seat at the bar about five stools down and allowed for a little adjustment time; finally, the few rubberneckers still looking my way made whatever calculations necessary about a white man in a black saloon and the volume picked up around me. The man sitting beside me got up and walked down the bar in a type of walk that involves pelvic thrust; cops call it a pimp roll. No bartender came over, and I could see two of them, one a dark-skinned Latino, busy washing glasses.

Well, to business.

I drew out my photo of Annaliese and prepared my story. I set a twenty on the bartop and waited. The black girl at the end of the bar gave me a long look and paused to adjust the top of her go-go outfit behind me. When I swiveled enough to take her in, she smiled at me, very relaxed and a little cocky. "Buy me a drink," she said. It wasn't a request. The bartender who had been maddogging me from twenty-five feet away a moment ago appeared at my elbow with a drink in his hand for her. "What can I get for you, sir?" was what he said to me.

"I'll have what she's drinking," I said.

"Right," he said, "another champagne." He scooped my twenty away.

She spluttered a bit of the liquid, a few drops of which hit my sleeve, and she brushed at it with her fingertips. "That'll wash off," she said.

"I hope so," I said. "They say that a fine vintage champagne will always leave a stain. I hope my coat isn't ruined."

Big teeth, eyes almost pinned from whatever drug she was on. "Baby, you for real or what? This shit about as close to champagne as you to Mars."

"Really? But—" I sniffed at the drink in front of me in mock dismay, "I thought you ordered us champagne."

She laughed again, her long arm resting lightly on her hip. "You are for real, I can see that now."

"No, but I'm not a cop, if that's what you're thinking."

"Baby, you was a cop, that boy over there, Nathaniel"—she nodded toward the giant bouncer— "he big enough to eat apples off your head. No way he let your narrow white ass by him. House rules, baby."

"I can see that," I said. "He's a big guy all right."

"Better than that," she said. "Nathaniel, he won one of those—whatchacallem things? Tough Man Contest."

"My, my," I said. "Well, now that we covered Nathaniel's biography, I wonder if I might persuade you to have a seat next to me. Got a question for your lovely self. Maybe even—" I tapped my inside pocket suggestively, "make you a couple dollars for your kind help."

She did. She looked all feline grace in repose. "Like what kinda questions?"

"Well," I said, "I'm looking for this young lady. I wonder if you might have seen her around." I dropped the photo between us.

"Mmmm, lemme see now. How much this information worth to you?"

"Well," I said, "It really depends."

"Depends? Like, say, on what?"

"Depends on how long we sit here negotiating. The longer the time, the less money it's worth."

"Then maybe you won't ever see this, uh, young lady again." She craned her neck to look at the photo and then turned her bright eyes and smile on full.

"May I ask what your name is?"

"Name's Serreta. With two *r*'s."

"Serreta with two *r*'s. That's a pretty name. Here's what I'm thinking, Serreta. There must be twenty guys in here who could use a twenty right now. But not one of them is going to talk to me in this place. So I figure if I go outside and wait, see who comes out, I just might get that information for all of twenty dollars. Might take a while." I let that hang in the air.

"So, man. How's about I give you some information—" she tapped the photo with a nail— "and you keep nice and warm, don't have to go outside in the cold night air."

She gave me a pouty face that was supposed to look sexy.

"OK. For that I'll pay forty dollars."

"Fifty."

"Why?" I asked

"Cuz you disrespected me, motherfucker."

The smile never dropped a notch.

"Sixty," I said.

Then, if anything, her teeth got bigger and she laughed in my face; silvery notes bounced all around me.

"There she is, Mister De-tective. She dancing at the end of the bar. But she got a boyfriend already."

That long, painted fingernail pointed the way like a signpost.

I swiveled my neck very slowly to take in the dancer. Being myopic does has its disadvantages, but I could see well enough that the girl on the built-on platform abutting the bar could very well be Annalese. Rather than stare, I turned back to Serreta and slipped three twenties into her hand.

"Another drink on me," I said.

She had the money already folded and placed inside her G-string. The sound she made passing me was a whisper.

I kept my eyes dead and sipped at my drink. I put another twenty on the bartop to buy a little more time. I never expected to find her. *Serendipity, the luck of the draw*, I thought. Once in a while you just do get lucky. Trouble is, I'm never that lucky. The hairs on my neck were tingling like tiny alarm bells with a single message: *notrightnotrightnotright*.

There was a potential problem if Marcus, in fact, happened to be around. Could be difficult to do anything in this place, and I had just about decided to follow her after closing time when I felt a hand squeezing my shoulder. I turned around hoping there wouldn't be a suckerpunch to go with it, and looked into the moon face of Nathaniel the bouncer.

He left his hand where it was and said, "Drink your drink and get the fuck out of here, motherfucker."

Without looking at his hand, I said, "Fine. I'll just toss this down and go."

I stood up to leave. I heard laughter around me. I almost made it to the door too.

The first punch went to my kidneys. The second may have been a kick, I'm not sure. The third caught me on the neck, and the fourth, if it landed, snapped my head back but didn't seem to have anything behind it. The reason, I knew, as I faded into black, was that I was losing consciousness and wasn't able to feel much.

The lights came on, and I next remember feeling cold and then seeing a woman's face above mine looking down at me. *Serreta with two r's*, I remember thinking.

She was smiling with those enormous teeth and saying something with her mouth, but I couldn't hear it because there was something, some urgent force pulling me up over the lip of something and pushing me down. Then I was falling. That was all I remembered until I awoke in the ambulance on my way to Beth Israel, with an oxygen mask over my mouth, and, of course, without wallet or papers to tell anybody who I was or what I was doing lying in a gutter at dawn in East Boston.

CHAPTER 4

The hospital they hauled me to had a sculpture of the Virgin Mother and seven arrows or swords piercing her heart. I was jabbed with sedatives and pain killers but coherent enough to tell the uniform beside my bed enough information to help him fill out his incident report.

I listened to two nurses behind the curtain speaking of a patient's cancer. One said, "If it's lymphatic now, like they say, she'll be dead of brain cancer in a month. You watch."

The officer spoke to me:

"What were you doing in East Boston, Mister, uh, Hoffman?"

"Looking for someone, officer. That's *Haftmann*, with two *n*'s."

"You know who beat you up?"

"No idea. I was hit from behind."

"Were you inside the Gryphon that night?"

"I had one drink and left to look for a cab."

"So you have no idea who gave you the beating?"

"No, officer. No idea at all."

"What were you doing in that area at that time of night?"

"Looking for someone who asked me to look a person up."

And so on and so forth. He wrote. I responded. Neither of us kidding the other, but I understand paperwork because I did my share of it. Police are a paramilitary organization and paperwork drives the system. I'd give him more information if he pressed, but he seemed uninterested in probing beyond the basics. I was a white man in a black area; obviously, my purpose could not be reputable and therefore what happened was a natural consequence of being in the wrong place at the wrong time—a cliché I have often emended mentally to read *at the right time*. I didn't want him to see me as a victim.

He was around twenty-five, swarthy complected, muscular in the shoulders and biceps. He said, "You got yourself a first-class beating but nothing broken. The doc says a couple hairline fractures above the eyebrow and your cheek. The rest are lacerations and bruises from your fall, most likely." He touched his right side for emphasis. "If you don't mind me saying so, Hoffman, it looks like that wasn't the first time somebody worked you over."

I told him I didn't mind his saying so.

"If you think of something else, call the precinct. Here's a number and an extension; you can talk to the detective handling the case. Name's Detective Cooney."

I glanced at the card and put it on the table next to a plastic water jug.

"You don't mind, I'd not go visiting that section of town after dark. It's all dopers and drug dealers. You have a safe trip back to— where was it?—Iowa?"

"Ohio. Thank you, officer."

I used to say the same thing to dumbass johns who got themselves into trouble looking for action away from the refurbished Warehouse District in Cleveland. Going on a toot in some darktown bar away from the lights downtown or the Flats, where the pubs catered to college kids, was a surefire way to wind up like me. I felt like telling him I thought I'd drop by Trinity Church as soon as I got out, say a prayer for the lost souls of Boston. He wouldn't have appreciated it.

Trinity Church is one of the ten most architecturally beautiful buildings in America, they say. But I don't waste my time praying to air in or out of buildings these days.

After that, I had time to think. I needed to get back to the Gryphon as soon as possible. I didn't know whether the beating was connected to my search for Annaliese or whether it happened because I had hung my ugly white face out in a black bar where Caucasian faces aren't welcome. One thing I knew: there wasn't time to lose now. I had Annaliese in my sights. I got lucky, despite the trimming last night, and when luck is good, you go with it as far as you can before the wheel of fate turns. As it always does.

• • •

"Let me explain something to you, Haftmann, so that you're very clear in your mind. I want you to understand me," said Detective Sean Cooney of the East Boston PD, precinct one-five. "We can't even keep count on the number of people these guys have killed. We got about nine people who are going to plead down on these drug-related murders and about five more who could get the death penalty."

"I know you're busy as hell, Detective," I said and tried on a hum-ble-pie look .

He didn't look impressed.

"You got plans to get this girl, this Annaliese O'Reilly, out of the Gryphon? That's fine. That's your job. But you do it fast and get out quick because there's a whole long list of people this Nathaniel Craft has popped. I'll bet even he don't even know how many."

Cooney was East Boston right down to his argyle socks. I'll take an educated Mississippi accent as the zenith of spoken English, for the lilting beauty of its cadence, every time. Boston English, educated or otherwise, is the nadir—it grates on the ear like slow torture: Death from a Thousand Cuts, a murder of crows feasting on roadkill, fingernails on a blackboard.

I was deep in some depressing reverie at the moment, not eager for a lecture from someone I would have called a brother-in-arms once upon a time.

He walked over to my window and pulled the drapes aside. "How about some light in here?"

He must have noticed me wincing. "The light bother you?"

"Just a little. I'm down to one good eye, and right now it doesn't feel particularly good."

"Yeah? Anything happens to that one, and you're really fucked."

"I've given that some thought on long winter nights back in Ohio."

"Good. Because I was beginning to wonder if anything I've been saying for the last twenty minutes has been getting through."

"I'm listening."

"All right. So I hope you understand this. That shaved-head street fuck is a very dangerous person. We'll pick him up tonight or tomorrow, but it won't mean shit. There are no witnesses, so we've got less than nothing on him, but that I assume you do know . . . besides, we don't really want to louse up a federal case amounting to maybe sixty, seventy murders just to give you a little justice."

"So what *can* you do for me?"

"We know this much on your boy, he hangs with two knuckleheads, a couple brothers from South Boston. Tarvarius and VonShae Holley. Street names "Bones" and "Psycho." Stone killers. They'll pop you just as soon as look at you. They work for a major dealer, call themselves Best Friends."

Best Friends. The blowjob photo, the writing on the back.

"These characters blow away rival dope dealers the way you step on bugs. We got dead gang members all over the city. They took out a whole gang on the east side run by a dude name of "White Boy Rick" Wershe, Ed "Big Ed" Hanserd, couple others named "Hollywood" and "Big James." Got two of them in a house and two in a taxi a week afterward. Not that we care all that much about these guys, of course. Killed the taxi driver too, as if that meant shit. Your boy Craft is one of the real shooters. They'll do anybody, anywhere for about $10,000 to $30,000. A low price of $5,000 if you're just a street yo, not a player. These guys are murder-for-hire."

"So why don't you do society a favor and get them off the streets before they kill more people?"

"You know what AVANHI means, Haftmann?"

"Yeah." *Cop slang: Asshole Versus Asshole, No Human Involved.*

He had his back to me and he was thumbing through a copy of the complimentary autobiography of the self-made millionaire founder of the Marriott dynasty. He tossed it on the desk top near the window overlooking Cambridge.

I glimpsed a metallic sheen between high-rises and brownstones—the Charles River.

"Bragging sonofabitch, ain't he?"

I assumed he meant the hotel founder, not Nathaniel Craft.

"We need one of these shitbirds looking at serious prison time to roll over," Cooney said. "You know how it goes. We're squeezing one right now, in fact. Need a little more juice on him is all."

"Obviously, you're not looking for my help."

"As a matter of fact, no. I'm only being a little extra courteous to you because you were homicide once. Normally we'd be having this conversation downtown. I don't give a shit about private eyes, as a rule. Mostly jerkoffs, window peepers."

"Thanks."

"You're welcome, Mister Haftmann. By the way, we did pick up your girlfriend for questioning."

"Serreta?"

"Yeah, only the name is William Wilkes. He dances under the name Serreta. A tranny. Good-looking she-male.

Serreta, a transvestite. A knot of hot bile rose in my gorge.

"You do know what those are, right, being from Ohio and all?"

I was concentrating hard on holding down the urge to vomit, but I heard Cooney's words from the doorway clearly enough.

"Have a safe trip home and don't let the door hit you in the ass on your way out."

• • •

I didn't have the energy to get up and close the drapes. I don't know how long I stared at the smudge of gray light coming into the room, but I must have fallen asleep. I dreamed of Micah. She was pregnant, standing in the living room of her house watching me stumble drunkenly about the room. I kept falling into things and knocking over furniture. Her face creased in a look familiar to me, she guided me by the hand upstairs and put me to bed. I told her my face was burning so she brought me a cool washcloth and covered it. I knew she was gone when I heard a noise from the next room, bed springs going wild, and her honeysoft moaning came through the wall, followed by a man's voicing cooing, "Take it, ooooh, take it, take it."

One side of my face was wet with tears, the only socket able to produce them, and I knew just before coming fully awake in my room in a yellow twilight that Micah was straddling him, her belly jutting out and her breasts exposed, the tips swelled with blood. Betraying me. I could visualize that glistening snail-track of sweat coursing down her back and disappearing into her buttock cleft. I put the edge of the pillow into my mouth so that no one down the hallway could hear me scream.

• • •

I washed down the Percodan with coffee, ordered a cab because I didn't trust myself to drive in the organized mayhem of Boston traffic. and headed for the elevator. I planned to check out, relocate to East Boston, a flophouse near the bar if possible, and then stake out the place all day until she showed up.

I would speak to her and tell her what I had to tell her. I had some options in mind if she were to show up with Marcus, or whoever it was, in tow. If the latter case, then Plan B: follow them both after closing, see where we wound up, stake out the place, and wait for him to leave. I had three years' vice experience that comes in handy now and then. If I had to, a little B & E was another and remoter possibility. I had fake ID's for insurance and bill collecting that would not be amiss in that neighborhood. Lots of ways to get people out of places with phony messages and lures, so I was pretty sure that isolating her for a few minutes wouldn't be impossible.

My cab driver talked continually at me, except for periods of throat-clearing that sounded like a horse nickering, all the way to East Boston. He had the Boston cabby's homegrown expertise on a variety of subjects, such as crime in the streets, the Bosox chances in the AL East, niggers, right-hander Daisuke's chances of bouncing back, politics, the cost of living—especially gasoline (thanks to those "fuckin' towelheads in Libya")—the best pussy, and Bill Belichik and the Pats' glory years.

Once in East Boston, he careered down one-ways and blew past stop signs as if they were symbols in an alien tongue. Apparently I had punctuated his monologue at the right intervals with sufficient nods and grunts because he kept the chatter up.

I found myself dumped in front of a corner store off Chelsea, a dented red Coca Cola sign with Arabic lettering down its pockmarked side. His patter beat sounds inside my concussed brain like raindrops on a tin roof. I fought bile rising as I watched him speed off, my suitcase rocking on the sidewalk, and I could see his mouth still moving in the rearview mirror.

I spent an hour checking out the neighborhood, circling the block. I stopped in a couple small markets and gas stations and showed my photo of Annaliese to a few proprietors. A neighborhood kid thought he had seen her around, remembered her because she was white and "hangin' with a black dude."

"Did you ever see her in a car?"

"Nope."

That was good because I had no options if they bolted in a vehicle. I would make my pitch for her father, and then I was going home.

I found a motel by asking around. I wound up in a brick hotel in a section of East Boston with a lot of PRs, illegals from the DR and Mexico; the place didn't have much of a descent to go before it found its level as a flophouse.

I walked in past those old-fashioned swinging glass doors. The glass was smeared from top to bottom with hand prints. I saw a flyer on the front desk that said one of the local Irish churches was sponsoring a boxing event in the gymnasium next to the church. Several young men with chiseled physiques were hanging around the lobby who might have been boxers. Some local boys wearing starter jackets and reversed baseball caps were in attendance. I was three blocks from the Gryphon, but it wouldn't have mattered if I were across the street. Too far to see anything, even with two good eyes, but it gave me reason to be in the neighborhood. There were young mothers strolling down the street with infants.

The sun was bright but not enough to take the chill out of the air. The Percodan made me woozy and nauseated, so I cut the dosage. I walked to the corner store with the Arabic lettering and bought some sandwiches and coffee to take back to the room.

Haftmann's rulebook says eat when you can on a surveillance job. I got one sandwich down, but the coffee made me vomit it all up. That exertion left me with a ragged pain and a ringing in my ears; it felt as though someone were teeing off behind my left eye socket, so I lay on the bed for a few minutes to get my bearings.

What I thought was a few minutes turned out to be three hours, and when I finally found the strength to hoist myself from the bed, I knew that the neighborhood had changed with the dying of the light. Slingers and their white customers (Jack used to call them city goats) and young men with muscled torsos wearing bandannas or corn rows met and dispersed in threes and fives all over the street. The women and children were off the sidewalks.

OK, I thought, *time to check out the nightlife.*

I made my way unhurried and as unnoticeable as any white man can, and headed straight to the Gryphon. I scoped out a walk-by routine that should keep me well-hidden from passersby. Any threats from the neighborhood's rogue males should be visible, and I had a mental map of danger points where harm could come and, if worse did come to worst, then I had a few escape routes. I had no gun. Truth is I couldn't hit a building, and I never intended to bring one with me. Ninety percent of my job is attitude. Just then I had a sickening dread of taking another beating. I had my nose broken in an alley fight once, and I distinctly remember the pain as well as that voice in my head that told me to flee, don't take another shot on top of that. The better part of valor, from my viewpoint, is not discretion but coward's wisdom to know when to get the hell out of Dodge.

I made a dozen passes from across the street and saw clearly three out of every four people entering the Gryphon. It was almost ten thirty by now and the wind had a bite to it. My nose leaked and my legs knees were stiffening. I had not seen any white women enter yet, but six or seven white males did. The distance and clothing made it difficult to be sure. No sign of the giant bouncer.

Then *she* came around the corner. The hair and eyes convinced me. She was with a black male who could have been the Marcus that Brenda Holbacher described: about five-nine, 150 pounds, light-skinned. I wondered: what is Marcus's connection to Best Friends? Was he pimping Annaliese?

She seemed in a hurry compared to his casual stroll about five yards behind her. As the door opened, I noted that angry rap had replaced the Caribbean lilt of reggae I heard in my earlier passes.

It would be a long wait until closing. I had to make a decision: stay or go? There was no place to settle in nearby and stay out of sight. I was no TV private eye who would have hidden between dumpsters or disguised himself as a homeless man in an alley. I had neither youth nor courage for it.

I had to walk five blocks to hail a cab. Back in my room, I peeled off my clothes and lay on top of the bed. I set my internal alarm clock. My body ached. My vision was still blurred; the wind now piercing in this blighted cityscape of grime and poverty made dustdevils with the city's debris. I wondered, too, if I might be interfering to no purpose in a young woman's life.

I awoke in time to hit the shower, dress in my darkest clothing. I checked my money and made my way down the stairs. Someone off the lobby was hacking out his lungs in a smoker's cough. Before I was old enough to do it, a man my grandmother hired used to come over to start a fire in the furnace; he smoked Pall Mall's, "plain ends," and on those blue-black February mornings his hacking would resound throughout the house from the ductwork.

I shortened my walk this time and leaned into shadows whenever cars passed; the city was shrill with noises and occasionally topped with the hi-lo of cop cruisers, the Nazi bleat of urban ambos and their occupants, the tough EMTs making their runs for the city's dead and wounded. The sounds of human catastrophe.

There was a spot between two parked cars directly across from the bar where I planned to be at closing time. At 1:30 in the morning, I was stamping my feet from the cold and waiting for the neon sign in the window to go out; by 1:40 the bar had emptied its last customers. One or two dancers and the bartender who served me the champagne cocktail followed them twenty minutes later. It was 2:15 by the time she came out with Marcus—whether it was he or not. I followed them from across the street, my stiff muscles slowly coming back to life.

If they made a move to get into a car, I was going to confront them on the run and hope that I could stall them with enough patter to keep him indecisive and immobile. The man would be the one to deal with, so I had to get my hook into him somehow, smile big, mention money—whatever it took to keep the man glued to the spot. I worked my jaw around to get the smile ready and began to close the distance. I was angling at them so that we would arrive at the corner and be under the streetlight and within sight of any passing cars.

He made me before I got close, whirled, and put his right hand under his leather coat. "Who the fuck you following?"

He was wearing shades at three o'clock in the morning. The wings of his nostrils were the only part of him moving. His hair was done in "twigs," each spiky tendril wrapped in a rubber band in the latest gangster style. I resisted the temptation to look at her.

"I'd like to speak to you for a minute. My name's Thomas Haftmann. I'm a private investigator, and I'd like to talk to you both."

"Fuck off, white boy."

I've always found that one a little hard to come back on, so I just stood there in the chill wind of a pre-dawn Boston and smiled to appease him. I even held my hands in the air and waved them gently about. That worked like a rubber crutch.

"Stay the fuck away from me, motherfucker." He said it in one breath so fast it sounded like "fuck" twice. He was holding the gun in his fist now, a blue-plated .25 automatic.

Worse and worse.

"Look, my name is Thomas—"

"I don't give a fuck who you are, motherfucker. Move and I'll put you down for the set, motherfucker."

I was pulling all the stops on my appeasement *shtick* now; all systems oozing goodwill in his general direction. "Just let me speak to Annaliese—"

"I'll fuckin kill you, motherfucker."

I believed him. Out of the corner of my eye I could see her moving closer to him. I was radiating fear by now.

"Marcus, is it Marcus? I'd like to just explain—"

The gun moved up to sight my face. "I know who you are. I know what you want, racist motherfucker. You got a message the other night but you didn't listen to it."

"That was a misunderstanding. No harm done."

That brought the shades off with a single swipe of his free hand. "No harm done? You dumb motherfuckers don't listen. I know you been stalking me. I'm gonna fix you so you don't have no legs to stalk with."

Christ, the knees. He's going to shoot me in the kneecaps.

"Marcus, just listen to me for a minute. I'm only here because of Annaliese's father. He just wants to know that she's OK is all."

He wasn't listening. I could see him stiffening up his resolve. The gun was inching down my midsection. "Listen, Marcus, please, I'm just—"

"Marcus, don't, baby."

Annaliese was clutching his gun arm now but he shook her off. "Let him go."

"Baby, get the fuck away from me."

"Listen to her, Marcus. I'm just a private investigator working for Annaliese's father. Nobody's going to bother you."

"You right about that, motherfucker."

"Let me talk. Just a few minutes."

I turned to Annaliese slowly and said, "Will you let me explain what I'm here for and then I'll never bother either of you again? Take just a moment."

"You can go to hell and you can take my father with you. Leave us alone."

Marcus smiled in a way that didn't go all the way to his eyes. "You got your word now, motherfucker. I ever see you again, it won't be a beating next time." He stuck the gun in his pants and hustled her by the arm down the street. I watched them go until they disappeared around the corner.

That was it. My knees were still weak. I waited for my heartbeat to return to something like normal. Game over. Her father could take what solace he could from her parting words. I had found her but you don't bring people back who don't want to go. I'm not that crazy. I'm not that dedicated. I don't need the money that badly.

Aw, fuck.

I could no more abandon this case than I could have flown to the moon. To be just a few feet away from her, to see the woman of the photos, and then go home with my tail between my legs and Cooney's smirking jibe ringing in my ears?

No taxi would pick me up at that hour so I walked the way back to my hotel. I had a lot of thinking to do now. My size eleven shoes were pinching the hell out of my triple-E feet by the time I made it to the street where my hotel was. A patrol car on its way somewhere slowed down to beam me. I stood there in the blinding light and raised my hands in a hapless gesture of defeat, an actor with stage fright, when the light suddenly snapped off and the cruiser sped away, its turquoise and cherry lights flashing.

Round one was over. I had taken a thumping. Before round two commenced, I had to go home. I had some unfinished business at the office that could not wait. I even had to get out of a bench warrant for failing to appear for jury duty at the county courthouse in Jefferson. Most humiliating of all, the desk clerk at my fleabag hotel informed me that the charge for the room had been rejected and I would have to pay cash. He handed my card back as if it were radioactive. I paid him from the depleted funds of my fee from O'Reilly. Considering where I was sleeping lately, I wondered how much farther from grace a man can fall before he finally hits bottom.

CHAPTER 5

I read the *Globe* headlines, sipped a coal-black Starbuck's espresso, and waited for my flight to be called at ten-fifteen. Elizabeth Taylor had died while I was slumming in East Boston. My getting home at dawn and managing three hours' sleep had lulled me toward numbness. I usually enjoyed watching the parade of people coming and going. So much activity, like a beehive and everybody with a cell phone clamped to their heads. I'm here, come and get me. I'm in an airport and I miss you. I'll be home soon . . . Some physicists believe time doesn't exist; they just don't know how else to explain the fact that everything doesn't happen at once.

I was thinking of my grandmother. I had returned from the ore boats with a terrible wound to bury her; that's when I asked Micah to marry me. That's when I entered the police academy. She was eaten up by her cancer and lived only a few days after my return. The pain was horrifying to behold. A little song she used to sing in German came back to me: *Ich bin hier, da bist du*. I heard her singing it in my dream last night and when I awoke, I realized I had been humming it while reading the paper.

Ozzie's Black Sabbath tune went off in my pocket. It was Detective Cooney. I didn't remember giving him my cell number.

"Where are you, Haftmann?"

"Logan," I said. "Waiting for my flight."

What he said took a moment to get through, but when it did, I felt that lurch inside you whenever life throws a suckerpunch and puts its hip into the blow: Annaliese O'Reilly was just found dead, murdered in a motel room in East Boston. I had to delay my flight home to answer a few questions.

One dead actress with a tabloid Hollywood history does not change the misery or the happiness quotient of the world's population. A hundred million people scraped from earth's bulk might, but not an aging prima donna much less a young woman who intended to turn her back on her sordid past. I riffled the pages for the crime beat section: she hadn't even made the news yet.

I watched the crowds of people lining up in rows or coming

through the security queues. I felt like a man falling through a trap door. Annalese was dead. How? Why? Had Marcus killed her? Was I a cause of it by showing up as I did?

Cooney had a unit coming out to fetch me. I was to remain at the Delta gate and they'd send security down to retrieve me. When I hung up, the tiredness I felt was gone. My hand was shaking. Had I been able to pry her away from Marcus, maybe she'd still be alive. I wanted to get far away from the sanitized and slightly scented air of the concourse.

I sat still and waited to be called back.

Existentialists are by definition above superstition. There's no God, no Grim Reaper whetting his scythe—just a ticket in your back pocket or your purse that says on such and such a day and at such and such a time, you're going to be canceled. Finis. Yet I had a raw feeling in my stomach and on the back of my neck that something big and mean was glowering at me just then.

● ● ●

"Haftmann, I'm not saying you weren't a good cop in your day. I'm just pointing out that things are a little different nowadays, is all. We'll pick up Marcus Gordon and that'll be all she wrote," said Cooney over the phone.

I told him about my short meeting the night before. I also told him that, based on his description of the murder, Marcus didn't seem right. I talk to him and less than three hours later he stabs Annaliese in a frenzy? That dog don't hunt.

"You're goofier than a bag of dicks if you think these guys actually premeditate their crimes, Haftmann. The guy was out of rock, he was desperate, he starts fiending. She said something—hell, she didn't need to say *anything* to get sliced up like that."

I couldn't disprove Cooney's theory. I've seen a crack addict left with his own baby tear his place apart looking for one more rock to keep the high going. He did a real fuck-o tracheotomy on the kid's throat and used a straw to suck out the infant's insides because he thought the kid might have put one in his mouth.

"I know what you're saying, Detective," I said. "He fits. He's probably right. But something's off. What time was the body found?"

"M.E. can't say but the congealing of the blood—some technical bullshit about blood and sere separating, whatever, she says maybe between three and five, latest."

"Check-out time is usually eleven."

"True but this place they're staying is a notorious party place. Booze bottles lined up like tin soldiers in the hallways, bed bugs—not exactly four stars."

I didn't bother to tell him I was staying in that kind of place. People mind their own business in these kinds of motels. I said, "It'd be unusual for someone to complain then, right?"

"Normally, but in this shithole, I guess they have standards or else they made a helluva lot of noise. Victims generally do when sharp objects are being thrust into them."

Cop humor. "The timeline still bothers me." I said.

"Don't worry about it. We'll grab the little fuck soon. They always turn up."

"I can guess the next part," I said. "Don't leave town yet."

"Be a sport, huh? You're a material witness," Cooney said.

"I want to see her," I said. "The father will expect me to."

"She's being posted this afternoon at four. A little back-up problem with stiffs right now. Fuckin' bodies are falling all over the city."

"Life and death in the big city," I said.

"It's either a full moon or the Red Sox lost three straight at Fenway."

"I've already checked out," I said. "Stay put until your ride gets there. When they drop you here, take the elevator to third floor, turn left. Help out with the composite, huh? He's down there doing the sketch right now. This Marcus doesn't have a recent photo in his jacket anywhere, can you believe it?"

"Cooney, my bags are already on the plane," I said.

"So use your credit card and buy some clothes and shit, what the fuck."

Nothing's ever easy.

At the precinct desk I was given a message to call a number. I figured Cooney had forgotten something. A voice answered on the first ring and a breathless male voice said, "Who this?"

"My dime," I said, "but your number."

"You know me," the voice said.

Jesus H. Christ. Marcus. What balls.

"Why are you calling me *here*? How did you get my—"

"I don't have time for fuckin questions, man. I'm getting out of here, so don't bother with any bullshit right now. Just listen. I called every hotel in town and left the same message. I just want to put out the word on this, case I get bagged."

"You want *me* to alibi you, asshole?"

"Just listen to me, God damn it! I didn't do it! I didn't kill her! I don't know what the fuck's happening but you—you put yourself in the middle of this. Now you gotta listen."

"Why me, Marcus?"

"Because you came after me, remember?"

"What do you want from me?"

"Fuck, I don't know who *them* is, man! I don't know. Something's been happening. I thought you were working for them—"

"Who's *them*?"

"That's the whole fuckin' thing that's so crazy, yo. We was stalked, man! People watching me. I don't fuckin' know why. I thought it was the fucking cops, you know? Watching me, like, you know, in my business and shit."

He meant drugs obviously.

"Look, man, there are people I know with some, uh, legal-type problems. I happen to know those people, see? You walk into that bar the other night, see? Like, see, a lot of people were *expecting* something when you showed up."

"I'm not interested in your bullshit and your fucking crimeys," I said. "I want to know what this has to do with Annaliese's murder."

"Man, I'm telling you. I don't *know*, man. I had to make a run, I come back fifteen, twenty minutes later, and I see wall-to-wall cops, sirens—all that shit. I loved her, man!"

Some lover, I thought.

"That doesn't square, Marcus. The killer was in the room long enough to tie her up and rape her. Were they looking for you and found her there?"

"Fuck, man, I don't know. Don't nobody want me dead that bad. Little business rivalry here and there, you know?"

A drug dealer's life, a mixed bag of problems.

"What do you expect me to do for you?"

"Shit, man. I gotta—I gotta just, like, tell somebody. Just in case."

"I can't help you. I haven't heard anything yet that convinces me you didn't kill her."

"Listen, motherfucker. I loved her. I really loved her. I would *never*—"

"You used to slap her around."

"Fuck you, you been talking to that Brenda bitch, I s'pose. She hates my fuckin' guts. Man, she had a lesbian thing going with my old lady."

"Listen to me. You're wasting your time. Every cop in the city will know what you look like by the second shift."

"I'm real good at not being found."

"You're better off coming in, clear your name. You want to get who did it, right? Did you hear how she died? What they did to Annaliese?"

I heard the slow susurration of breath. He knew. "I'll take care of that myself. I have friends."

Cooney told me Annaliese had shallow, defensive cuts all over her face and hands. She was tied to the bed post and bruising around the vagina and anus suggested she was raped and sodomized.

"Marcus, you said somebody was stalking you. Who?"

"Man, I keep telling you I don't know! Lots of white dudes hanging around. Ain't real."   I tried to remember: his eyes last night, jumping and bulging, but was it over the confrontation with me or the user's paranoia?

"Why don't you meet me somewhere tonight?" I suggested.

"Shit, man. You could set me up," he said.

"If you run, the trail to the killer gets cold. You'll be the one they'll nail. They never close the books on uncleared murders. You'll be looking over your shoulder all your life."

"How do I know I can trust you?"

"Give me a time and place or get the fuck off the phone," I snapped.

The push in my voice must have done it. He gave me an address in South Boston, the Sobin Park, at the entrance at six in the evening, near Necco Street and Mt. Washington Avenue. I was to look for three trees by the gate, he said.

I had to fill out a sheet of information at the front desk to get my plastic visitor's card and wait for Cooney to come get me. It was four-twenty-seven when he stepped off the elevator and crooked a finger at me.

"Let's go, we're late," he said.

We took the elevator down to the parking lot and Cooney showed me to an unmarked Crown Vic, standard cop undercover car. These things are so well known in the hood it's almost reverse psychology to use one on surveillance.

He drove through Boston without the siren. It wouldn't have worked anyway. Traffic in this city borders on third world. We were lucky it wasn't rush hour.

"You don't like our fair burgh?" Cooney asked at some point while swerving between lanes. We were near Copley, the jewel in Boston's crown.

"I'm closing my eyes because I didn't get much sleep," I said. The glare from the high rises and the chrome glancing off all the shiny high-end SUVs, sleek foreign jobs, Bentleys, and Porsches was bothering the nerve muscles around my bad eye.

"Got anything like that in—what city you say you're from?"

I looked up. A shimmering turquoise Trinity Church was perfectly replicated in the massive glass panels of the Hancock Building beside it.

"Amazing," I said. "Let's stop and I'll see if I can get a postcard."

"Fuck you, gumshoe," Cooney said.

● ● ●

Most people think morgues have to be in the basements of buildings. There's something in us that almost requires a subterranean resting place for the dead, especially those who perish violently. The M.E.'s office was on the fourth floor. By the time we got there, the Y-incision had been made, the organs and tissue samples extracted, and the bone saw was busy slicing off the top portion of her head. Her skin had already been pulled over her face in preparation for the removal of the brain.

From where I stood, I could barely hear Cooney's voice above the saw. He followed the pathologist around the body, talking all the while, but keeping a distance from the spray that dotted the pathologist's smock. He and the doctor had a good rapport, it seemed, because both made animated gestures and I could see the doctor's eyes show laughter above the mask; occasionally she ignored Cooney and attended to her work on Annaliese. When the doctor set the brain in the scales, Cooney leaned over her shoulder and said something that made her laugh. The doctor made frequent notes on a clipboard set off to the side and, finally, began peeling off the latex gloves.

I approached as Cooney was finishing a story about an M.E. who had misdiagnosed a killing because he couldn't find the bullet holes in a victim's face.

Cooney introduced us and I shook hands with her. She gripped my hand once, shook it, and let go. Cooney thanked her and wagged an eyebrow to me to signal that we were all through here.

"Just a minute," I said.

I asked the pathologist if she would pull the scalp back so that I could see Annaliese's face. Without hesitating, she put on new gloves and grabbed the skin on both sides of Annaliese's head and pulled it back over her face. There was only a little sag.

The knife wounds were many, mostly short and shallow cuts along both cheeks and bridge of the nose. Some ran laterally across her face. There was a rusty trail of blood from one ear hole. I juxtaposed the newspaper photo of her onto this face, and I could see that three years had been a long time for her.

"C'mon, Haftmann," said Cooney, leading me off.

Back in the parking lot, he said, "Fucker played tic-tac-toe on her face with a steak knife and then he put the barrel right in her ear."

That bothered me. A killer's savagery and then to do a coup de grace like that—why?

She was a long time dying.

"The slug's flattened out, no good for comparison purposes, but without the gun, the slug doesn't matter anyhow, and we'll not get the gun, most likely, right? Or do killers do it differently in Ohio? Like leave the gun lying around on the coffee table, make it easy for forensics."

"Sometimes," I said. "I've never known killers distinguished for brains."

I was getting a headache and losing patience with Cooney's wisecracking and attempts to get my goat. I just wanted to sleep, clear the cobwebs, pretend last night never happened, that Annaliese wasn't in a chilled steel tomb upstairs, hollowed-out like a cored apple with crude black stitching across her chest. I started out thinking I was on a mission to bring a daughter home to her grieving father, a family re-union, tears of joy and hugs. That changed and now this sordid ca-tastrophe—a daughter viciously slaughtered, a father who would never see her alive, never ask her for forgiveness.

"Fuckin' .22's. They bounce around too much. That's the prob-lem with them."

"None of the knife wounds deep enough?"

"Nah, too shallow. No vital organs. He did put a couple in her *post mortem*. For fun, you might say. Deep wound channels. Enough to kill her if she weren't already dead—nearly severed her liver, the doc said."

I almost snapped: *I was right there.* "So what are we looking for?"

"Not *we*, Haftmann, and not what. *Who*. Marcus Fucking Gordon. Who else?"

"You get any leads?"

"Better. Got me two witnesses. A waitress at the motel cafe saw a slender back male walking across the parking lot as she got out of her car at 5:45 A.M. Got a back-up witness who says he spotted the same figure walking very fast just northeast from the motel five minutes after the waitress says she saw him. Trouble is, the second wit's a pipehead. He got up early to score. But we're still canvassing. Even without more witnesses, that puts him at the scene just inside the time-frame the doc figures on."

"She was in rigor on the table," I said. "I saw the effort it took to move her arm."

"So what? Fuck rigor. Too many things affect it. Body size, heat, room temperature—"

"Twelve hours. She must have been seen alive checking in with him. He leaves right away. Your witnesses didn't see blood, right?"

"No."

"Maybe Gordon was just leaving and the killer came in right after. He comes back twelve hours later and finds the body."

"Yeah. Maybe he stepped out for a cigarette break, give his arm a rest from all that stabbing. One thing, Haftmann. We sure as shit ain't going to take the spotlight off him at this point on any flimsy hunch from you. You're a guest here."

"I know it. Have you called her father?"

"Yes, I left a message this afternoon. I'm calling back tonight."

"What about phone calls to and from Marcus's room?"

"We checked. The telephone company says one call. To the room. From a Beacon Hill exchange."

"Who?"

"Book publisher. A pay phone in the lobby. Knock it off, Haftmann. You're not assisting the case. In fact, your flight is leaving soon, am I correct?"

"Who would be calling a hood like Marcus Gordon at that time of the morning?"

"Maybe somebody who wants to sell him a fucking book."

"You send anybody up there to check?"

"Fuck you, that's it."

● ● ●

I called O'Reilly, told him how Annaliese died and that the police were close to arresting the suspect. His voice broke when he asked about the body's return, because I told him that as long as the investigation was open, the coroner's office had to keep Annaliese's remains.

He concluded our conversation by telling me he knew all along this was going to happen and that he tried to prevent it, didn't he do everything a father could be expected, Haftmann? I agreed. He said she wasn't really his own daughter, and then I heard racking sobs, oddly high-pitched like nails being pried out of wood, come through the line. I would be returning to Ohio the day after tomorrow and I would talk to him then. I was sick of the man and sick of trying to fix broken lives. Mostly I was sick of Boston, and I wanted to go back to my grubby office in a third-rate resort town on Lake Erie. Drop by Tico's, play mah jongg, work out again. *Sometimes, Jack used to say, you get the bear . . .*

The room phone rang while I was packing my shaving gear. I answered it on the third ring. Silence. I said hello but heard nothing. I knew someone was on the line. I could feel it. I said, "Marcus?" Nothing. Dead air.

I had an hour to kill before meeting Marcus. It would be my last contribution to the case. I took out my deck of Solitaire and cheated on every hand.

This time the taxi driver was a woman in her twenties. She said nothing all the way to South Boston. I had her drop me off about a hundred yards from the park entrance Marcus had told me to find. He had said there were three oak trees with crossed branches near the brick entrance. I wondered if witches were hanged elsewhere besides the Commons. The oak trees were all gone, nothing but tourists and vendors selling baseball caps and T-shirts.

I found a park bench about fifty yards inside and read my newspaper and waited for Marcus to show. The *Globe* and *Record* both ran retrospectives on the fifteenth anniversary of Jackie Kennedy's death with photos. *Onassis* had been dropped from her name throughout the article, and her brother-in-law, the late senator's funeral oration was quoted again.

I saw a figure in sweats moving toward me, about Marcus' size. He was walking in a crazy-legged fashion that suggested a drunkard's movements. Marcus staggered up to me and sat down. His forehead was beaded with sweat. Summer had come all at once, out of nowhere, so I thought he had been jogging a long way in the heat and was exhausted.

He said nothing, staring straight ahead, not looking at me. Two strangers sharing a park bench. Then he slurred something, maybe a name, but I couldn't make it out.

"What did you say, Marcus?"

He snorted through his nose a couple times and turned to face me and repeated a word that sounded like *priest*. His breath was rank. The front of his navy-blue sweatsuit glistened where Boston U was lettered, and then I heard him say, "Oh." By some crazy associational logic, I thought a sewer close by had erupted and then I realized that Marcus had voided his bowels. His eyes were half-shut, and he stopped making that chuffing noise through his nostrils. I put my hand on his neck and felt the worm of a pulse. I pulled open his sweatsuit and saw the holes: three of them, dime-sized, stippled with black around the circumference. Contact wounds. His head lolled forward and that was when he died.

I sat there longer than I should have, but I wanted to make a choice. I knew that someone, maybe the killer, was setting this up. Maybe I was even a part of it. I was sure that Marcus, whatever else he had been, was not the killer of Annaliese O'Reilly. A rage in my guts fought with great fear and made me grasp the ends of the bench and squeeze until my knuckles were white.

Carefully, very carefully—I stood up, pretended to tuck in my shirt while I scanned as far down Mt. Washington as I could see. *Christ, Christ*, I whispered, a useless mantra under the circumstances. Dozens of late-model cars parked on the street, moving traffic on Necco Street. Nothing unusual to see, and no one was looking in my direction. Couples holding hands, joggers, families out walking on this balmy spring afternoon. I folded my paper and regarded the dead lover of Annaliese a final time before walking all the way to West Broadway for a taxi.

● ● ●

I called Mr. O'Reilly's father in Roxbury. First, I told him of Annaliese's death. He said he knew it, read it in the paper that evening; there was nothing in his voice that registered any emotion I could fathom. "What else you want to tell me?" he asked.

"Has anybody called you for information about Annaliese's whereabouts besides me? Anybody at all, Mister O'Reilly?"

"A priest, he called my wife. He dint give no other information but he say to her Annaliese was safe now."

"What else did this priest say?"

"He said Annaliese was all right now. He said: 'Annaliese is safe from the pollution of this world. She will be in her father's arms soon.'"

Jesus fuck. Priests again.

"Mister O'Reilly, listen. When *exactly* did that priest call?"

"He called day before yesterday. Very early. I was asleep. He woke up my wife and he told her Annaliese was dead but not to worry no more about her doing bad things."

"*Bad things*? This priest said 'bad things'?"

"He said she's all right now. She was at peace."

Jesus Jumping Christ.

● ● ●

Marcus's death was buried at the bottom of page five in the *Boston*

Globe under a boldface heading barely larger than standard type size proclaiming that a suspected drug dealer and "associate gang member," had been found on a park bench by some children playing.

He was shot at close range by a .9 mm automatic. There were no witness, no suspects. What the police beat reporter left out was that there was no real investigation. I suspected as much because Cooney never called me with the news. This was going down on some unlucky South Boston detective's caseload as uncleared, a real whodunit. Unless somebody turned up to give any description to homicide, always a possibility. But Cooney would clear the Annaliese murder with Marcus Gordon and go on to the next shooting or stabbing in rotation. I couldn't very well jerk his chain without implicating myself, and there wasn't much I could do from Ohio. Someone knew the angles. I thought about that silent caller just before Marcus called me. Could it be the same person impersonating a priest to old man O'Reilly?

I had nothing left but questions and not much time. How far had Marcus walked with three slugs in him? It's a myth that you have to fall down when you're shot. People get it from TV like everything else. You can walk a long way with bullets in you unless you take one to the brain stem or spinal cord. Even a clipped aorta will allow you fifteen minutes of life before you die. Marcus wasn't bleeding that much. When I pulled his clothing aside, I saw a fragment of bone protruding. The bullet must have smashed a rib bone and gone on to do other damage without hitting a major organ. If a major artery had been hit, his heart would have pumped his blood out in a couple minutes. It told me one thing: the shooter placed the gun carefully—he wanted Marcus to live a little while. Otherwise, a head shot, gang-style.

Maybe the killer wanted Marcus to keep his appointment in the park . . .

● ● ●

I slept on the flight to Cleveland Hopkins. I remember coming out of fitful sleep to see the interior of the cabin suddenly plunged into darkness as we streaked through clouds the size of skyscrapers. The dappling of light awoke most of my dozing fellow travelers too, and I beheld us all in a chiaroscuro beyond time and motion that lasted and filled me with utter dread until a flight officer with gold chevrons on his sleeve walked past to the tail section. I heard somebody behind me cough and I drifted back into an uneasy sleep.

I was grateful that no one in Cleveland found my car worthy of stealing. I cranked it up and trailed a cloud of blue smoke out of the long-term lot and pointed it toward home. On the Shoreway near East 72nd, I spotted two husky figures carrying objects in their hands midway across the metal walkway above the Martin Luther King, Jr. underpass. I watched them to be sure they didn't stop. The objects in their hands cylindrical—graffiti artists. I'd investigated a couple homicides where a gang initiation required dropping rocks from there onto cars traveling at seventy-five miles an hour.

That's when I knew I was going back to Boston. Jack would have called it an epiphanic moment. Two boys walking across a bridge on their way to paint gang graffiti somewhere, maybe go down to the lake's edge, roll a drunk, terrify some citizens. Last week a man fishing off the breakwater was sodomized by three males. It all made no sense, any of it. Nor did going back to Boston.

I pulled off Interstate 90 at the Mentor exit, the humid air rank with rotting fish, bought a sandwich and coffee at the local McDonald's, and called O'Reilly. No answer. I drove to his office but one of the maintenance staff told me had not been in all day.

"Had some bad news last week," one man said. "Told the foreman he wasn't coming until the end of the week to sign checks."

I called his house from there again but no answer; the recording machine wasn't on. Ever since I ceased being a homicide police, I have tried to reacquaint myself with other people's notions of privacy, but it is a hard habit to break. I hoped that he was—despite what little he gave off over the phone—grieving Annaliese, and I decided to get my business with him done while he was susceptible. I wanted him to bankroll me for another week, send me back to Boston, and let me get closer to the truth of what happened to Annaliese.

I didn't dare risk his saying no over the phone because I couldn't afford to return on my own, and I thought a face-to-face conversation with him was necessary. Convince him to bankroll me a week, let me get this thing squared away so I know just a little more than I did then about the circumstances that caused a young girl's life to go leaking onto a motel floor. *Butchered.* The pathologist simply confirmed Marcus' word for it in polysyllabic jargon: *Exsanguinated.*

He lived in an antique brick-and-wood, two-storey structure set far back from the highway. An expensive landscaping job out front was in progress; a small hill of fresh soil and dozens of bags of peat moss lay next to the house. I saw a Lexus and a Camaro occupying both slots in the garage. The ass-end of the Lexus stuck out too far to close the door, so I figured O'Reilly was coming or going. I practiced my smile climbing the steps, something harder to do every day in this abattoir of a civilization.

No answer. Lights on, nobody home, as they say. *Fuck this.*

I banged the back door hard enough to wobble the glass panes. Walked the perimeter, looked in the windows. Gave it five minutes of shouting and knocking. Nobody even close enough to hear me.

Contrary to TV, you don't always use a credit card to slip a latch. You can take off your shoe and hammer the glass, or, as I preferred, a large pipe wrench for emergencies I keep under my seat. I call it Henry. Short for Henry Lee Lucas, serial killer, who with another sleazebag named Ottis O'Toole crisscrossed the US in a killing spree a few years back. I had heard that the ragtag warriors facing Caesar's disciplined legions used to name their spears before going into battle.

I wrapped the wrench in an old blanket I kept in the trunk and picked my window. Some French windows in the front would enable me to climb through without a lot of muscle. I broke all the glass right down to the glazier points at the top and bottom, reached up, thumbed the lock back and let myself in.

I entered a spacious den. A lot of wood. Ceiling fan. Large-screen TV. The furnace was on despite the warm weather. I traveled from room to room downstairs and went upstairs. Halfway up, it hit me: the smell. I debated whether to leave my jacket on because it's a smell you don't get out of your clothes that easily, but it wasn't bad enough to strip.

Much hotter upstairs. None of the ceiling fans on.

He was in the master bedroom, trussed up in a leather outfit. The faint, sweet smell strong now, a few black flies hovering around his mouth. One had already laid maggots in the corner of his left eye. I watched one walk into and out of his mouth. The heat was accelerating decomposition, but there were large purple splotches on the exposed skin of his lower back and behind his thighs where the blood had settled; another day or so in this heat and the blood would break down, as would the gases insde. His lips had drifted back from his teeth. An empty bottle of Glenfiddich was on the floor.

Both arms were tied in front of him with nylon flexties. The cord around his neck, fastened to an eyebolt behind the door, looked like silk. His bare legs were splayed out in front of him with the bottoms of his feet touching; the rest was suspended a few inches above the floorboards by the cord stretched taut and biting through the flesh of his neck where it had turned black.

I figured that I had time for three rooms. I did all the drawers, bottoms first, in all the dressers but found nothing except some unused cellophane bags under a shirt drawer. There was no bag on the bed or on the floor. No bag anywhere else that might have come off his head if he had flailed around at the last moment before he died. Why, I wondered, would the killer leave so obvious a clue? It made no sense. Everything else said autoerotic asphyxiation. I calculated the time from my Boston call. He drew his last unsober breath on this Earth 36 hours ago.

I did two other rooms and came up with one more item of interest in a secretary with those clever little sleeves secreted behind ornate carvings. O'Reilly sent a considerable amount of money to white supremacist causes, including $500 to the Byron De La Beckwith Defense Fund. There was a personal note of thanks from the defense committee folded around the canceled check. De La Beckwith had even scrawled a spidery "thanks."

I was beginning to feel as if there were wires to me too. Wondering who could be holding those wires raised the hackles on my neck.

CHAPTER 6

Feature this: I'm coming out of my office on the Strip, haven't had a client in five weeks; no rich daddies looking for their wayward kids. The credit cards are maxed out and the bank account is as dry as the Gobi; my credit's shrunk to zip everywhere but the one place where I have a friend left in the world who will stand me to a drink. I was waiting for Marta to turn on the neon sign to open her husband's joint, and concentrating on his neon sign to light as I began weaving between cars to cross the street. I nearly get clipped by a convertible and I look up in time to see the gold-toothed smile of Mike Tyson looking down on me. He was seated in the back of a Mercedes convertible with Don King. This is after Robin Givens and before he lost his title to Buster Douglas in Japan. Before the rape conviction and prison sentence, before two more wives, eight children, his cocaine arrest, that goofy WWF wrestling stint, and his IRS woes.

Tyson was the wunderkind of boxing, its brightest star, and elected grand marshal for the opening-day festivities at Jefferson-on-the-Lake. He had come in with King for Memorial Day. Tyson waved to the crowd and tipped a baseball cap with Arabic writing beneath an Islamic logo. His vast manor house down Route 534 wasn't far from King's former training camp in Orwell and had IRON MIKE scrolled into the metal arch above the gate. In those days, before Tyson swung on America's favorite buffoon for stealing him blind, King was vainly trying to keep Mike from all that temptation in New York. That day, antsy and depressed as I was, something so unnerved me about his sudden presence I lost my desire for drink, turned on my heel and went back inside my office and had a long fitful nap full of bad dreams. Existentialists don't have heroes, but they do have epiphanies and Mike was mine. I think of all that he had done since his boyhood in Bed-Stuy to his conversion to veganism on the *Ellen DeGeneres Show* and I realize that, my own petty life in comparison, it all ends the same. In a hundred years, none of it matters.

One week after finding the body, I was summoned for another round of questioning by Det. Sgt. Ronald Jones. Jones was an ex-state trooper and one of that five percent of all cops who would have been a criminal if he hadn't become a cop. I used to wonder how he could give up the fascist black so enamored by the state boys. His message on my machine was polite enough, but if you scraped away the veneer, it was blunt cop talk for "we want to see you now."

I greeted Phil on my way upstairs and nodded toward a few cubicles to some of my former colleagues who weren't ashamed to acknowledge me.

Chief Millimaki, as uncouth and unkempt as ever, waved me into his office, so the interrogation was going to be anything but routine.

"There's a man come all the way from New York City here. You know him from the last time you dragged some business our way."

On cue, a dapper, fiftyish man with wavy silver hair walked in from the outer office. Trim in his double-breasted suit and a tie I should have thought too loud for the FBI gun-club network of good old boys, I extended my own hand to meet his coming at me.

Special Agent Booth. Damn it.

"Thomas Haftmann, ah, a pleasure to see you again. How many years? Four? You're looking well."

"Three," I said.

"Yeesss." Dragging it out three syllables as if he couldn't recall. "The bureau keeping you busy?"

"I've just returned from a temporary posting in Puerto Rico. Minnesota before that."

"That's Pine Ridge," I said.

"Not many people would know that." His teeth were still gleaming but I could hear the wheels turn, assessing me. "I headed the regional office in New Mexico before that."

"Gee, they've been moving you around a bit," I said and made my own smile big.

"They sure have," Booth said.

Silver tongue to go with his silver hair. Pine Ridge Reservation was the biggest shithole in America outside the South Bronx. Leonard Peltier and the Oglala Sioux Nation have a long memory for the FBI and with good reason. Booth must have stepped on some important toes, or as the feebs say, his elbows got too sharp.

We grinned at each other like two fuckwits. Truth is, Booth should have hated my guts, and he had every reason to. Crap postings in Albuquerque and San Juan, not to mention South Dakota—the toilet for a senior agent whose career parabola had been flawless before he hooked up with me—could only mean one thing. When Booth was agent-in-charge in the hunt for Ohio's most notorious serial killer, he had given me too much slack and failed to rein me in, and even though the killer was put down in a firefight, he must have been unofficially reprimanded in true FBI style by those sideways promotions to places that rookies out of Quantico got as first assignments.

I thought of the two dead state troopers on the floor of Perry Nuclear Power Plant, one of them sprawled across me, dripping blood in my face, feeling the metal of the gun secreted in his ankle holster *so close to my hand if only I can reach it, ah, there, there, got it, that crazy fucker seeing me now . . .*

I snapped to and heard Booth, dapper as ever, cut his eyes slightly to Chief Millimaki and dismiss him. Millimaki took the hint, not gracefully, and shifting his signature cigar around in his mouth with a wet, plopping noise, took leave of us in his own office.

"Well, Thomas," said Booth, "we seem to be star-crossed lovers, you and I."

"So it would seem," I said.

"I'm glad to see you're recovered. I hope you'll forgive me for saying this, but I wasn't altogether sure you were going to pull through your ordeal when I saw you last."

"I don't think much about those days," I said.

"I understand," he replied.

"Are you here to discuss the great themes of life and art or do you have something else in mind, Special Agent Booth?"

Then, as if noticing for the first time, he said, "Aren't you about twenty pounds lighter than you used to be? I remember seeing you run. Half-moons of sweat under your arms, your belly hanging over your belt—"

"I've cut back on the Scotch and bourbon a little. You know, I believe I'll take a jog around the park right now."

"Knock it off," This said with a bit more snarl than he meant.

"OK," I said, "what gives?"

"Ever heard of the Phineas Priesthood?"

Priests. Oh shit. Boston. Here we go again.

• • •

And so he told me. Not all of it right there. Booth was no fool, and he didn't trust Millimaki as far as he could throw him. Out of his presence, he used to call him "the fat one," if memory served, but FBI agents are taught to work closely with local law enforcement. Never alienate street cops because you never know when you might want to use them again. The operant word being use.

It was about racism. Organized murder, to be precise—a movement to create chaos and civil disorder on the scale of nothing ever seen in the country before. Not like the civil rights nor Vietnam protests, those organic movements of the people, but a combination of alliances of top and bottom of society, although the bottom would never know it. Through the well-greased system of legal corruption in which politicians are willingly bought or rented with lobbyists' cash doled out by the richest and most powerful, the impossible becomes possible. When the dust settles and the people demand order, they'll get it all right—but it will resemble the Ordnüng of Nazi Germany more than anything.

I looked at Booth as if I were hearing one of those conspiracy theories from one of our local juiceheads at the bar.

"You're crazy," I said. "Doesn't the FBI have anything better to do now that bin Laden's sleeping with the fishes?"

"Our purvey is domestic by law, Haftmann. That's the CIA's job, not ours," Booth replied primly.

"OK," I said, "I'll play along. Tell me how this organized chaos begins."

He did at length and through three sloe gin fizzes to my sparkling sodas and a St. Pauly Girl.

He said it will start with secret funding of racist groups and hundreds of acts of violence all over the United States.

I interjected: "We still vote in this country, right?"

"Of course," Booth admitted, "but what's the significance of that when the entire propaganda machine of the media is overwhelmed by money to influence the direction people will vote."

"We're not sheep. People still think now and then," I said. "Reporters dig up stories. You can't buy everyone in the country, for God's sake."

"Don't be naïve, Thomas. You just need fifty-one percent."

According to Booth, one group in particular had surfaced in recent FBI reports that had for years been documenting and tracking white supremacist groups ever since the assassination of Medgar Evers in Mississippi in 1963. This was a secret society that called itself the Phineas Priesthood.

"Come on," I said. "We've got a black President of the United States. Nobody pays any attention to those Neanderthals nowadays."

"You're wrong. Haven't you been listening? Where were you when a few Wall Street degenerate gamblers nearly took the economy of the United States over the ledge in oh-eight? This isn't a dying twitch of Southern racism from the civil rights days. This is a new federation working behind the scenes while the entire country is obsessed with Muslims next door."

"That's why the whole country is fed up with you federal police," I said. "Paranoia, Booth. Didn't you people learn anything from Waco or Ruby Ridge?"

"It's *because* of Ruby Ridge and Waco we're so hamstrung now," Booth said. He sipped his drink and made a face. Tico's wasn't known for serving bonded Scotch.

"It was a dying movement, but these are the very conditions that make for non-violent coups d' état."

"I'll concede this much: the Midwest is like Appalachia now. We're a dying breed and none of you in Washington give a shit."

Booth grinned.

"What's so fucking funny?"

"You just proved my point," he said.

"Look," I said, "it's too much. Congressional hearings on Muslims in America as a smokescreen for big business or whatever it is just so a few rich people can grab what's left? A few rednecks joining the Tea Party or falling for that Birther nonsense—come on, that dog doesn't hunt."

"Greed," Booth said smugly, "has no bottom."

"You're Thomas Aquinas now," I mocked.

"You should read *City of God*," he replied.

"I don't need to," I said, "I've read Dante." Actually, I skipped *Paradiso* and *Purgatorio*. Everything I needed to know about human beings is in the *Inferno*.

"Then I shouldn't have to convince you that rain is wet. Read history. Hitler didn't get to power because he wasn't helped every step of the way. Bankers and politicians did more to assist the rise of National Socialism than the commies."

"I still say, so what? Just because Donald Trump goes on television and demands the President show his birth certificate," I said, "doesn't mean he's an unwitting tool of a conspiracy of braindead racist thugs and the conservative establishment."

Booth stared into his drink, pushed it aside, and then ordered another sloe gin fizz. I remembered that drink from high school; it was a girl's drink then.

"I just don't believe that's possible," I said. I barked a laugh: ludicrous.

"When you put powerful people, money, and a common cause together, things can happen."

"Oh really? I suppose you have evidence of this?"

"We do and we didn't need warrantless wiretaps to get it. Look at this."

Booth handed me the case file and told me to read it all and not ask any questions until I was done. By then it was midafternoon and we were still sitting in Tico's Place. In the few short weeks I had been back from Boston, a cold spring had flip-flopped into a hot and muggy early summer.

I was tempted to ask Booth if he appreciated the irony; we had nearly come to a fistfight in the station house once when I learned that he had finally wearied of my demands for information, files, and updates and had told everyone to freeze me out of the investigation.

While I perused, Booth gazed out the window over a periwinkle blue lake, watching the gulls wheel and dive among white caps at schools of early shad. By late August, they'd swim to shore to in their annual massive die-off, millions of them. The odor of rot would be everywhere.

And so I read names, dates, and facts that went back thirty years. Much of it was familiar to me from newspapers and having lived through those times. Some of the names rang bells like Byron De La Beckwith, for example. The killer of civil rights leader Medgar Evers. There was a faded newspaper clipping from the *Knoxville News Sentinel,* dated September 17, 1973, in which Beckwith was arrested for carrying an armed bomb into New Orleans. He did three years in solitary confinement at the Louisiana State Pen in Angola. I scanned one of Beckwith's letters in 1986 to *The News-Free Press* in Chattanooga on sodium fluoride in the public water system:

'So also does constant dosage work on the human mind to
stifle normal resistance, to say, tyranny, and also, of
course, to greatly diminish wholesome resourcefulness.'

I found an envelope with a return address in Signal Mountain, Tennessee, to the local water board. Inside was a letter from Beckwith making the same complaint, and noting that "queers/perverts, and even a few innocents with AIDS, die much faster drinking fluoridated water." He had added: "So, there is a great scrambling/shifting of population to non-fluoridated water. Well, if fluoride kills AIDS-infected perverts, en masse, then that to me is great—God orders the same (using stones)—or have you read your Bible lately?"

Other clippings detailed his shadowy life and affiliations with hate groups beyond his obsession with fluoride and AIDS. Twenty-five years after killing Evers, the *Jackson Daily News* quoted a Mississippi attorney who demanded Beckwith be tried again for a murder he publicly bragged about.

I looked up to see Booth calmly sipping his drink and gazing out over the water.

"What's this?" I asked.

I showed him membership information on the American Pistol and Rifle Association. Booth barely glanced at it. "That's a military survivalist outfit near Benton, Tennessee. Remember an extremist group called The Order, early 1980's?" He rattled off names: Ardie McBrearty, Randall Rader, Richard Scutari, Andrew Barnhill. Netted four million from armed robbery and counterfeiting. Murder, bombings. They first met at Benton during a three-day survival hike.

I riffled brochures with titles like *Jews Are of Their Father, the Devil*, advertisements for various Christian-survivalist groups where one might learn the "truth about Martin Lucifer Coon," the black race, the real goals of international Jewry and "Jewsmedia"—and enjoy a little firearms practice on the side. Beckwith himself operated one for a time called the Rod of Iron Christian Mission. Pamphlets from para-

107

military and revolutionary organizations of all kinds like the Southern National Party claiming the South never surrendered at Appomattox ("This is a popular misconception encouraged by liberal academics and the left-wing media, but it is completely false") and Tom Metzger's White Aryan Resistance. I had seen Metzger on a talk show once. He referred to blacks as a "mud race."

I had to stop when the shooting pains behind my eyeball became too bad. "So what else is new, Booth? Most of this stuff is old garbage. Except for the cross-burning and baseball-bat wielding, there's nothing here that isn't covered by free speech. Just your garden-variety Klansmen and Neo-Nazis—or am I missing something?"

"You are, as a matter of fact. But so haven't a lot of people for a long time."

I didn't know whether I should pity him or laugh at him. Looking for a comeback on the strength of the rise of neo-Nazis in America. I had once admired him though we didn't get along.

"I'm having tissue samples from O'Reilly sent to Basic Sciences. We've already done this for the daughter. It's a big case, and getting bigger all the time."

I reached for something to say. "So old Doc Harris fumbled another one?"

I myself had a long working relationship with the conservative and pugnacious Jefferson County pathologist. Harris wouldn't sign off on a corpse with a knife sticking in its back and call it homicide unless the killer's hand was attached. I had made the turkey wattles under his neck vibrate with indignation more than once when I chivvied him about some point of forensics. He was arrogant right up to his polka-dotted tie and down to his Oxford wingtips. He'd no sooner clap eyes on me than he would leave the office and order an assistant to walk me off the premises. During one especially acrimonious exchange, I told him he could fuck up a baked potato, and I saw the tips of his handlebar mustache quiver with rage.

"What did he miss?"

"We won't know for sure until the results come back. Maybe something from toxicology that Harris's rinkydink lab couldn't find."

Booth being coy. "C'mon, Booth. You know Harris would send anything he couldn't handle to Cuyahoga County especially with you leaning on him."

Booth sniffed and smoothed his silver pompadour with one hand. "Let's just leave it at asphyxiation for now. That's what the death certificate says."

"So why Annaliese too? What are you guys looking for?"

"You were in Boston. What did you think?"

"I don't know," I said and winced at the ugly memory. "She bled from every orifice."

"We found out one thing," he said. "One of the bullets bounced around inside her skull and made a mess before exiting, but she was clubbed too."

"Clubbed?"

"Her brain almost fell out of her head when they lifted her onto the gurney."

"All right, Booth. Stop simpering and tell me what you came here to tell me."

That's when he got to the part about the Phineas Priesthood. Before Beckwith died, he was a kind of ambassador-at-large among hate groups. He knew them all and despite his public buffoonery, such as walking into a courtroom with his Celtic cross dangling from his withered neck and shading his eyes to scan the jurors for blacks, issued moronic statements on race, the water, and AIDS. But he held some troubling influence nonetheless.

One of the FBI documents was a prison guard's testimony about the people who came to see Beckwith in prison; someone had apparently angered the old man because he described the change in Beckwith's demeanor as staggering: a great snaky vein popped out on his forehead and he raged at this man, some underling or messenger: "Be very careful because I have more power in jail than you have out there."

Some interesting people kept the former candy salesman on their personal Christmas card lists dated back to the early 1960's when, according to Booth, the FBI had already documented over 300 separate acts of violence from the White Knights of the Ku Klux Klan in Mississippi. Only one of which happened to be the assassination of Medgar Evers, shot in the back by a sniper using a 6x scope, as he stepped away from his car coming home from a rally at the New Jerusalem Baptist Church in Jackson.

I flashed back to the cover photo from *Life* and segued to the infamous triple murder of three civil rights workers. I was sailing on the ore boats at the time, aboard the *J. Burton Ayers*, my first steamship as an ordinary seaman on the Great Lakes, and I remembered Max, the watchman I had killed in that alley in Lackawanna, New York, mentioning to me that a nigger, a nigger-lover, and a Jewboy had been dug up near a levee somewhere in the deep South. "You look like a nigger-lover to me, boy," he said. We were headed into Duluth harbor with a load of taconite. "That right, Haftmann?" When I turned from coiling one of the ropes on deck, I saw him grimacing at me in that open-mouthed smile of his, all rotten teeth and rank breath. *You a Jew-lover too, Haftmann? Faggot cocksucking college boy nigger lover . . .*

Booth recited some names and organizations from the Beckwith file—a *Who's Who* from that darkened corner of our history that finally numbed us to public murder. I was one of millions born into the promise of the world after the Second World War and one of those who watched it turn to shit. My pathetic little wheel of destiny was also turning in those days before all promises withered including my job, my marriage, and hardest of all, the children I'll never father.

Micah, always Micah that ripped inside me with her claws.

I snapped to and heard Booth reciting names, some of them from yellowed newspaper clippings like Sam Bowers, Imperial Wizard of the Ku Klux Klan; Pastor Richard G. Butler, founder of Aryan Nations. I read his fan letter to Beckwith in prison and of course he signed it with an "88," meaning *Heil Hitler*; Pastor Dan Gayman of Christian Identity (Beckwith, ordained a minister in 1977, wrote a prison letter thanking the pastor for his inspirational tapes); J.B. Stoner, founder of the National States Rights party; Metzger from California and David Dukes from Louisiana hailing him a hero and "selfless patriot" . . .

"Haftmann, are you following me?"

"Yes, continue, Professor."

That drew a scowl and a swipe at the silver hair. "OK, I'm boring you with ancient history. Let me cut to the present. Beckwith's a liquid, but let me throw one more name at you, another close friend and supporter. His name is Richard Kelly Hoskins of Lynchburg, Virginia."

I said, "Means nothing to me."

Booth, ever the lecturer, said, "Hoskins isn't one of your wigged-out types, spewing racist filth in all directions. He stays out of the lime-light mostly. But he did one thing of interest. He appointed himself historian of a secret society—"

"Your Phineas Priesthood," I finished.

"Exactly. Read this." He handed me another sheaf of papers.

"Jesus, I feel like I'm cramming for a high school test."

"Just skim it then," he said and muttered something about me being a "one-eyed Cyclops."

I sighed and signaled the bartender over. Tico's son Cesar used to be a hot prospect of a welterweight who trained with Kelly "The Ghost" Pavlik in Jack Loew's Southside gym in Youngstown before he busted his hand up. I ordered a shot of Jack and a beer chaser.

Booth looked at me.

"I earned this one," I said, "listening all afternoon to your con-spiracy theory."

I read on.

Hoskins was a follower of the Christian Identity movement be-fore he got the writing bug and began recording the history of the Phineas Priesthood. "Here, read this first." He handed me a Bible, and I looked up to see Tico giving me a big grin with his gold tooth. He made a thumb's-up sign to me. Tico was as devout a Catholic as I was an atheist.

"Uh-oh." I said. "When Tico shows that gold incisor, it means something. I'll be hearing about the day I got religion in Tico's Place for the next ten years. Next time, use the xerox machine." To Tico, I said, "Wipe that shit-eating grin off your face, you wet-backed spawn of Satan and bring this man another drink while I peruse the Holy Word."

Booth was not amused: "Don't be a clown, Haftmann. Read the part I marked. Right there, number twenty-five."

What I read was a mini-action narrative, a double homicide, if you will, but not a whodunit. A certain Phineas who felt himself inspired by God skewered an Israelite and then rammed the same bloody javelin into the man's woman. It seems he disapproved of race-mix-ing, she being a Midianite woman. God chose to reward Phineas with the covenant of eternal priesthood.

Marcus' last word before collapsing onto the park bench. Old Man O'Reilly's caller, a priest: '. . . Annaliese safe from the pollution of this world.'

Booth, downing his third sloe gin fizz under the staccato whir of Tico's broken ceiling fan, turned to me and said: "John Wilkes Booth, who by the way, is a distant kin to me, and Jesse James were members of the Phineas Priesthood."

That's why I'm an existentialist. Life surrounds you with so much absurdity that, half the time, you don't know whether you're on foot or horseback.

• • •

It didn't surprise me that O'Reilly died intestate. I'd seen other busy men, well off like him, leave the little detail of passing on to the last minute because they assumed they'd be spending that last minute in a four-poster bed talking about stocks and bonds to their grandchildren. *Let the state have it*, I thought, since Annaliese wasn't going to inherit anything beside the small space they had packed her remains in somewhere in downtown Boston. I on the other hand was beat out of my time and expenses by the Grim Reaper. I couldn't afford to sit around brooding. Business has never been that good for me.

And thanks to those Wall Street sharks who brought us this long, drawn-out recession, I have been dwelling in the driest off season I've ever known. Money was scarce. So when I left Booth in Tico's he was about three sheets to the wind and telling a very bored Tico the only proper way to make a White Lady. I knew our conversation was merely interrupted, not finished, but I also knew how Booth's cagey mind worked, and I wasn't at all surprised to be sitting in my office the next morning checking my messages and tossing a few missed opportunities into the circular file when the phone rang and he asked to meet me for lunch. "Pick the place, Haftmann," he said, "this is your town, but nothing too squalid, please." I told him fine, that I'd meet him at the Bavarian House at 1:00 p.m. sharp.

I don't know why I picked the House because I had stopped going in there, even though Fat Augie DeDomenico wasn't the owner. Augie used to be my bookie, and everyone else's, for that matter, but he had been caught skimming. Two years ago somebody put two bullets in his head, thus severing for all time Augie's connection to the Youngstown Mafia. My fracas with Augie during that violent summer of the serial killer hunt earned me a trimming from a couple of Augie's goons in an alley outside the bar.

I was sitting at the bar when Booth came in on the trot and had a ginger ale ordered before he sat down.

"How do you young men do it?" I asked.

"Shut up, Haftmann. I know for a fact you used to hear the chimes at midnight on occasion." Booth didn't know all of it, of course, but he had seen enough of me, red-eyed, unshaven, and hung over in the mornings to know I once had a serious drinking problem. One big reason he wanted me cut me out of the last investigation.

I said, "I've heard those chimes at seven in the morning."

"Being a problem drinker is nothing to brag about," he said with that sanctimonious look.

"I never did have a problem drinking, Booth," and hoisted a glass in his direction.

He ignored my cheap wit and started pulling out more papers from his inside pocket.

"Oh shit, no," I said. "No more homework until you fill me in all the way, daddy-O."

"Annaliese O'Reilly, or did you lose too many brain cells from that maniac's clubbing to figure that out by now?"

I stared at him.

"Sorry," Booth said. "That was crass."

"Forget it."

"They called me in on this because, as you know, I've got some experience organizing field investigations. This one was originally assigned to the head of the Boston bureau, but Washington co-opted me into the operation three weeks ago."

"Pull my other leg. The one with bells on it."

"OK, here's the truth. One of our agents spotted you sitting on a park bench waiting for someone. That someone was being followed and that someone sat down next to you and that someone died a short while after. You piqued the interest of the surveillance team. You were investigated. Your file was retrieved. Thomas Haftmann, private investigator, ex-homicide detective, Cleveland, and, once upon a time, part-time special investigator for the Federal Bureau of Investigation."

"You took away that I.D. card back before I was out of the hospital."

"What did you expect? We had to extricate ourselves from possible embarrassment. ”

"Booth, kindly get to the point." *Bureaucrats. They should have their own gang slogan—We don't die, we multiply.*

"Ah, let me see. You were the subject of much animated discussion at the table, as I recall it. We discussed several options for, uh, dealing with you. The one we chose was, I feel, the right one. We aren't going to pressure you as we did last time because I have seen how you react to pressure. I know how fast you can muddy the waters, so to speak."

He took a long pause to eyeball me before saying: "This is a big investigation, Haftmann. It's what you cops sometimes call a red-ball. We think the Phineas Priesthood is killing white girls who have involved themselves with blacks or Hispanics. Annaliese was killed by one member of this society in particular who is responsible for at least fourteen women."

That sobered me fast. "So how can I help you?"

"Our VICAP profile says he's a bona fide sociopath, dangerous, acting out fantasies, and too organized to be caught by stupid mistakes. He has eluded every trap we've set for him."

"Why Annaliese?" I asked. "There must be hundreds of girls to choose from in every big city. Race-mixing isn't even an issue today."

"Don't bet on it. The people I'm talking about dislike—how shall I put it—that kind of Social Darwinism more than ever. We want to know everything from the time you sat on the bench waiting for your dope-dealer friend to the moment you boarded your flight back."

"Why didn't you take me in for questioning in Boston?"

I'll give Booth credit. He doesn't flinch from delivering bad news.

"We were hoping you would lead us to him."

Here it comes, I thought. "Exactly how . . .”

"We think he's watching you, Haftmann."

"Uh, *who?*"

"Don't know yet."

I didn't hear another word. Was this some kind of cosmic joke? Booth was nattering on but I didn't hear much of what he was saying just then. I felt like the world's biggest fool. Micah and her books and her quotes—but I could hear her voice in my head as clear as crystal: *A man may smile and smile and still be a villain . . .*

I tuned back into Booth:

". . . we have the record of the phone call to you at the hotel. It's the same phone from which a call was made to the motel where Annaliese and Marcus Gordon were staying. The phone is in the lobby of major publishing house on Beacon Hill."

Cooney telling me the call was made from the book publisher . . .

"Booth, why didn't you guys bring Boston homicide into this?"

"We decided against it. Two reasons. First, the publicity would hurt us more than help us right now. You remember the Strangler panic? Second, gangs and drugs are preoccupying homicide. Besides, we know there's a big problem with information leakage in the Boston police department. One of our informants tells us that he paid off several cops over the drug murders going on right now. Charming young man with the street name 'Bones.'"

"He has a brother, 'Psycho,'" I said. "They call themselves Best Friends. I met one."

"I already know that from the file on you. I was right to bring you in."

"Why? Because I'm a magnet for drawing bad people?"

"Just do your part and stay within the guidelines—"

"What guidelines exactly? The FBI guidelines for stalking horses?"

"What's wrong with that?"

His mug hanging out over his drink was so deadpan I wasn't sure if he were kidding me.

"I don't want to get back into this," I said. "I had one go-round and that was enough for me. I'll tell you what I know, Booth, but that's all I want. Understand me?"

"OK, fair enough. Now tell me everything. Tell me how you got involved with her. Tell me everything you can remember from the day her father approached you . . ."

• • •

Booth never did believe in sharing information, so I had to pick and prod and piece things together afterward. I managed to get one big concession from him, however, and only because I said my life might be in danger: he agreed to let me read the VICAP profile on Annaliese's killer.

I remembered the one they did on my serial killer five years ago.

What they didn't know about his motives and habits wouldn't fit inside the circumference of a shot glass. The only time they came up short was in underestimating the scope of his fantasy. The fucker actually made it into the bowels of a nuclear power plant where he planned to blow the pipes in the water coolant system and trigger a meltdown. Kill everybody in the northeastern part of the Ohio from Toledo to Erie, Pennsylvania. Before he beat me into unconsciousness, I remember the look in his crazy eyes as he shook me like a rag doll. Gibberish was spewing out of his mouth, but I heard two words distinctly: *power* and *light*.

I had another phone call that day. O'Reilly's ex-wife in Pittsburgh called me to say she was coming in for his funeral. She knew that his body wasn't going to be released because I had explained to Ingrid what the state does in uncleared homicide cases when I told her about her daughter's remains. She nonetheless spent her own money to have a memorial plaque made up for him out in Kingsville and arranged for a simple service that would be performed above an empty grave. I promised to meet her flight in Erie and drive her in that evening. I went home to a TV dinner.

I couldn't remember the last time I played Russian Roulette on a Sunday. The black dog of depression was off howling in the distance instead of nipping at my heels. I met Annaliese's mother and we drove in silence except for the sounds she made into wadded balls of kleenexes. She wore a navy blue outfit that reminded me of the photo of her daughter fresh out of high school and on her way to work at the county courthouse. The air was humid, the night still muggy from the eighty degrees, and she had a line of perspiration above her lip. I put her up at the local Holiday Inn, and then went home to shower and shave (my habit of many years was to shave at night). I lay awake for hours, also a habit of years, and waited for the bad thoughts to stop.

I had no reason to expect that night's dreams to be less fearful than any other, but I wanted, for some reason, to think about Annaliese. It had been a long while since I'd cared about another human being, or thought of anyone except Micah, and I wanted to get to the bottom of this feeling. Why her? Why now? Something in me wanted me to get into this investigation. Why, I wondered, had this dead girl suddenly become so important to me? I tried very hard to think of her as I had glimpsed her before I saw her stretched out on the stainless steel autopsy slab with the constant dripping noises and the hoses washing away the blood and gore. I had the vaguest flashback of her on top of the bar, a freeze frame of a dark-haired young woman with a pretty oval face. Her breasts and groin obscured from view by the heads of the men at the bar. I did not look at her when I confronted Marcus in the street later, and I regretted that, because her voice was easy to recall—clear and soft in the chilly night air. Then the dark drew me into its vortex, and I was as good as dead.

• • •

Booth is nothing if not persistent. I thumbed off the connection three times already and the day wasn't over yet. I told him not to surveille me, and I told him if I saw any of his buttoned-down boys within a mile of my office on the Strip, I'd go over his head and complain. Like any government servant with at least a GS-12 rating, Booth dreaded the official reprimand. I'd burned him once before, and there was no love lost.

The only problem was that neither of us had a plan to catch the killer. The assumption that I was followed to Ohio was, I told Booth, ludicrous. We both let that hang in the air awhile because we both knew that the Jack-in-the-Box killer had done precisely that—moved into and out of the county despite every law-enforcement agency in the state on his trail. Even added to his body count with a woman in Canton and a young couple down in Tuscarawas County; he had pulverized their infant child's head against a wall as an afterthought and tossed its headless body in the river.

Trouble is, I began to get nightmares all over again. I'd feel my palms sweating just like the old days when my body's refrigeration system had to work overtime to get rid of all the booze. It was fear. I had that sick feeling a woman must get when she knows there's a deranged, obsessed male waiting out there for her, watching her every move.

I called Booth at the motel on Erieview. "All right," I said. "Let's finish it. I want to know the rest."

We met later that afternoon in his room. He pointed to three stacks of papers, each about eight inches deep, on his bed. I read the top page of the first stack. Technical mumbo-jumbo.

I sighed. "Booth, just give me the short version."

He did. I let him talk.

"Annaliese O'Reilly, we think, was killed by a man who is killing women associated with black males. She's the fourteenth woman between fifteen and thirty-seven years of age to lose her life in the Boston area between 1991 and 2009. We're talking about Boston metro mostly, but one professional woman, Marcine Windham, lived in Wollaston Beach and was killed in the parking lot of the Squantum Yacht Club. One body was dumped in Franklin Park, one apiece in Winthrop, Chelsea, and Somerville. There's no classic pattern of organized killing, no fantasy fulfillment. He's taking no trophies, no body parts missing, no articles of clothing. The bodies are not being positioned or touched after death. We've dusted eyeballs to be sure. The breast slashing appears to be of a piece with a victim's defensive wounds in the stabbing deaths."

"And Boston PD doesn't have any idea these murders are connected?"

"They asked us for a profile fifteen weeks ago," Booth noted, "so they are beginning to suspect a serial killer. Nobody's organized a task force or given out anything to the media."

"Why the one exception, that yacht club woman?"

"So far she's the only one not covered by the similarity of the victims' low socioeconomic status. The one exception. A professional woman, a book editor, stabbed in a parking lot. We're not sure about her. She had mace in her purse, so it could have been a random mugging."

"She had a black male companion, I assume?"

"Correct. Her husband is a graduate of Howard University, supervises underwriting in the John Hancock Building. Makes ninety thousand, married right out of college, two kids, no marital problems."

"How does she fit?"

"She doesn't—except for the biracial marriage. All the rest had black boyfriends, lovers, husbands too. But they were expendable types. Twelve had police records ranging from prostitution to petty drug charges, child endangering—that kind of thing. None of the families had clout or, like your girl, were drifters or runaways far from home. The killer or killers may have known that and it could be a calculated and acceptable risk."

"Why?" I asked.

"Because these are throwaway people, not real victims. She stood out. A gratuitous killing, we think. He wanted her, even though he had plenty of other potential victims who could have been disguised by virtue of their being nobodies."

"No, I meant why did you say 'calculated'? How do you know?"

"Crunch the numbers, probabilities say the common factor of these fourteen killings is the single fact of their being associated with black men."

The locals called them 'coalburners' and worse names.

"If there aren't obvious data linking the crimes," Booth added, "we tend to exclude them unless there's methodology pointing toward deliberate randomness, a kind of X factor we program in to keep the clever ones from hiding their personalities too deeply. The thing is, as you know from our common experience, true psychotics *must* reveal themselves. They have to leave something at a crime scene to satisfy the inner compulsions driving them."

"So he's a serial killer without a fantasy life?"

"He has a fantasy life, all right. We just don't know what it is yet."

"But you're thinking he's a member of this Phineas Priesthood?"

"If that is the case, and if he's disguising his dementia under the ritualized killing of women guilty of miscegenation, then it's troublesome."

Troublesome—another coy Boothian term for *Shit, meet Fan.*

"So he could be killing for his own reasons," I said, trying to understand what Booth was telling me, "not so much for those ideological reasons you told me about?"

"Yes. It's possible. Right now, we know that killings of white women are increasing in all major cities—this blends with traditional white flight, so it's not a glaring statistic at the Department of Justice. But it's working toward that perfect storm of civil disorder and chaos I spoke of."

"I'm guessing here, Booth, but isn't the incidence of murdered white women associated with black males high anyway?"

Booth said, "About five times. There are social reasons for that. We're trying to find the proverbial needle in the haystack in a nation where domestic killings and murder by stalking are making it possible for great numbers of women to be killed without the public suspecting that racially motivated murders are being carried out all over the US."

He grabbed the middle pile of papers from the bed and handed them to me.

"Look at this, Haftmann. Check the statistics."

I looked at the statistics: Tampa 20% higher rate of homicide for women with black men, Baltimore 26%, Washington, DC 23%, New York 19%, Chicago 11%, Detroit 17%, Boston 67%. Every big city, but Boston was off the charts.

"This Phineas Priesthood is responsible?"

"The Christian Identity movement is being revitalized and we've either infiltrated or have informers on every skinhead, white supremacist, Klan outfit in the nation. We know what the lowlifes in the movements are doing almost before they know themselves. But two years ago, something happened. It was as if these wackos were deliberately lying low. The Southern Poverty Law Center discovered hate crimes dropped momentarily."

"You think somebody made a difference?"

"We think that somebody new was taking over the Phineas Priesthood and that somebody was giving it a new direction. You did your homework last night, I trust."

"I did," I lied. "Not the most fascinating biography I've read."

It was Byron de la Beckwith's sanctioned biography and it was called *Glory in Conflict*. The page Booth had marked had two yellow highlighted passages. Beckwith, under a thin veneer of humility, declined to lead an unnamed group with "roots traceable to antiquity" because he felt that he was not qualified "intellectually or spiritually." It was gibberish and I closed the book after twenty pages. Booth was staring at the closed drapes as if he were scrutinizing the weave pattern.

"Here is a man who has been a busy little chatterbox his whole life," he said. "Bragged everywhere, even in print, of murdering a civil rights leader, threatened people in and out of prison, written hundreds of letters professing every word or deed he has done—a defense attorney's worst nightmare. Yet now, for the first time in his life, this racist cretin is conspicuously silent. We think he knows what's going on:

"Oh, he's become in death some kind of Saint Paul to the racist movement?"

Booth ignored the sarcasm. "We infiltrated a Seattle skinhead group last year and obtained copies of some private correspondence of one of their troubleshooters. This man hinted at a 'priesthood' in the vanguard of the coming race war that was going to make *der Führer*'s four-point genocidal program against the Jews look like amateur hour."

"So bring him in and shake him down," I said.

"He was shot in the back of the head and dumped in the desert. April, last year. Unsolved homicide. No leads."

"What convinces the FBI this is for real now?"

"One segment of it is highly organized. We keep hearing whispers of this secret society gearing up to make its move. We don't know who the real brains behind it is, but we keep coming back to Boston and the killing of these women is a prelude to a larger plan."

It didn't make sense to me how white women sleeping with blacks fit into Armageddon.

"All we know for sure is," Booth went on, breaking his own curtain reverie, "that some very prominent people are being attracted to racism in one form or another."

"Booth, I think there's something—maybe a lot you're not telling me," I said.

Booth sighed theatrically, an old habit of his. I had the one functioning eye but he regarded himself as the one-eyed man in the kingdom of the blind.

"The cities are teeming with poverty and drugs," he said. "There are no jobs. Washington politics is mired in gridlock. The Nation of Islam grows more followers by the day. Whites are flocking to the extremist groups. Who's going to stop it from boiling over?"

"There's fear in the streets," I countered, "but things will never be that bad we can't fix it."

"When did you turn optimist?" Booth snapped.

"I don't know, Booth. There's just too much even for diehard conspiracy buffs."

"Then consider this. One of those think tanks did a prediction study two years ago that was quietly buried in some DC warehouse. They do war-games scenarios, only they use data on the demographics, technological and social factors instead of missiles. They forecast the lid is going to come off the top because we have put such strains on the economy—hell, the middle class is already convinced the woods are burning."

"Bullshit."

"I'm telling you that the top people in this country are scared witless of that report. Five years, they give it. Society is fractured along lines of race like never before, Muslims around the world are openly preaching anti-Semitism, anti-Crusaderism and if this recession doesn't abate or, worst case, teeter into a depression—well, the biggest predictor of imminent disintegration is the rise of white supremacy. This isn't a Mississippi phenomenon anymore."

Not here, not here. Having a German surname made me a target for young toughs in an Irish-Catholic neighborhood. Nobody believed a runt with a funny-looking moustache could rise to power but he did with the help of politicians, patricians, and bankers.

Despite my cynicism, I knew Booth wasn't blowing smoke and I was no longer convinced he was trying to make himself important to headquarters. I threw religion and God away a long time ago, and I never understood people's obsession with explaining why there is or is no God. Although my own existentialist fervor was cooled the day I bumped into a Sartre essay about the difference between *en-soi* and *pour-soi,* I don't need Sartre or Nietzsche to know the world is a shitbucket. I just can't explain it in words of more than two syllables. Booth was still talking, droning like a pesky mosquito in my ear lobe.

" . . . half the conditions have already been met. Rand and Carnegie did their own and corroborated the original study. It *can* happen here."

"C'mon, Booth. Those pinheads are jerking you off!"

"How can you tell?"

"They're just dipping their snouts in the public trough at taxpayers' expense," I said. Playing devil's advocate to Booth wasn't my idea of a fun afternoon, but I didn't want to give him the satisfaction of agreeing with him. I know what's going on in the world is sickening. I've seen Bosnia on the news too. I was drunk all through Vietnam. Everywhere today is Bosnia. Or a Rwanda waiting to happen. Shitholes like Haiti are metaphors of the human condition of the future— a world of tribes eager to stick a tire of gasoline around your neck or hack you to pieces with a machete.

"So why me?"

"Because you happened to take a stroll in a park one day in Boston. We had Marcus Gordon all staked out because we finally had a lead on one of these Phineas Priests. We figured their Boston man was an out-and-out psychopath. He isn't killing for a race war. He's killing because he enjoys it so well."

"I don't know, Booth. It's just too fantastic."

"What's fantastic, Haftmann, is your naiveté. Study history. You yourself know from your police experience that there are too many jurisdictional problems in police work. You don't know what the homicide bureau in the next precinct is working on unless you run into another detective and he tells you. State computers can't quantify data with as much sophistication as we can at Behavioral Sciences—"

"Je-sus, Booth. Just tell me why you're so sure of all this. Tell me why the killer is taking a calculated risk."

"We think he's simulating a serial killer by leaving us disorganized crime scenes one time and organized the next. If these are meant to be religious executions, the killer has so far been flawless. Now it's as if he's trying to leave us clues at the crime scene that point in all directions."

"So this Phineas Priesthood is responsible for him?"

"We think he was initiated somewhere at one of these survivalist camps in the Southwest. They usually recruit from those places. They're using the Priesthood to enforce order among all these supremacist groups. Someone is putting together a machine in anticipation of bigger things."

"Bigger things being the collapse of moral order?"

"Haftmann, you dope, organized fundamentalist Christianity is a hair's breadth from organizing train rides to Auschwitz." He snorted contempt. "Do you really think Joe Sixpack is any more enlightened than a citizen of Germany seventy years ago? Do you think these idiot teenagers give a hoot about anything besides facebooking for five hours a day? School shootings, bullyings, a culture drenched in sleaze."

I couldn't argue with him there. We were just twenty-five miles from Kirtland where that Mormon psycho slaughtered a family of followers.

"The problem with a conspiracy theory," I said, "is too many people would have to know."

"Not if these think tanks are right," Booth said. "People mobilize fast these days with social networking. Look at Tunisia, Egypt. It's easy to imagine the entire Caucasian race united against crime when it's an ethnic minority doing tattoos on white skulls. It's happening in Great Britain."

"So what's their plan? Get the entire US media under their control?"

"It may be easier than you think. The country runs on dollars, not good will. Insert a few prominent people into high office here and there until the time is right. Converting the masses can be left until the end. They're already there. Most people are convinced that Mexico and illegals have reconquered the American Southwest without firing a shot. You can run for President on that plank alone today. Get them to swallow the big lie. Television has been doing a wonderful job at exploiting our worst fears and stereotypes. Hollywood has only just stopped demonizing the black man. Even so, the polls show the average white Caucasian male believes that African-Americans comprise forty percent of the population, not the actual thirteen."

"Stop lecturing me, Booth. I had a wife who was good at that. Perception is truth, blah-blah—and so what? I still don't understand why he chose Annaliese."

"Nothing gets into a racist's craw more deeply than miscegenation. Homophobia is nothing to it. You told me that Annaliese was half-black. Maybe that attracted him to her. That's where I need your help. He's so good at avoiding patterns. We thought at first he was choosing them indiscriminately. It could be there is a pattern and we just can't see it. We've checked as many names as we've been able to gather on white supremacist and skinhead groups from all over the country, especially in the Northeast. Run them all through the computer. Nothing so far. Every possibility we had checks out. Not exactly your average citizen but nobody who looks good for these killings. Take these files with you and study them."

"OK, Booth. I've been around the block before with you. I know these files are the sugarcoating to make the pill go down easier. But what's the pill?"

"I thought you guessed. We want you to go back to Boston. Pick up where you left off. We've cleared it with Cooney so that you can work with him on the O'Reilly cases."

"You said 'cases,' plural."

"Oh, I forgot to tell you. Yesterday morning Cuyahoga forensics called me with the autopsy results. O'Reilly's alcohol content was point-oh-two but there was a trace of succinic acid in his bloodstream. High levels of ammonia, lactic acid and histamines. A dangerous drug family, they tell me. I'm having them send it on to Quantico for a full spectrum analysis."

"Just tell me what it means."

"It means he probably ingested the drug with the whiskey. He was doped, incapable of movement, but fully conscious, and able to feel pain. He knew what was being done the whole time. He was bagged and suffocated. They found lint fibers when they scraped his throat. The killer used a cellophane bag at the bottom of one of his drawers. The fibers match one of the shirts in the drawer. He should have left it on his head, but he must have thought it wasn't necessary. The death certificate would have said heart attack."

"So who did him?"

"I'm hoping you'll help me find that out, Thomas. I really am. I don't have much time because there's a plane ticket back to South Dakota with my name on it, if I don't get this one right." He locked tired and old, suddenly, not the dapper man whose worst problem before he met me was how to keep a Glock from snagging the silk lining of his imported jackets. "You know anything about Pine Hills?"

I remembered AIM, a place called the Running Bull Compound where two FBI agents were shot to death, and a name: Leonard Peltier, still in prison. Tribal warfare, Native American style. Government-friendly Indians backed by gun thugs who killed dozens of traditional Indians, usually full bloods.

"Except for a mix of Kiowas and Lacota Sioux, there are twenty-five thousand Oglala Sioux on that godforsaken reservation, Haftmann. You've never seen poverty and misery in this country like this. I don't want you to cock this one up the way you did the last time, because I know for a fact that not one of those Indians in the Pine Woods casino can make a decent sloe gin fizz."

• • •

I read the homicide reports, the supplemental reports, the VICAP profile, and a stack of other papers that had to do with the k.a.'s of promi-

125

nent racists in the United States. Booth had xeroxed portions of the history of the Phineas Priesthood for my "edification and amusement." It was an international society, secret like the Masons, and probably as old. They believed it necessary to kill anyone guilty of race-mixing. They also believed, as Byron De La Beckwith and the Christian Identity movement so often professed in the tumultuous days of the civil rights era, that Caucasians alone comprise the Lost Tribes of Israel. God's word was to them, and He had given them charge over the mud races who occupied the same spiritual plane as animals and, like animals, lacked souls.

I drove to the Holiday Inn and picked up Ingrid, who was standing in the carport with her hands crossed in front of her. I thought of apologizing for my car, but changed my mind.

We drove to Kingsville, about six miles from there, and made small talk the while. I learned that her husband in Pittsburgh had left her and that she and he had never actually been married in a civil ceremony. It turned out that he had a wife in Joplin, Missouri.

"What was she going to do?" I asked. She replied that, for the time being, she wanted to stay around Jefferson, see those places where her daughter had lived before going back to Pittsburgh to settle affairs. I asked her about her ex-husband and whether he had ever evinced a taste for bondage. Her translucent skin flushed, and I could see the white outline of her nose in the contrast. But she answered my question by denying that he had ever been given to "that sort of thing." I described how he was found, the leather paraphernalia and the bondage magazines under the bed, but I left out the part that it was I who had discovered the body.

She turned full face to drill me with her eyes. "Mister Haftmann, I would prefer not to speak of my former husband." I said I understood but that the investigation of her husband's death might assist in the case of her daughter. "How?" she asked. Eyes brighter, cheeks still flushed. "OK," I said, free-wheeling it, "it's possible they may be connected to each other."

"How so?"

"First, I'd like to ask a favor of you."

"All right."

"Now, as I understand it from the police, your husband—"

"We were not married."

126

"Yes, forgive me. Your ex-husband. He was—"

"Mister Haftmann, please."

"Yes?"

"Is it considered routine for private investigators to assist in police investigations?"

"Well, not exactly."

"Then I would prefer not to discuss my former husband's death with you."

"I understand."

"I don't think you do."

"I see."

That was pretty much it for conversation until we arrived at the Greenlawn Cemetery in Kingsville. The man she spoke with on the phone was there to greet us at the chapel, and explain things to us. Some business associates of O'Reilly showed up for the services. A photo of him was placed on a small oak table, one of his company's own products, we were told, and the services commenced. I looked around but no one seemed out of place, and I recognized a face or two among the mourners. Chamber of Commerce types, a local politico who came to work the crowd and gladhand for a few minutes after the service. I watched him shoot his cuffs and depart. I wondered if the stained glass in the chapel was real. The upkeep of the place couldn't be much, I figured, because there was only the chapel to maintain—no tombstones to work around. A brush hog in late spring could do the whole area without expensive manual labor involved in trimming or cutting around edges because the burial plaques were depressed in the ground.

At last the proprietor ushered us all into the late afternoon sunlight. I heard small talk begin around me, someone mentioned a blowout at Progressive Field last night, and then I felt the slight pressure of Ingrid's hand on my bicep. It seemed strangely quaint to walk across this green landscape of the newly with her hanging on my arm.

As we walked to the car, she told me that my distance from people was evident, even when I was looking into their faces and smiling or nodding. I hadn't realized it, but I knew she was right.

I'd always had a gift for tuning people out. I remembered my grandmother saying much the same thing in her broken English, that peculiar Berlin accent she brought with her to America, when I was a boy just entering my teenager years. The prison shrink told me it was one of the best symptoms of incipient schizophrenia, this kind of detachment. I remembered that summer of the hunt when I had nailed a murder map to my ceiling and stuck brightly colored pins on it so I could lie on an old velour couch and stare at it. Fix all those places the Jack-in-the-Box killer had been in my mind so that it would be the last thing I would see before sleep. I remember how the edges of furniture had started to blur, and it was becoming difficult to see people's faces without their noses or mouths shifting right under my gaze. I also remembered telling the prison psychiatrist to get fucked.

I said to Ingrid, "You're very observant, yourself. Most people don't care enough to notice whether others are listening or not."

Then she staggered me: "You seem like a sad man. Like someone who's waiting for something to happen and hoping at the same time it doesn't."

I stopped short of the car and turned to her. "Your daughter is dead. I was supposed to find her and bring her back. I didn't do that because I was either careless or stupid. She paid with her life for my mistake."

"You're wrong, Mister Haftmann. She was my responsibility. My husband's and mine. We bungled it, and I'll have to live with it for the rest of my life. Don't you dare take my grief from me! It's too selfish, it's too selfish!"

At that, her face transfigured itself into a blood-darkened mask of misery and suffering that stunned me, and I felt her heave with great, racking sobs she could not suppress. I led her to the car and we drove home in silence except for those terrible sounds she made. *That's me*, I thought, *Mr. Fix-It*. There ought to be about a million fewer in the world just like me.

CHAPTER 7

The mail brought me a check for five hundred dollars. It was sent by a former client of mine who was currently doing a three-to-five bid in another state. He had stiffed me on the bill and skipped town. This was shortly after I had provided explicit proof that his wife was unfaithful to him. I have often had occasion to show men photos of their wives in the embraces of other men, but I had never before shown a man a glossy of his wife having a champagne bottle inserted deep in her vagina; her lover, an imaginative coworker, gave it a good shake first and rotated it slowly up until the neck of the bottle disappeared. I also had photos of her and a large dog that I ripped up because I figured he didn't need more than the champagne douche to convince him. Maybe, like so many cons for all the right and wrong reasons, he got religion in the joint and wanted to square his debts.

I paid some bills and then I made a phone call. I had a stack of mail to open when I returned from Boston and there was a short note from a couple from Sandusky who looked good. One photo enclosed. She was big and blonde and wore black high heels and nothing else. I called them and made a date for that night.

I met them for dinner at a restaurant near Cedar Lake. We agreed well enough among ourselves after dinner that we would return to their house. Did I mind if they smoked? I thought the question strange because they both smoked as soon as we arrived at our table, but then I realized she meant dope.

"Not at all," I said.

"I like a little dope that you can reason with," she said and thought that very funny because they both laughed.

I had her from behind while the husband was in front of her. They had the air conditioning off and rubber sheets on the bed. We were all sweating. I watched drops of sweat collect in the sacral dimple just above her rump. She had a very high and shapely rear.

The room was redolent of the musky smell of sex and marijuana. My head kept pummeling me with unbidden images of Annaliese's blonde mother having sex with a black man. I imagined Annaliese too, simpering at me while she performed fellatio.

Safe from the pollution of this world.

These terrible images kept me past my point of endurance, all the more unusual because I had not had sex since the motel couple in early spring. I was locked into my own twilight zone, oblivious to this display of masculine staying power. At one point she disentangled herself from us and came back with towels to wipe our sweating faces. The husband had been gone for a while and I hadn't noticed. He was a dentist who specialized in orthodontics. The rhythmic slapping, the mindless stroking was beyond sex. She had quick, easy orgasms: a spasm, a moan, and then back at it. She turned her head to regard me from that angle, but her eyes were slits, barely visible, and clouded by the effects of the grass. She wasn't a natural blonde. Her pubic thatch of dark, tangled curls was slick from perspiration. She was still looking at me but I couldn't tell what she was saying. Her husband came back into the room and she said something to him. He came closer to me and said, "She said you need to finish this marathon. She can't come anymore. But she said she'll suck you off. We've both got to get up early for work."

On the ride home on the Shocknessy Turnpike, I remembered Old Man O'Reilly's words: *She'll be in her father's arms soon.* I was thinking he meant our heavenly father. The man who called him must have been the killer, mocking him with his perverted priesthood, predicting O'Reilly's own imminent death. I had an image of O'Reilly on the bed, rigorous death's head grin, rotting in his leather outfit, his arms cinched upwards toward the ceiling and his lifeless hands drooping in mock supplication.

• • •

I got in at three and slept until seven. My cell phone on vibrate: Booth. God damn it.

I ignored it and slept until noon. On my way out the door, I saw some white-crowned sparrows flitting about the empty feeder. I'd been neglecting them lately, so I threw a whole ten-pound bag on the ground and waited a moment to watch them gather and feast.

I drove to the Strip for a meal at the Boar Room where they scorched my eggs and took the chill off my steak. Filling up the inner man, filling in the lacunae of my life between choices. I took my notepad out and reviewed every page since O'Reilly had walked into my office eight weeks ago; there was a single bright thread connecting my mental snapshots of three people now: Annaliese, O'Reilly, and Lawrence Gallatine, the Vo-Ed teacher.

Sex.

And now there was racism in the mix. Gallatine's flaxen-haired blue-eyed Jesus paintings resurfaced in my mind. Time to pay another visit to northeast Ohio's favorite academic martyr.

I had plenty of time on the way to formulate a plan too. I believe in planning; plans are signs of intelligent action. The trouble is, I didn't have one, and when I saw Gallatine's expensive car in his driveway, I lost it. I stood on my brakes so that my rustbucket of a Plymouth stopped about an inch from his Porsche's outside fender. The sound of spitting gravel was something out of an old World War Two newsreel where you expect to see guerrillas dying against a wall in a hot fusillade of lead. I slammed the car door and saw Gallatine looking out his front picture window regarding me. The look on his face was not welcoming.

I put one fist against the door and drew it back over my shoulder because I intended to dislodge the little half-round pane of decorative glass, if at all possible. Gallatine, however, opened it, before I could and then opened his mouth. Before he uttered a syllable, I had him firmly by the lapels of his suitcoat and in one fluid motion, I whipped him past me the way you might see kids do on a playground. His arms flailed, he lost his balance and went down in a heap.

My next thought was purely rational: I hoped that he didn't keep a varmint gun on the premises and that it was being trained on my back right now. I heard him scream to his wife to call the police. A door slammed behind me.

Good. Plenty of time.

I was on him in a second, had him hoisted upright so that my face was right in his, and then I gave him one hard shot to the solar plexus. A whole bunch of nerve endings join up there. It's a little bonus in law enforcement that it doesn't leave a bruise.

He gagged and began retching out ropy strings of bile. That was good too because it meant lots of nausea. You hit a guy and he starts that projectile vomiting bit, and you'll be lucky if he can remember his name on the fifteenth try. I couldn't be sure there wasn't a cruiser in the area, so I figured we may as well begin with the fifty-thousand-dollar question:

"What's his name?"

He was on all fours, not even looking at me or attempting to move. I kicked him in the same place. That got the heaving going again, and then a rancid spume erupted from his mouth and burst out his nostrils. He tried to stop it with one hand and steady himself with the other, but neither effort worked; he tottered and then nosedived into the ground. He lay there and made sounds like an old lawn mower I couldn't get to fire up.

I kneeled next to his head and said very closely to his ear, "If you don't tell me what I want to know, I'm going to hit you in the stomach again."

He wagged his head from side to side. His eyes were full of fear. "No. Don't. Hit. Please. No . . . more."

"Tell me who you talked to in Boston." I had sized Gallatine up at our first encounter; he was strictly middle-management. Somebody a whole lot bigger was behind him pulling his strings. There had to be. I knew it in the deepest cockles of my heart this guy was a nobody. A rotten nobody but no sadistic killer. I could hear my ex's mocking laughter when I accused her of cheating on me, calling it one of my hunches, a lucky guess.

"Can't. Tell you. Name."

Fuck. Valuable seconds were passing.

I tried another angle, "How did you meet him?"

"Sent me information. Got . . . my name . . . from a list."

"You knew O'Reilly, the father?"

He spat out a little blood. "Yes, yes."

"How did you know him?"

"Met him at Klan rally in Painesville. I was there with some students to study crowd reactions. Noticed him. Arranged to meet him later. Meetings together."

I shook him a little. "What kind of meetings?"

"Christian Identity."

Byron De La Beckwith's radical white supremacists. The gun-toting kind.

I thought of the FBI profile of the killer. I had to put on that mask and be emotionless for a moment. There was no time. I jerked his head upright by the hair and slapped his face with a loud cracking sound.

"Who is he, Gallatine? Tell me who organized these meetings. Who is the Boston man?"

He shook his head from side to side. "He'll kill me."

"I'll kill you right here, fucker. Tell me!"

This time he looked right in my face. "No. You could . . . never do to me . . . what he is capable of. Beyond imagining . . . beyond pity."

His eyes started to cloud over and he groaned, so I slapped him again. *Craaack!* "Give me his name!"

Nothing. Two more, a backhand to finish. Tears streamed down his cheeks. I twisted his hair harder and wrenched his face closer. The irises of his eyes were flecked with green. "Tell me!"

I drew back for another one and let him have it on the meat of his swollen cheek. Spit and a little blood flew. "Tell me, God damn you. What's his fucking name?"

"Can't tell you. Don't know name. Just number. Only number to call."

Bingo. "Where's the number?"

His mouth was swelling up too much to talk but it sounded like "briefcase."

"Get me the briefcase."

He tried to get up, and I saw him grope around in the direction of his pockets. *Keys*, I thought. I patted him, felt his keys in a pants pocket and dug my hand for them. My mitt too big. So I ripped the pocket open and let the keys and coins fall to the ground.

Shit Piss Fuck. My magic triad wasn't going to tell me which of the dozen or so keys on his ring was the house key. Sirens in the distance.

"Gallatine, which key? Which key! Don't faint on me, you miserable piece of shit. Which fucking key!"

He tapped one in my open palm, and I ran to the door.

The wife and two daughters were staring at me, eyes enormous with fear. The headlines were shaping in my brain, and I could imagine the words in that type-point size they use for declaring wars screaming in my brain, tomorrow's *Jefferson Gazette*: PSYCHOPATH ATTACKS FAMILY IN ANDOVER, BEATS FATHER SENSELESS BEFORE WIFE AND CHILDREN. *Forgive me for what I am about to do.*

"Mrs. Gallatine, where is your husband's briefcase? Tell me, please! Where is it?"

She stiffarmed the air toward another room. The den, I hoped.

His office at home. The sirens were whooping close now, too close.

I found myself in a utility room. Crazed, I ran back toward the mother, but I heard the door slam just as I got there.

I could see a Sheriff's car just cresting the hill. A hundred yards.

I tore from room to room. Nothing downstairs that even looked close. The back door opened to a redwood deck and a lot of woods where I could make my getaway. Call Reggie Stevens to intervene for me. *Shit! Upstairs. Run!* The sheriff's car was in the driveway; the gravel spat by the tires pinged a hubcap. I bolted from room to room—bedrooms, theirs, closets, bathroom, girls' room, bunk beds. I stopped in my tracks and looked out the window. The deputy, a young man in his twenties was keying the mike and looking up at the house. Gallatine was being comforted by his wife and daughters. The little girls were crying hard. I could see their mouths working. I thought, *well, game over. I tried, Annaliese. I'm sorry.*

Then I glimpsed a corner of it. Just visible from the hallway beneath the bed in the master bedroom: Gallatine's briefcase. What to do now? I made my way down the stairs and slipped around back through the kitchen. There was a second deputy, older, circling out back with his weapon drawn. I hadn't even heard the second car pull in.

I walked out the front door, my hands up, the briefcase dangling from my right hand. The young deputy roared at me to stop. He put himself in a two-handed stance and walked toward me. "Drop the briefcase! Now!"

I did.

I thought, *keep calm. Slow down the breathing.*

I felt the second deputy coming up on what I call my near-blind side.

Please let him put the barrel against me.

As if he were reading my mind, he did—squarely in the middle of my back.

It was a crazy thing to do, with all those people standing around, and hoping the young deputy wasn't the panicky sort. I had a moment more to think, *Please, Jack, let this work . . .*

I spun toward the deputy holding the gun snug to my back and slapped his arm away with my momentum. Some part of my brain registered the shot.

I felt nothing, but I was clear of the gun. Before he could swing it back toward me, I closed in on him, and caught him in an embrace so that my arm could curl around his gunhand. I held it against me so that he couldn't move his arm. Then I shoved the heel of my hand under his nose. I telegraphed the punch too obviously, so he managed to twist away from the blow. My back was wide open to the other deputy. Whether there was screaming or talking or whatever, I can't say because the tunnel vision was so intense that I could count the hair follicles on that deputy's nose, but I couldn't tell you if anybody spoke any words during the whole time. My second shot to his nose broke it. Then, steeling myself for what came next, I clasped my arm under his elbow, locked my wrist and jerked upright, once, hard.

I didn't hear his elbow breaking, but I know it did. He just crumpled from the incredible pain, and I let him shield me from the other cop as I lowered him to the ground and grabbed his gun. The young deputy had me in his sights, an easy headshot. He could have blown my brains out my ears from where he was. Impossible to miss. I could see his knuckles whitening beside the trigger guard. This time I heard the words, he was screaming at me to drop the gun. Get away from his partner. Just screaming. Words coming out the hole in his face while I concentrated on my next move. The deputy was close to my body, but he was in a dead faint, and his body weight, although about one hundred seventy pounds was like twice that much on a bench press.

"You drop it," I said.

He just stared at me. He couldn't believe this was happening, I suppose. I could see him thinking, *goddamned domestic calls, the oldtimers were right, you never knew about these, always the worst.*

That's when I went into my spiel, told him my name, profession, just gabbed to get time—and a little closer to him. "I'm going to set down your partner," I said. "Here's the gun, I'm not going to shoot." I kept repeating: "Here's the gun, take it." He should have backed up, but he watched me come on, my patter soothing him. He was still tight and a touch would set the gun off. I nearly burst into hysteria when I caught sight of the family standing there taking it all in like some kind of virtual reality playacting. They looked like cardboard cutouts to me. Gallatine was on his feet, eyeing me. His wife's mouth was open in a perfect circle.

This is ridiculous, ridiculous.

"He's hurt," I said, "I think his arm's broken."

As if on cue, the older deputy moaned as I made to set him down. That's when the deputy lowered his vision, and that's when I made what must be the luckiest move of my life. I threw the deputy toward him, and, sensing the ruse, the young deputy raised his gun to fire. The bullet made a sucking noise next to my ear.

Before he could get another shot off, I deflected the barrel with the edge of my hand and raised his gun with his fingers locked. With my own gun, I brought the butt around in a long arc that caught the deputy right under the jaw. The blow didn't disarm him, but it sent off two more shots overhead. I clubbed him over the temple, harder than I intended, and his lights went out. He toppled sideways and lay motionless. The skin over his eyebrow was split and blood was pumping out hard.

I told the family, "Take care of these men."

I walked up to Gallatine and put the gun to his head.

"Did you kill O'Reilly?"

"No, no, please—I—I watched. God help me, he made me watch it!"

I fetched Gallatine's briefcase, tossed it onto the front seat with the deputy's gun, and did a three-point turn across his lawn. I floored it down the driveway, reckless of me at this point, but the adrenalin was churning in me too. Before I was out of the township, I pulled off to the side of the road opposite a row of mailboxes and tossed up what I had for breakfast. Some cars, I remember, passed me and saw the grotesque apparition of a man's head leaning out a car door a foot from the ground. Out of Andover, I took back roads all the way back to Jefferson-on-the-Lake. No sirens. No police cars passed me or saw me. It was like a dream, a very crazy dream. I was following the loneliest hunch of my life, and I had never yet played a long shot to win in all my gambling years.

• • •

Two miles from 531 I found a dirt road and pulled behind a deserted homestead to take stock of things. My back was stuck to the seat where the bullet had creased me. Jack used to practice that move on me with an empty revolver when I was a rookie. We'd drive down to the docks behind a warehouse where the night shift used to drink after the bars closed. If the gun is touching the body, it can work if you're fast. The last time, a few beers too many, Jack hadn't emptied the gun, or thought he had, and the instant I cleared the gun and swatted his arm, I heard the explosion.

Five cop cars, some drinking, a few cooping on company time, were instantly screeching tires and roaring off. Jack just looked at me. "Well, kiddo," he said, "you just never know."

At dusk, I put on a radio station playing classical music and heard Mozart's *Requiem*, the *Lacrimosa*. A fitting end to a disastrous day. I had the briefcase, though, and it confirmed my suspicions of Gallatine. I dismissed him as the killer of John O'Reilly, but I had no doubt that he knew who the killer was; at the very least, he was himself involved enough as a coconspirator. I had studied Booth's VICAP profile. Gallatine didn't fit. He was too well alibied, according to my sources at the station house. A favorite quotation of Jack's, often trotted out at a cop's bar where no captains or colonels were permitted, about ambitious men: *He doeth like the ape. The higher he climb, the more he doth show his arse.* I couldn't see him as part of this murderous priesthood. He had been sleeping with Annaliese, and he may have handed her over to this society when she turned to Marcus Gordon, a black man.

These reasons I could only guess at; he may have incurred favors, or possibly he wanted to ingratiate himself more deeply in the secret society. I found his briefcase full of odds and ends, some of which hinted at his dark interest in the white supremacy movement; nothing however that couldn't be explained by a sociologist. I saw a thumbed copy of the legendary tract *The Protocols of the Elders of Zion* among school papers, the book by Hoskins, historian of the Phineas cult, *Vigilantes of Christendom*. A flyer that said PRAISE GOD FOR AIDS was folded in half and tucked inside the book.

There were two portions of ripped pages from the *Boston Globe*'s classified ads section, one dated three days before I found O'Reilly dead in his house; the second was a smaller piece of the *Globe*'s same ads section, ripped less evenly and showing only a portion of the personals. Most of the ads were identical to the dated one; however, there were some personal ads mixed in with the business-like ones offering appliances or looking for labor. One was a biblical quotation in the dated piece that looked to have a matching quotation in the second.

I found his appointment book in a sleeve compartment at the bottom of the briefcase, in which Gallatine had logged school business, appointments, and reminders. On the back he had a phone number and above it a quotation had been penciled in italic handwriting; it said: *"Let us make game of those who make as much of us."* The number's area code was Boston.

I waited until shift change for the Lake patrols and drove in. I pulled into a parking lot near Little Minnesota and watched the action. One of the bars that appealed to a gay-lesbian clientele featured a famous crossdresser who did Bette Davis on talk shows. I could hear him vamping over the loudspeaker: *When You Swish upon a Star*. The girls were already working the crowds, darting in and out of traffic, checking out drivers and asking one variation after another of the same question: "You wanna date tonight?"

I saw some veterans out tonight; these were favorites of Chief Millimaki. They would kick back a portion of the night's earnings. The others would be hassled until they learned the system. Mostly blondes, sixteen, greasy under the neon in their make-up and tight clothes. Once happy hour commenced, the nightlife along the Strip took off. The earning hours were limited by the whore patrols. I watched one girl for a while, discarded her, chose another, and finally settled on one who seemed right.

I left my car in the lot and walked over to her. I explained to her what I wanted her to do, gave her the car keys and fifty dollars and told her I'd be in the bar across the street waiting for her. I wrote down the address and her instructions. She took the fifty, looked at the bar, and said in a whiny little girl's voice, "You a fag, huh?"

I said, "Would it matter? My money's still good."

"Nah," she said. "I'll do it for you."

I went inside, ordered a club soda at the bar, and sat in such a way that I hoped the body language worked, if body language can say "fuck off" while you're hunkered on a bar stool.

She tapped me on the shoulder twenty-five minutes later and handed me the papers and the envelope I told her was in the third drawer, right-hand side. Her own body language, when she realized she had brought me a packet of money, was a fatalistic shrug. She'd get that playing the skinflute a couple times. I gave her another fifty dollar bill, and she turned and left. I asked her if there was a patrol car across the street from my office, and she said yes, two. One unmarked. Millimaki giving me VIP treatment. Sending his best boys to bring me downtown.

I didn't want to, but I had a vestige of regard for Booth, so I called him and explained the situation, how it looked anyhow. He said little, but his grunts were enough to tell me that Booth knew when to cut bait. I was, I suspect, very malodorous to the neat little man right now. I didn't feel it, but I said, "I'm sorry, Booth. We don't have the same agenda. You want a big case. Headlines. A ticket to New York. I just want the killer of Annaliese O'Reilly."

He said without rancor: "You don't know yourself. Those nightmares you had in prison the shrinks told you about afterwards? You were damned near catatonic at one point. You'll never make it, Haftmann. They'll pick you up in Boston."

"Just don't help them out. Stay out of it. I can hide for a while. I just need a little time, and Booth, help me with Cooney. Fix him for me. Use your juice one last time."

"Why the hell should I, you crazy prick. I can see them cutting me a ticket to South Dakota before I get off the plane. Why should I?"

"For auld lang syne. Just do it, Booth. I can find this guy. I've got a lead to him."

"Fuck you. This is a crusade for you, isn't it? You're a walking textbook of diseases of the mind, Haftmann. You've got some kind of messiah complex—"

"Booth, please."

Long silence. Then: "A dog returneth to his vomit." He broke the connection.

My next call was to Micah. I got her husband and asked for her. I could hear the muffled exchange of voices before she came on the line.

"What is it?"

"I need money for an emergency. A couple hundred dollars if you can spare it."

"I thought you stopped gambling."

"I did. This is something that came up, a real emergency. Please, Micah."

"With you, it's always an emergency. Your whole life."

"I know, I know. Like old man Wallenda used to say before he tumbled off the high wire: 'Life is lived on the high wire. The rest is waiting in the wings.'"

"Tom, this is not a good time. I've got a baby coming. We're spending a lot of money these days."

I thought of their house in Roaming Rock Shores, the yacht, the tennis club.

"I know. I'm sorry, Micah. If I weren't desperate—"

She snorted. "When have you not been desperate whenever you've called me?"

"Micah, you can have the house as collateral. In fact, you can have the house. This is the sale of a lifetime. Just a couple large bills, a couple hundred, to see me through this. I won't be needing it anymore because I'm leaving town for good."

"I don't want the house."

"Micah, listen to me. I swear I'll never bother you again. You'll never see me again."

"No, Tom, I can't. I won't."

I could hear his voice in the background. He was urging her to hang up on me.

"Micah, if you hang up on me, I'll be waiting for that slimefuck husband of yours—"

"You rotten sonofabitch," she said. Click.

Jesus shit fuck, what is wrong with me?

I felt sick to my stomach. The air was greasy with the smells of frying food and cotton candy in the night air. Mixed with the offshore breeze of dying fish that kept coming ashore in suicidal waves, I felt dizzy and nauseous. My hair was slick with sweat.

One more call, one I didn't intend to make until I dialed the number. She picked up on the first ring. "Yes?"

"It's Haftmann," I said. "I'm going to Boston. I'm going to find the man who killed your daughter."

What she said next didn't surprise me, but what I said did: "Take me with you."

"All right."

Go figure. You live your life looking for a semblance of order in the chaos, some light at the end of the tunnel that isn't a freight train or the whole woods going up in flames. What was I thinking of—dragging this woman off to Boston on such a flimsy pretext?

I told myself, a one-eyed man driving a rattletrap Plymouth from Ohio to Boston makes as much sense as a rat copulating with a grapefruit. But, hell, she can drive.

CHAPTER 8

Fuck. She couldn't drive. Not a lick.

Sat behind the wheel of a car exactly once in her life. I must have looked at her the way the woman at the state license bureau looked at me when she asked had my vision changed since my last renewal. I told her I was practically blind in my left eye and couldn't see that well out of the right.

"What?" she asked, skewering me with a sideways look behind her own bifocals.

She thought I was joking. She wrote down "astigmatic myopia" and gave me my new laminated license without changing the information.

"I'm not kidding," Ingrid said. "I never learned to drive a car. John didn't want me to learn. He took me driving once and swore he'd never do it again."

Eighteen hours, give or take an hour, is a long time to spend in a small space with another human being and not get to know them. She was a curiously beautiful woman, not to everyone's taste, I guessed, but a white-blonde hair and skin that is so much the opposite of Micah's olive-complexioned Jewishness. I thought my heart would stop beating the day I saw Micah for the first time. To this day, I don't know whether I was in love with her or whether some imprint in my brain said I must have *this* woman and no other, I must mate with her.

Like most men of my generation, I blundered toward the American Dream, expecting that sheer persistence would get me my share and maybe a little bit more. Micah was the centerpiece, the axis of my own dream, and whichever way she tilted, I followed. I did not realize until too late that we had wholly different dreams. The job had come between us by then. It was all wrong, of course, but I thought I could make it right if I stayed true to it long enough.

Once, she dozed while we were passing the Syracuse exits, and I heard her whimpering in her sleep. I realized that her dreams were tarnished, if not broken, and that, like me, she was coming to that lonely middle-age where you find yourself companionless, childless, adrift in a strange country where you keep wondering how you got here but you can't find anyone to stamp your visa so you can get to another country. I didn't think that I had the strength to leave anyway.

We stopped and ate at one of those roadside franchises on the Dewey Thruway. Like me, she drank coffee stout, and I saw her wrinkle her nose in distaste at the watery brew. The compress she had put on my back was healing the infection of my back wound, but it was still oozing pus, staining my shirts and sticking to the car seat. I asked her about some names of things in German, words I recalled from my grandmother. I asked her about Berlin. Had she ever been there? What was it like? She told me that she had been there twice, but that Berliners were snobs and spoke a slangy dialect. I didn't tell her about my mother. I wondered about her sometimes. Just a girl in a world ripped apart by a world war. Everyone dead. Having to fend for herself in a new country. I wondered what that would be like. I thought that, maybe, it wasn't such a bad thing to be childless. How could you keep a child safe from harm in a world like this so full of monsters?

We slept at a Days Inn and drove at night. I awoke once and she was stroking my forehead. A bad dream. She was saying something in German, but wouldn't tell me what it was. I wanted to touch her then, but I was afraid to. She moved off my bed, as if she sensed this, and lay down on her own. She wore an old-fashioned peignoir that tied across the neck. I could see her nipples under it, like eraser tips.

A moment later, I heard her say: "If you find this man, will you kill him?"

"Yes," I said.

"Then what will you do?"

I said, "I don't know."

I didn't tell her that my last bad dream full of amorphous sounds and dark images and colors that bled into one another in a kaleidoscope of furious chaos was the final resistance of my will, my lifeurge to cling to being over nothingness. This life of mine which, for so many years, had become a nonlife, an existence without meaning or shape or destiny. The sexual gluttony of recent years had been a way to find something and fill up the hole in my life that was every day a yawning abyss. I couldn't remember any of them clearly, their faces, the bedroom scenes, the positions, the dozens of ejaculations into mouths and wombs.

I doubted that Gallatine would want to press charges because he had every reason to want to distance himself from O'Reilly's death. There was a record of his call to Boston. Otherwise, I was the only one who could implicate him.

But there was no way for me to escape jail time for what happened to the deputies back in Andover, and fleeing a felony was aggravating it. My name was already entered in the National Crime Index Computer for what happened years ago, and not even Booth had the clout it would take to whitewash this one. I knew I was in too deep; besides, he and I were quits. I hoped he was good for his word and it wouldn't ruin things with Cooney. I was going to need Det. Sean Cooney on this one.

I knew this much, I thought: *at the end of it, when I come face to face with him, I'm going to kill him. Then I'm going to do myself. One take away one is zero.*

Ingrid surprised me, interrupted my interior monologue, and set my heart thumping; it was as if she had been reading my mind all the while: "Thomas, after you kill him, I want you to kill me too. I've never been afraid of dying. It's life. It's life that you have to be afraid of." I said nothing and then we both slept the afternoon away in the curtain-dimmed room where the sun was steaming the pavements outside; inside was the faint antiseptic smell of formaldehyde and sheets that seemed to burn my skin.

She made me find a pharmacy once we exited the toll and crossed into Massachusetts. The wound on my back had begun to fester and smell a bit foul when I pulled the bandage off. I had a slight fever, but my real problems were the blurring of my vision from the night driving. I chewed aspirin by the handful for the throbbing headache.

I looked at her, "We'll be in Boston in a few hours. Are you OK?"

"I'm fine," she said.

"Me too," I said.

It was the biggest lie I had told yet.

●　●　●

I found us a room in a two-story brownstone off Cardinal O'Connor just up the street from Massachusetts General. My head was aching from the strain of driving, and the fatigue of the last two days, so I asked Ingrid to hold the fort while I slept. "Any cops try to come in, you have to disarm them," I said. She herself was too tired to acknowledge the stupidity of the joke. *Why is it*, I thought, *that fictional private eyes are always cutting up and cracking wise at the worst of times and everybody thinks it's funny?* I slept like a dead man.

Ingrid awoke me gently at nightfall and held out a cup of black coffee in a McDonald's cup as I shook off the residue of sleep. She said that I hadn't moved the whole time, and she checked my breathing to see if I were still alive. I remembered nothing but the sweet blankness of oblivion.

"You try a feather?" I asked.

"Hunh?" she replied.

"You hold a feather to someone's lips to see if they're still breathing."

She stared at me as if I were deranged.

"Forget it," I said, "that was my last excursion into sidesplitting wit."

I had no clean shirts, nothing to clean the gun, and I was afraid to count the money I had in my wallet. Money was one form of pressure; time the other. How much did I have before the cops pulled me in? Would Cooney sic the dogs on me once he knew I was in town? Questions that would be answered. The ones that weren't had to do with finding the man I came here to kill.

I saw Ingrid playing with the handle of a silent butler. I hadn't seen one in years. "Look, Thomas." Her eyes were flashing with delight.

Who could believe, seeing her at play in that moment, she was a woman resigned to dying in a city that mutilated her only child?

● ● ●

I told Ingrid what we were going to do. She understood the term long shot, so I didn't explain to her what the odds were. We had the number, and if Det. Cooney of Boston's Violent Crimes Unit didn't get his knickers in a twist, we'd have a source of information. I'd worked with cops before; Cooney's feelings for me were typical: a cop would rather suck shit through a straw than share information on a case with a private investigator.

Cooney was out on a case, they told me. "Who's calling?"

I gave them a phony name; let them think I was one of his CI's, a term that every cop considered a logical contradiction.

We went down the street. I made some clothing purchases at a store that advertized "experienced clothes." The store owner wanted me to haggle over the price a bit, never my strong suit, and seemed disappointed I wanted to pay the sticker price on some shirts and pants.

We hit a K-Mart on the way into town for underwear and socks. Another thing that you never see TV private eyes do: buy underwear. Ingrid bought tampons. She tried to give me some money in the checkout line.

The black dog of depression was all about me at that moment; I felt how impossible this venture was and how limited my abilities to do anything right. I get a little paranoid at times like these, so I was wearing the gun in my pants—I was afraid of getting stopped in the parking lot this close to Boston. I told her, right there in the checkout line amidst mothers and their squalling progeny, that if it came to that, I'd spend her money too. She asked what we'd do if we ran out of money first. I said nothing, unable to come up with a halfway decent lie. She nodded her blonde head a couple times and glanced at my beltline where the gun was secured. Her way, I guess, of saying she understood that failure or success was irrelevant. I looked her full in the face to see if she'd flinch. Limpid pools of washed-out blue like deeply frozen ice; she calmly held my stare.

We had no phone to call Cooney, so I did a little recon of the streets. Looked for ways to disappear fast if we had to. Noted traffic patterns and streets where harm might come first. I had a hundred spiral-bound street maps lying all over the backseat of the car, indispensable to my surveillance, and I dug Boston out of the pile.

Finally, we took a walk and found a small restaurant squeezed between two office buildings near the hospital. An Afghani or Pakistani couple owned it and he took our order while she went into the kitchen to prepare the food. Ingrid asked me if I liked curry. I said I'd never had it before. She smiled like that time I caught her playing with the silent butler.

I found a pay phone and dialed Cooney again.

"Who the fuck do you know anyway, Haftmann?"

"What do you mean?"

"I mean, Jesus Christ, I got the head of VCU telling me with a lot of winks and nods to give you a hand on this one. The CID commander had his arm twisted too. Even Dooley, that prick of an assistant state's attorney, is bowing like a fucking Chinaman. Just who the fuck are you?"

"You know somebody named Booth?" I asked.

"No. Who's he?"

"A fed. I asked him to intercede for me. I'm in a little trouble back in Ohio right now."

"Whoever he is, he's got real muscle. So OK, big shot, what do you want from me?"

"Right now, I've got a phone number I want you to check for me."

When you've got a lucky streak, you have to ride it. I knew Booth wasn't the type to blow hot and cold; it seemed I had a temporary reprieve. But right then Cooney's words had none of the hostility he sent down the wire; they were the governor's words announcing a stay of execution to a man who's been shaved and cinched into the chair with the electrode plates slapped onto his greased skin.

As Jack used to say before a long stakeout, it was time to begin the beguine, so I called the *Globe* and had them place the ad in the following day's paper.

Then we waited.

Chapter 9

Ingrid brought me the paper. I had taken some Tylenol 3's I was saving up for the inevitable migraine and overslept by an hour. I must have fallen asleep playing solitaire because some cards fell to the floor getting up from the couch. A jack, a ten of spades, a red queen were face up. Looking for my fortune but seeing nothing.

In the paper, I found it, the finished quotation from II Corinthians, 14:

For what fellowship do righteousness and lawlessness have?
Or what sharing does light have with darkness?

If the material in Gallatine's briefcase made any sense at all, it had to do with this simple code. The quotations I found in the briefcase were Corinthians, so I didn't stray from it in case this was his assigned patch of the bible for summoning the Boston High Priest of Phineas. Unless Gallatine tipped him some other way, he would assume Gallatine placed the ad, his answer completing the quotation would appear the next day, and the contact via phone would proceed. I had the number, but I did not know whether a certain time was appointed for the call itself. That too could be important, but there was nothing in Gallatine's briefcase to infer a specific time after the ad appeared.

I called Cooney again and got him. "What now, Haftmann?"

"I gave you something to check for me, remember?"

"Oh yes, fuck me, I forgot. Seems these damned homicides keep interfering with my important gopher assignments."

"C'mon, Cooney, what the fuck, give. Did you do it or not?"

"It's the lobby phone of a little publisher next door to Houghton Mifflin—"

Got you. You motherfucker, got you now, going to put my gun in your mouth, you slimy fuck. . .

"Haftmann,? Listen up, we need to talk. Come down to the precinct—"

"Thanks, Detective. I'll be in touch."

"Haftmann, God damn you—"

"What is it?"

"You better not be running no vigilante bullshit in this town—"

Click.

Adios, Cooney. See you when I see you.

• • •

I had the maps, two bags of quarters, the plan, but not much time—
the time between the paper hitting the streets and the phone call to the
Beacon Street publisher next to Houghton Mifflin. If there was a fall-
back contact, I didn't know it, and the killer would become suspicious.
I patted her hand, told her not to worry: "Just call every hour. If anyone picks up, remember, you're not to say a word. I'll be watching.
You know what to do then?"

"I take a cab back and wait for you to call me."

I drove south on Charles. Her hands were twisting a scarf around.

"That's right. It may be a while before you hear from me, OK?"

"Yes, I understand. I will wait for you."

"That's right. You'll be fine. I've left you some money. Just wait by
the phone."

She said nothing more. The noon traffic was intense in the eighty-
degree heat. Cabbies leaned on their horns and pedestrians scattered
like fish. My hands shook on the wheel. The smoke from my tailpipe
was more visible and darker; if oil was getting mixed in the gas, this
clunker wasn't going to make it much longer. I wanted to toss up one
of those mindless prayers to the gods, but there was such a rage inside
me I felt like choking. I nearly missed the Tremont intersection because the flow of traffic from Boylston sent me into the wrong lane.
I took the turn anyway and heard the caterwaul of horns erupt behind me: *Fuck them.*

We drove north up Tremont east of the Commons. The park was
filled with people walking in antlike clusters down the center of some
of the most important acreage in American history. Vendors were
hawking items at them from every direction. I took Tremont right to
the end: Beacon Street. I showed Ingrid, off to the right atop the crest,
One Beacon Street: the stately firm of Houghton Mifflin publishing
company. Next door, like a tagalong sibling to a big brother, was the
specialty book publishing firm of Fabrice. A pair of names etched in
a silver framed plate above the massive oak door said: Nigel and Bob
Fabrice, Prop. The brass kickplate at the bottom looked spitshined to

a high polish.

"That's it," I said. "That's where I'll be."

I drove down Beacon past gold-domed state house, past the statues of poets inside the iron gates—"Look," I said, pointing to a black marble statue of Quaker woman with knitting needles in her lap. I didn't have to read the inscription to know she probably earned her distinction by swinging from an oak tree across the street; we drove past the row the mansions with their names chiseled into the stone. The rulers of nineteenth-century America once lived on this street—the financiers, industrialists, magnates, empire-builders. The same ones who ran America today.

I looked at her. Thus endeth the Haftmann tour of Boston's blue-blood district.

I hit the brakes hard. There, right there. A battered-looking pay phone just inside one of the park's entrances, one of the few left in the age of cell phones. Not a thousand yards from the top of the hill.

I jammed the tire into the hillside curb and walked her past a bas-relief of a Civil War scene honoring Major Robert Gould Shaw who led his all-black 54th Regiment into the Civil War. I jotted down the phone number in my notepad and gave it to her. I handed her one bag of quarters and a sack of food I had picked up at the corner deli.

"It may be a long while now," I said. "Just do what I said, and everything'll work out."

She took the bags and reached up to grab me by the shoulders to pull me down to her; then she gave me a hurried kiss on the lips.

"Be careful," she said.

"You too." I walked up the hill.

The building was bigger than I thought; it looked like a German castle transplanted from the Rhone Valley. It had two opposing turrets with crenellated edges on the towers and gadroons beneath the oval windows. Out front, the massive square columns with Corinthian pilasters made an imposing view if it weren't for the soot-blackened capitals, which looked as though the building had been scorched in a fire. Apparently the architect had changed his mind in the middle of construction and opted for Romanesque over Gothic.

I saw a pair of protective gargoyles leaning down toward the sidewalk. I was tempted to put a scuff mark on the kickplate but didn't. I found myself in a long corridor with small offices leading off on both sides. There were names and titles stenciled on the pebbled glass. This corridor widened into a triangular-shaped area with elevators and paneled doors with brass knobs and led toward a wide marbled stairway. A curved walnut desk with ornate images of gods and goddesses frolicking while shepherds pipes to their goats occupied the large space beneath a massive curved stairs. Oil paintings hung on the staircase walls—dour men, a few with long white beards. The Fabrice patriarchs, I guessed.

I found myself in a long corridor with small offices leading off on both sides. There were names and titles stenciled on the pebbled glass. This corridor widened into a triangular-shaped area with elevators and paneled doors with brass knobs and led toward a wide marbled stairway. A curved walnut desk with ornate images of gods and goddesses frolicking while shepherds piped to their goats occupied the space beneath a massive curved stairs. Oil paintings hung on the staircase walls—dour men, a few with long white beards.

A young woman with red hair in a French twist sat behind it and talked on the phone; a large plaque that said INFORMATION on it occupied the front of the desk. The first call was scheduled for noon.

I found a men's room just around the corner. The lobby consisted of vending machines and a telephone built into the wall. NO LOITERING placards were placed near the machines and above the phone. The public would not be expected to go beyond this point. I had a story, but I was saving it. I saw no security people. Even shaved and passable in my best clothes, I've never been inconspicuous; it wasn't going to be long before someone came along and enquired about my business in the building. As lunch hour approached, people were milling about from all directions; secretaries appeared from the stairways and elevators greeting one another and making plans for lunch. It was enough to cover me for a while. Five minutes to noon. I took a seat in the lobby and opened a magazine and stared into it.

The phone rang. Ten rings. No one seemed to notice it in the confusion. No one answered it.

Twelve-thirty. The same thing. I waited five minutes and called her back.

By one o'clock, most of the secretaries and typists had returned to work. The young woman behind the polished walnut desk looked up at me again. I nodded and smiled at her. This time she didn't smile back. The phone went through its ten rings and even with one good eye, I could see several people in the vicinity pause to take note of it. At one twenty-five, a man with a bald spot like a tonsured monk came out of an office to flirt with the receptionist. She had said something about me to him because he turned and stared at me for a moment before he returned the conversation to his real interest. I heard her voice go up a couple octaves and they both laughed at something he said. I got up, stretched and yawned, looked at my watch, and then walked into the men's room. I paused inside the door to listen. The phone rang. On the eighth ring it was picked up.

I came casually out and saw the man with the red suspenders saying "hello" several times into it and then hang up. He walked back to the receptionist's desk and resumed his flirtation with her. I took my seat.

She called over to me, "May I help you, sir?"

"No, thank you, Miss. I'm just waiting for someone."

I returned to the magazine as nonchalantly as I could. I felt the .38 snug against the middle of my back with the two-inch barrel digging into my spine. A hard place to reach but also very hard to spot and easy to miss on a light pat-down. I had wrapped several rubber bands around it to keep it from moving or sliding down. I knew Red Suspenders was looking at me. A few moments later, he went upstairs, singing off-key, and the sound echoed around the stairwell. He called down to her, "I'll call you tonight, hon. Give security a buzz meanwhile, OK?" She must have nodded because I heard nothing.

A snatch of buried memory came floating back with his oafish singing: *Nor in thy marble vault shall sound/ My echoing song.* Words I heard in a literature class in my only semester of college before aborting and joining the police academy in Columbus. *What was it called? Carpe diem. Seize the day.* I thought of Annaliese inside a stainless steel drawer in a room smelling of putrefaction and disinfectant. Then I thought of Micah putting on her game face for court. Something she used to say before walking out the door: *Let us make sport of them who make as much of us.*

Two o'clock, two thirty. The ten rings. Nothing.

At two forty-five I left the building so that I might not be confronted by the security guard ambling toward me from the far end of the corridor. At two fifty-eight I was back in my chair in time. The receptionist looked up from the man she was speaking to and stared in my direction. I pantomimed a routine with my watch and shrugged as if to say, my appointment had been neglected. She seemed to buy it. The rings came and went. I never looked up from the crossword puzzle I appeared to be doing.

Three thirty. The phone rang again. The receptionist looked at it through each ring as her forehead creased in wrinkles. She got up and walked off. While she was gone, a woman with gray hair and eyeglasses dangling from a silver chain on her chest walked over to her desk and dropped off a stack of papers. I tried to be helpful and mentioned that the young woman had just stepped out. The woman scowled and went into an office.

Four o'clock, the rings. I called Ingrid back and after she hung up, pretended to be in conversation with a business associate. Whether the charade helped or not, the receptionist stopped staring at me. But her resolve to ignore me broke at the half-hour calling because she launched herself from her desk, banging a leg against the corner of it, muttered *Shit* in passing me and caught it on the fourth ring.

"Who is this, please?" she said.

I only smiled up at her, but she gave me a look that said she understood there might be a connection between me and this incessantly ringing phone. I flashed her a big grin: "Shall I rip it out of the wall for you, Miss?"

That got a thaw in the chill, and she said, "I snagged my skirt."

I clucked my tongue in sympathy.

Sweetheart, he'd bash your pretty face in too.

The workday was ending at five. I was thinking of words to say to Annaliese's mother. I needed something to make my own resolve stiffen, but I could think of no stick large enough to lash to my drooping spine for the day's failure.

At four-forty-five, after downing another cup of the liquid filth extruded by the button marked COFFEE on the machine, I watched the activity in the hallway pick up as people began closing offices and preparing to leave. One more time and then we would be back tomorrow. I was trying to think of something more convincing for the young woman for tomorrow's vigil when two girls emerged from a nearby office, and I overheard one of them say she couldn't wait for the day to end because Baldwin was finally starting his vacation tomorrow. I got up to follow them, preparing the story of Mr. Baldwin's and my prior relationship in mind and was ready to blurt out an introduction when I heard the lobby phone ringing its last toll. It stopped on the third ring.

Red-haired missy is going to be a real problem . . .

I turned back and made my way about twenty yards when I heard a man's voice saying hello. The suddenness of it almost made me totter on the parquet floor as I made my way back to the lobby as unobtrusively as possible. Approaching the receptionist area, I saw her regarding whoever must have answered the phone, and as slowly as I could manage, I swiveled my neck to take in the man who just then turned so that his back was to me. Which one, I wondered. Someone being a Good Samaritan or someone just tired of a ringing phone, or a killer of young women who happened to be a member of a secret religious society with its roots in antiquity?

Fucking-A, Jack, old ghost and mentor. Everyone wants to see what's behind door number three.

He was between thirty-five and forty, about six feet, two hundred, short hair streaked with gray at the temples, dressed like a successful professional, an attaché case between his legs. His suit was charcoal grey, pinstripes, his loafers looked like those expensive ones as soft as butter. *Holding the phone too long . . . Either he knows I'm behind him or—no, not that—she's talking to him . . .*

"I see," he said. Then he said it again. Then he said, "That's very interesting." And then he replaced the receiver and slowly reached down for his case. He turned down the opposite corridor from mine. I was not going to lose him if it meant tackling him inside the building and gouging out his eyes with my thumbs. No security guard challenged me as I followed out to the parking lot and down across spacious concrete steps into the late afternoon sunshine.

His walk was casual but brisk, with that shoulders-back, heel-and-toe action athletes affected. The saliva in my mouth had dried, but I remembered to piss right after the 4:30 call. I slipped my hand around to my back and dug the gun out of my belt. I tucked it into my pants packet and caressed the safety. My mind was emptying of thought, just letting go. There was no time to call Ingrid to ask her to explain that bizarre conversation, but I had to be sure this was the killer before I blew him away. I told her that if there was any way to kill him so that she could watch, I would do it, but if not, she would have the satisfaction of knowing her daughter's killer was no longer breathing oxygen.

Save one bullet for me, Thomas, I beg you.

He strolled down Beacon with me fifty yards and closing on him from across the street. He was already past the Shaw monument and would be coming up on Ingrid at the pay phone any second.

What the fuck had she said to this man? I crossed the street at a forty-five degree angle right at the park entrance where Ingrid was standing. I watched him approach her, stop just abreast of her, say something, and walk on. I crossed the street at a jog and cut down the entrance where Ingrid was standing near the phone. I grabbed her by the shoulders and shook her, "What did you say to him?"

He was about fifty yards ahead, about to emerge into a throng of people. "Tell me!"

"I said he was going to be killed for what he had done to Annaliese—"

I was running now. *Shit Piss Fuck.*

So much for the plan. Tailing him to a residence was unlikely, unless he hopped a bus or took the subway, but I knew that if he got into a car, I could give Cooney the license number and they could run the tag through BMV. I wanted to confront him on my own terms. Look right into his eyes, not like this, watch to see if he bolts, and shoot him from behind if he runs. I could see him ahead easily, as if he weren't trying to escape, or worried about anything. Could I pull the trigger on this man without knowing absolutely he was the killer? I had punched and stomped a man to death in an alley twenty-four years ago. I had lived with that guilt, not well, but I endured the nightmares and seeing Max's leering face every day since that summer I sailed aboard the *Col. James Pickands* and discovered there was ineradicable evil in the world: evil inside me. But I could not shoot this man in the back *unless I knew for sure.*

Just then he veered toward Frog Pond and I maintained a thirty-yard distance between us. Icy sweat was pouring down my back. If he ran, I could close some of the distance, take my combat stance and shoot. He was much younger, fitter. I'd never catch him. There were too many people around. I could not send off rounds while all these people—women, kids, elderly folks—were milling around. The sky so blue and bright it hurt to look at it. Not like then. Before. When I killed a man for the first time. In a darkened alleyway. Not even a cop. Just for me. Just to play God with a human life that I declared not worth living. The memory of stalking Max seared my brain: the wet, plopping sound of my fist striking his face (I had put rings on all fingers and wrapped my fist in duct tape); the cracking sound of snapping vertebrae from my steel-toed boots . . . *Oh Jesus, awful, awful.*

He took the path that turned down past the Soldiers and Sailors monument, and then—still walking leisurely, never looking back—he backtracked to retrace his steps. I had not yet made the turn onto the path that would expose me to him face-to-face, so I used the moving crowd for cover, dropped onto a park bench, and watched him retrace his steps. He did this twice, walking his isosceles triangle in what, I suspected, was the only place in the Commons that would expose a tail from any angle.

Then, as if he sensed me looking, he looked over to the bench and began walking toward Charles Street. I stayed forty yards behind and watched him cross the street and head straight for the bridge over the Public Garden pond. I figured he was going to come out at Commonwealth Avenue. At the top of the bridge I could see his salt-and-pepper hair bobbing among the heads in the crowd going south.

At the Washington Monument, he hesitated. I kept walking. I watched him gaze at it alongside a trio of rubberneckers, Japanese businessmen, snapping photos and clucking at one another. I made it to the Arlington Street entrance before I risked a look backwards. He was still there, so I took a bench and pretended to study a piece of paper I had picked off the ground.

For the first time since Ingrid had trashed the scheme, I felt good. I knew I had him. He had to make a choice. I tried to ease my breathing into a slow rhythm.

Then he was past me, going left at a good clip. I followed him down Arlington but I closed the distance to twenty yards. *Let him look,* I thought. I'd keep coming, walk right up to him and shove the gun in his nose.

He was about ten yards from Newberry Street when, timing his move for the traffic, he loped across and headed for the Ritz-Carlton. A tiny doorman wearing more gold braids and piping on his scarlet trousers than an organ grinder's monkey tipped his cap to him and held open the door. If his plan was to shake me this easily, I foiled it by jumping in front of an oncoming stream of cars and trotting right up to the doorman. I was keenly aware of my sweating and less- than-crisp attire, but I used my size to create an attitude and muttered something about enquiring at the front desk for the association dinner that evening. He grinned, an ancient homunculus of a man, and opened the door for me too.

The air conditioning was chilly the way rich, elderly people like it. My eyes boxed the room, a spacious lobby with a gold chandelier, but he was nowhere in sight. I heard the hiss of the elevator and looked over to see a woman stepping off. My insides were churning and the hand on my gun was twitching.

There, he was just disappearing into a doorway off to the right of the front desk. One of the clerks eyefucked me as I approached, my goofy grin in place but nothing in my head to say if this weasel wanted to bumrush me out of the joint.

I veered off to slip past the door, opened it and found myself in a narrow, dimly lit passageway that ran the length of the building. My neck hairs were standing straight up, and I could smell my own body odor in the close air. I began walking down this corridor, a claustrophobic's nightmare, and heard humming and whirring noises from down the corridor. A lemony light was spilling out.

I had the gun out now and made my way toward the light. My hand shook. The air was close and the humming noise grew louder. As I reached it, I threw myself against the wall behind me and risked being backlit to take a long look. The laundry room. The humming was from rows of dryers and washing machines. Huge racks of linen surrounded me. I saw a man in a white uniform wearing a paper hat and apron extending past his knees bent over one of the dryers, extracting and folding towels. I quickly slipped the gun in my pocket so I wouldn't alarm him. I walked right up to him because of the noise and was about to tap him on the shoulder to get his attention, when I saw them because there wasn't time enough to change or disguise them: a pair of loafers no hotel peon could afford. I drew the gun out and held it to the nape of his neck.

"Nice shoes," I said.

He turned to look at me but didn't bother to raise his hands. "Thank you, Mister Haftmann," he said. "Guccis, by the way. I have them handmade and shipped here. I have elongated second toes, you see—"

That's when I pistol-whipped him across the face. Blood spurted from a gash on his cheek. "Oh-Oh-Oh! That—that was excruciatingly painful. You didn't have to do that."

My second swipe with the barrel caught him above the eyebrow, and this time he went down hard to the cement floor. It didn't open up much, though, because I had filed off the sight to prevent snagging in my clothing.

I watched him get up. He groaned and then wobbled a bit once he was on his feet. "Aren't you going to read me my rights? Oh, I forgot in all the excitement. My sources tell me you're not a cop. Just a private eye." He dabbed at his cheek with a towel and looked at the blood. This time I used the butt to smash his nose. The blood spurted in all directions. In a few seconds, he looked liked someone had taken a machete to his face.

I waited a few moments. "Get on your feet, you fucking lowlife bag of human shit. I'm going to beat your brains right into your expensive shoes."

He lay there moaning and smearing the blood across his face with one hand, then the other. I pulled him up by the hair and waited for him to register. His eyes were suddenly bright, clear, and he was laughing despite the beating and the blood. "How's the . . . how's the mother in bed?"

I kicked him in the ribs.

He staggered to his feet and held onto the edge of the dryer. He spat out some blood and I heard a tooth skitter across the floor.

He started to babble something else, but I was past listening. I threw a left hook, which slammed him backwards into the dryer. I'd never seen a human being oblivious to pain before. His eyes reached my face.

"Reach too hard . . . and you miss . . . that toward which you strive." His eyes were glassy and his head wobbled on his neck.

"Why did you kill her?"

"Make clear . . . your antecedents . . . and pronouns?"

I looked down on him, slowly feeling my rage boil up again.

"Motherfucker, I'll give you a grammar lesson," I said. I went to smash him in the ribs, regretting I didn't have steel-toe boots, pulverize his vertebrae—but I held myself back.

"Annaliese O'Reilly, you fuck," I said.

He laughed without much glee this time. His voice—even through the pain I had just inflicted—was lulling, a fact which spooked me. It was as if we had met in the Commons and were having a quiet conversation.

"Haftmann. German, *Hautedeutsche*. One Hamburg whore said of middle-aged men attending her brothel. 'They fear the closing of the door.' What do you fear, *Herr* Haftmann?"

"Men like you," I said. "Men who are really reptiles inside."

A woman walked into the room just then, saw us, and screamed. He was coherent enough to think that funny. "Doesn't appreciate the esthetics of blood, does she? Blood is a rainbow. Like red velvet when it first flows, black in the moonlight . . ."

A red mist came over my eyes. I hit him again in the mouth.

He rocked back and forth on his feet like an old man, a lock of hair displaced.

He was mumbling incoherently now. His eyes were glazed like a dead bird's. Blood had spattered his elegant clothing.

This time I threw my shoulder into it, the gun butt an extension of my fist. He slammed into the dryer, his legs going in a crazy jig, before he toppled over. Then he began writhing and twisting in spasms on the cement making gargling sounds before reflexively vomiting up blood and tooth fragments. His eyes were half-mast now, so I kicked his head to the other side to keep him from choking to death. His mouth opened and closed around red jagged stumps of his front teeth. I just stood there watching him breathe, his mouth opening and closing like fish in an aquarium.

I didn't notice the crowd of people jostling each other in the doorway, everybody trying to get a looksee until somebody suggested it might not be safe to be jammed into a corridor while a maniac stood there watching a man drown in a pool of blood.

I suddenly felt very tired, drained of all emotion. I wanted to close my eyes. My stomach was nauseated from adrenalin. I thought of Annaliese and wondered what her last moments were like, were they bottomless moments stretched to eternity, like these? My arms were lead and the gun seemed to weigh a hundred pounds.

Shouts behind me—the cops, finally.

The first guys in were the SWAT team because they wore those iron hockey masks with slits like something out of those teen sta-bathon films. The next thing I remember was being thrown to the floor and bodies piling on top of me; somebody had a foot on my neck and my hands and feet were tied tight behind me. I was trussed up like a pig.

I must have said something they didn't like because one of the cops came over to me and swung the butt of his sawed-off against my jawline. Then it was a red mist followed by blackness, and I was out for the count for a very long time.

PART 2

*Wer mit Ungeheur kampf, mag zusehn,
dass er nicht dabei aum Ungeheur wird.*

(We who fight monsters must beware
unless we too become monsters.)

—Nietzsche, *Beyond Good and Evil*

CHAPTER 10

I was aware of the sound of a man alternately pissing and shitting. Then the interminable sound of metal clanking. Laughter. A guard stopped by and called to me: "Haftmann, visitor."

After the pass was signed and the pat-down, I walked down a lime green corridor to the visiting room. Because this was medium security, there were no glass walls and phones. You had to sit at opposite ends of tables and talk. You could not touch, nor could you accept anything from a visitor. Since this was my first visitor in the eighteen months of my incarceration, it was explained to me.

"Hello, Haftmann."

"Hello, Booth."

The small talk was brief, vapid, pointless. I asked him what brought him this way, and he told me. "Richard Lindell. He's getting out. His family pulled some strings and he'll be released in six weeks."

One hundred fifty millions of dollars buys a lot of string, I guessed.

"How can they do that, Booth?"

"Don't be naive. He was never convicted of anything. His incarceration in a mental facility was a voluntary act."

"What do you mean? The state isn't going to indict—"

"Indict how? You pistol-whipped the bastard and destroyed whatever chance we had of making a case."

"Why is he getting out? He's as mentally fit as a rabid dog."

"Maybe they cured him. The fact is, he's getting out soon."

I remembered the VICAP profile's description of his mental make-up. He was one of that rare breed of human being who is completely without the capacity to feel emotion. No pity, no compassion, no sorrow, no laughter. His type always learned to simulate the socially correct response to every situation in life; they simply did not have the capacity to feel. You might as well explain color to a person born blind. To survive in society, this kind of sociopath had to become a great actor to avoid detection. Now and then they would make a mistake, laugh or cry at the wrong time; people would stare. *You learned by doing.* The psychobabble was tortuously convoluted on the next point, but I know what it boiled down to: these vicious, sadistic monsters wanted more than anything to *feel*. They wanted the very thing nature denied them at birth, but there is no chromosomatic cure for this.

There is, however, the violence you can inflict on another person, and in that person's pain and anguish, you can feel something, escape the freakish horror of being trapped in a yawning abyss of emotionless sameness. The first one is like the first shot of heroin, and like heroin, it doesn't last, so you have to keep maiming and killing to recapture the feeling, redefining yourself by more and more vicious acts of violence against the flesh of other human beings, and only then, for a moment in time, can you escape the sterile wasteland of living. These monsters will continue to ravage as long as they live or remain healthy. Nothing will cure it, and it'll never stop.

"Tell me why it happened?"

"He asked for release."

"You mean the fucking state's attorney's office set no conditions—"

"Sure they did. His lawyer got them overturned as unconstitutional in a federal court two weeks ago."

"So he's getting out?"

"I thought having one eye affected depth perception instead of hearing."

"All right, all right."

Then, smoothing back silver hair that was never out of place, he asked me, "When is your parole hearing?"

"Next month, the fifteenth."

"The Ides of March," Booth said. "Fitting."

"I'm not the one who needs to beware, Booth."

"You get three to five for breaking a deputy's arm, and he does nineteen months in a mental hospital with more accommodations than Club Med. Fourteen murders, we know of. There could be bodies dumped all over the country."

"I can't believe you can't put a case together."

"The evidence is all circumstantial, Thomas. No forensics, no witnesses. His only mistake was keeping that contact code too long."

"What about O'Reilly?"

"We think we have a CCTV video of him from a motel off Interstate 90. But he's wearing a hat and the clerk's description of him is too vague."

"So enhance it. That's what your famous lab does, right?"

"We'll only enhance the hat. We need face to go into court. His legal team comprises of *Who's Who* of Harvard and Yale luminaries with family connections back to God. I don't need to tell you what your word is worth in a court of law."

"What have you got prepared for the day he gets out? How many teams are you going to have on him?"

Booth's look was a laser beam. "None. We're trying to stop the entire movement at its source, not one sociopath using white supremacy for murder."

"Don't tell me you're just going to leave him out there."

"We'll be monitoring him."

"*Monitoring* him. That's FBI slang for watching him eviscerate females while you build your case."

"Listen, you, and listen good. There's more going on than you're aware of. You ever heard the concept of teamwork? Seems we had this identical conversation before only it was in a West Virginia pen. Stay out of it now. Forget Lindell. You're done and that's official."

"I can't," I said. "He laughed in my face. You think he's done?"

"No, I don't think he's done. There's another reason I stopped by. We've been paying one of the orderlies to check him out from time to time. He's an opera buff and he was out of his room for a day and a half attending a performance."

"Opera? You tell me this world isn't deeply fucked up, Booth."

"The orderly found his journal and xeroxed some of it. It's not good. Of course, a shrink would call it therapy, curing himself through writing—"

"What's he planning?"

"He has a lot of information on Annaliese's mother. Where she lives, what stores she shops."

"Christ," I said and waited for him to quit waltzing.

"He's going to use drugs to keep her sensible as long as possible—"

"I'll fucking kill—"

". . . just ravings. They don't mean he's going to do anything."

"God damn it, Booth. Look where I am."

"Haftmann, will you stop acting like you're responsible for the moral order of the universe. She's safe. He can't get to her."

"Fuck your casual surveillance," I hissed at him. "Get her into witness protection."

"We can't," he said, and I knew he was lying. She was his bait. I knew the feeling.

"What else?"

"He wants you. He gets quite intense on the subject. Some of the description is very technical before it collapses into gibberish."

"I mean *her*, damn you. What about her?"

"She's working for a motel chain on Jefferson-on-the-Lake. Cleaning staff. Gets a free room, minimum wage. Hasn't she been to see you?"

I hadn't seen her since my sentencing to Lake County Correctional. She held a scarf in her hands the same way. I had forgotten how shapely her hands were . . .

"I haven't seen her since my sentencing."

"Never wrote, huh?"

"Why?"

"Lindell knows a lot about you. Knows all about your rather exotic sex life. My God, Haftmann, don't you worry about STDs? How many—you're like a dog in heat."

This last uttered with a nose-wrinkling of distaste. "Anyway, he rented an entire private investigation firm in Toledo. Their only assignment is you, find out all they can."

"Is that legal?"

"It's legal and he's got the cash."

"Booth, you didn't look into his face. He'll go after her. He won't care if you are watching her. It'll just make it more of a challenge for him."

He gave me one of his patented stares and then swiped at his immaculate hair. "Well, we agree on that much. The Basic Sciences people concur. He likes a challenge."

"Jesus H. Christ."

One of the guards entered to usher out a couple cons who had come in to see their families after I arrived. They gave me black looks as they passed. FBI clout.

"We fixed Boston as much as possible. The assault with intent and the gun charge is all they want. You've plead that down as far as the state's attorney's office will allow."

"How much time?"

"What's Ohio give these days? "

"Ten days good time for a month served. Three days every month on top of that."

"Not bad, considering."

"Not bad? Axe murderers don't do seven years. Can't you do something?"

"The only reason I didn't leave you twisting in the wind is that I did some very good creative writing on my field reports for Washington. They seem to be buying it. At least, I'm still in charge of the operation."

"If it weren't for me—"

Pouting, his face screwed up in a snit. "The Phineas Priesthood was your work."

"So help me. Just once more."

"You don't listen. I'll bet you've been told that more than any human being I know. But if you're worried he can get to you in here—"

"I can take care of myself in here."

"No, it isn't that. He's spending a lot of money to see to it that you're well taken care of."

"You mean in here? In this second-rate slammer? There are nothing but check bouncers and hit-and-run drunks. Hell, I did a skip trace on a couple of these guys."

"One of the guards told us. It's Boston he's looking out for. Had your cell picked out at West Boylston before the ink was dry on the extradition papers. He wants to be sure you come to no harm. It's an easier place to do a stretch than Cedar Junction."

"How can he do that? The prison board for the entire state makes that decision."

"He bought them."

"Booth, nobody buys a whole prison board—"

"Prison boards are sinecures. Political appointments. If you know the right people—"

"What is it that you're not telling me?"

"He's well-connected, untouchable. I'm going to send some information. You'd better look at it because I have to tell you that I've never seen anything like this in my life."

"You're still not telling me everything."

Booth looked to me at that moment old and tired, as if he were burdened by secret sins. "I've even felt the pressure. I didn't think anyone could reach this high for something this ugly. Things keep deflecting the investigation. I've had three agents working on him transferred out."

"Having a crisis of faith, are we? In homicide we used to call you guys Fan Belt Inspectors."

"Don't joke about the bureau to me. I've given my life to it since I came out of law school."

"Watch her, Booth. She doesn't believe me. You know?"

"I know it," he said and he raised a hand to signal time up.

I wasn't sure he believed me either.

• • •

Prison is like college. They both prescribe your behavior. They allow you to read books. They both give you time alone to think and time to discuss issues with peers. The difference is that prison is about the past, whereas college is about the future. An existentialist might see no crucial difference. I might have been content to spend months doing what I did with time on the outside—play mah jongg and solitaire, lift weights, and eat starchy foods—except that the future was somewhere beyond these walls. I had one course of study: Richard G. H. Lindell. Class enrollment: one. My degree program was Pass/Fail.

I had written Micah one letter but received no answer. I began writing Ingrid long, detailed letters asking her to write me, trying not to alarm her, but her letters to me were all short notes in grammatically skewed English, written long after her work was done, at (I imagined) a small utility table in the efficiency apartment. She never mentioned speaking to Lindell that day. I never brought it up in my own letters. I saw her in a room with no view, drafty in winter, airless and cheerless in summer; mouse turds in the closets. No matter what touches of home she tried to bring into it, it would never be a place where you could leave a mark or feel good about yourself. *Please come see me*, I wrote at the end of every letter.

She did. The day of my parole hearing. I did not expect her to, but she testified for me, and impressed the panel with a mother's grief and sorrow. My crimes, she said, were all a result of my trying to help her find her missing daughter. It must have wrung blood from her heart to have to tell her sorrow to strangers, but she did. Somehow, by the end of my session, I was painted as something less than the wild-eyed ex-cop trespassing, resisting arrest, and fracturing the bones of the law's sworn minions than as a blundering cretin donning a suit of armor too heavy for him to wear, too moth-eaten and rusty for use. I felt the invisible hand of Booth in the room.

Gift horses and looking into mouths, they say. Dante buried that guy deep in the Inferno, the one who lied to the Trojans about that big fucking horse in front of the gates. Me, I would have listened to the hollowed belly for the clanging sound of iron.

• • •

Whatever it was, it worked. The letter of conditions was spelled out with bullets and a numerical list. One of life's little absurdities intruded into my reflections: the only condition that mattered to me was getting permission to leave Ohio for Boston, but I would be leaving the state in the company of federal marshals who would be escorting me in cuffs looped to my belt to answer for crimes against the Commonwealth of Massachusetts.

Where could she hide? Where would she be safe? Every time I put my mind to it after lockdown and the lights went out, I could see no solution. His leering face blended with the face of the dead watchman until I had one twisted, grinning visage that mocked my every thought.

The day the marshals came for me was like every other day of confinement except that my cellmate told me I was laughing in my sleep instead of grinding my molars. An ex-con and outlaw biker named Fat Danny, in for stealing and chopping Harleys.

"What's so funny, man? Share the joy."

I told him I had a crazy dream of being back in homicide police. Before the crack-up when everything—job, marriage, life—went to hell. In the dream I was standing in the muster room when the day-watch commander came out and handed me a note. It said my old partner Jack was found dead in his apartment. "Ate his gun," the note said. Below that line: "We all gotta die." In the crazy logic of dreams, I go to see the shrink to have the note explained, although it wasn't a mystery to me. The shrink is the same guy I was forced to meet with

169

after my first shooting. He was an exotic little man with from some Southeast Asian island chain, now a Cleveland psychiatrist with an office in the Terminal Tower with the incredible name Matrooshian. The plaque on his door spells it all out in humorless gothic letters: Terd Porn Matrooshian. That was his real name, by the way. The shrink hands me another note. I open it and read it. YOU HAVE BEEN SENTENCED TO DIE, it says.

When I look up to ask what's going on, I see the shrink pivot in a balletic way, windmill his arm like in fast-pitch softball, and while I'm standing there with my gob hanging open, he plunges a shiv right under my ribs. "Oh, it hurts," is all I can say.

I gave a condensed version of this dream to my cellie. The low-riding slob laughed at the punchline.

• • •

The airplane flight to Boston was uneventful; a little chop had me reaching for the vomit bag a couple times. The late March sky above the cloud cover was clear and the sun burned above the scud. Logan was shrouded in a mist as swarms of waterspouts with upended funnels moved off the Atlantic; the air full of icy mist and stank of diesel fuel. The airport crowded with people snapping black umbrellas. Depressing. The marshals were in their thirties, neither spoke much nor asked me any questions, and I couldn't remember which name went with which man. I was just a job, but they knew why I had done time in Ohio, and they were not friendly.

Inside my new prison, I was strip-searched—all orifices checked for contraband and weapons, my hair professionally tousled, and my clothes replaced by white prison duds with blue piping and the name of the prison in block letters on the back. My loafers replaced with an ugly pair of black 12EE's. Block D, Tier 4, Cell 8B, said the next guard in line who read from a clipboard.

My cellmate was a small man named Donald, a homosexual who painted his fingernails and tweezed his eyebrows. "Defalcation," he told me; then he looked up at me to explain what the word meant. "Stealing company funds. Three years." He also told me that he belonged to a lifer named Frank in cellblock E.

"They've separated us right now," he said, "and I do worry about

Frank a little."

Apparently Frank could look out for himself. "Oh not that anybody would be stupid enough to mess with him, you see," he said without looking at me. "Even these dumbass niggers have enough sense to leave him alone. The same goes for me. Nobody touches me, so you're safe—as long as we're friendly and get along," he simpered. "It's just that he's such a stud he might go sticking that beautiful cock into one of those black butthole surfers while he's in that cell. The slim disease, you know? We fight all the time because I'm such a jealous little bitch." Then he gave me what I supposed was his coquettish grin: "Shall I call you Thomas or Tom?"

"Call me anything you like but don't call me late for supper," I said, recalling the ancient quip of sailors from my days on the Great Lakes. When I turned around, he was fashioning another loony grin.

"How about if I call you 'Sugar Britches?'"

Lindell, I assumed. Using his power and his money and connections everywhere to have a little joke to help me idle away the boredom of my captivity.

• • •

I dug into the prison library system for information on Richard G. P. Lindell. Naturally, in liberal Massachusetts, there was a sophisticated version of the "college for cons" programs of every state. Some of these shitbirds were knocking down more federal money to go to college than taxpayers. Go figure. Some do-gooder left the state's prison system money to purchase computers and provide a network with access to the Tufts library in downtown Boston for the advanced students. They classed me as an advanced student because I could read and write beyond a sixth-grade level.

The socialite stuff I expected. Photos of Lindell winking behind glasses of champagne held aloft celebrating this or that event or commemorative occasion. He or one of his clan seemed to be in attendance at every gala event in Boston over the last decade. Sometimes the events were strictly familial; having started in banking, they considered philanthropy "their real *raison d'etre," which I took to mean using charity as a cover to fuck people over in the business world.* His mug was all over the society pages. He had been affianced twice in the last five years. No follow up on either marriage. His family traced its lineage back to Adams—the Adamses of Massachusetts. He was destined for a career in medicine from birth; apparently, that's where the initials came in: *Galen* for the second-century physician of Asia Minor and *Paracelsus* for the sixteenth-century Swiss philosopher and physician. But Booth was right about his brilliance. The more I read, the more I doubted my own senses. He looked ten years younger than he was. I replayed the film of my beating him; his face lit by something beyond the power of drugs, its animation was grotesque, babbling through broken teeth. His incredible intellectual gifts were nurtured like a hothouse flower in all the right private schools, from Harvard *magna cum laude* straight through the College of Medicine, until his appointment at UCLA as one of the youngest research professors of medicine in the school's history. Wit and charm in abundance, never a blemish along the way, nothing to mar his progress. No one suspected what he was.

I googled his name to see what it had. His academic career testified to another age than our own with all its narrow specialization; it was a Renaissance portrait in miniature: articles on science, the humanities, sociology, psychology, and law. I did not think a man my own age could have been made to be so unlike me. He defied the axiom that there are only six degrees of separation between the highest and lowest of humankind.

At about the time one career stopped, his other began. I wrote down the names of his books and put in a chit for inter-library loans.

I read passage after passage from Lindell's books that hinted of apocalypse. Nothing so dramatic that anyone alerted to his intellectual proximity to white supremacist thinking would have been alarmed about, but as text followed text, he began to abandon his early interest in behavior modification through drugs. The earlier books on psychotropic drugs stank of the lamp; after 1997 he abandoned clinical research for the most part. He was interested in whole societies, their rise and fall.

I found a passage from his book on race mixing to be most revealing because he abandoned the tight-assed, pedestrian prose of a scholar and begins to digress lyrically from his thesis. The issue of race-mixing itself is one he approaches and avoids elsewhere; this time he drives toward it before pulling back into arcane matters of ethics or philosophy. At this time, according to the dust jacket blurb, he had been affiliated with the San Diego police department as a criminologist working on developing a deterrent policy to combat gangs. Most of it is cool, analytical, and—to this private eye—yawningly pedestrian stuff dummied down for the layperson until it comes to page 256. Then the little burst of radiance from an inner light infuses it and tantalizes the reader with what it could really mean. It ends as abruptly as it begins and merges back into the smooth wake of a discourse on the demographics of East Los Angeles and southeastern San Diego. I underlined portions, which I copied into my notepad:

He went on to speak of the abandonment of civilization, "as a result of the decay and pollution, abetted by the largesse of certain factions within America who control the information gathering from shore to shore." He concluded in solemn tones that:

AMERICA IS LOSING ITSELF, IS APPROACHING THAT CRITICAL MASS WHERE ENOUGH PEOPLE ARE PRIMARILY VILLAINS SO THAT ALL PEOPLE LIVE IN FEAR AND COME TO HATE, THUS INVITING SELF-RIGHTEOUS VIOLENCE. I KNOW I HAVE RUN ON HERE, BUT I AM SO TROUBLED BY OUR CHANGES, ESPECIALLY AFTER HAVING SPENT FOUR YEARS IN VIOLENT COMMUNITIES TRYING TO DESIGN MORE EFFECTIVE POLICING. THUS I TREMBLE FOR THIS ONCE SO IDEAL LAND. WE ARE LOSING OURSELVES TO THE CONSEQUENCES OF OUR MISSPENT IDEALS OF RACIAL EQUALITY. WE ARE TOO PLURALISTICALLY FACTIONALIZED, THE CHANGES ARE AT SPEEDS TO WHICH WE CANNOT ADJUST, BECOME ECONOMICALLY MORE RIGIDLY STRATIFIED THUS REALISTICALLY LOSING EQUITY, AND OF COURSE SUFFERING THE CROWDING OF BEHAVIORAL SINK AS WESTERN IDEALS, RACIAL HOMOGENEITY—ALL, ALL, I SAY—MUST PERISH IN THE MUD. PERHAPS THE ANSWER IS FOUND IN THE ANCIENT WISDOM OF A SECULAR PRIESTHOOD WHOSE GOAL IS TO PRESERVE US FROM OUR MOST BRUTAL INSTINCTS AND THE PREDATORY URGES OF THE UNFIT, SUBHUMANS EAGER TO DEFILE WITH THEIR FILTH THE UNPOLLUTED MAJORITY.

Mud races. Was this the turgid ideological manifesto of the Priesthood of Phineas or one intellectual's lament, another variation on that chord first struck in Dallas in 1963? Now that I had time to reflect, I remembered how the city had been in mourning for a murdered President's wife.

My ex-wife was right about me and the moral order of the universe: I wanted to save one person from catastrophe and I had failed.

I hoped the astronomers and physicists were right and that there was a parallel universe out there where you got to make all different decisions.

• • •

I closed my eyes and slept twelve to fifteen hours a day, every day, for the next three weeks. Det. Cooney came to see me in late April; he was en route to Suffolk Superior Court to testify in the Best Friends drug-murders. He told me he passed his sergeant exams and was now working directly under one of two lieutenants at the One-Five.

"Congratulations," I said, into the phone when his words about the promotion finally registered and I realized he was waiting for a response.

"Skip it," he said. "You got trouble, Haftmann."

His voice was muffled, as was mine, I supposed, and the plexiglass was filthy with scratches. Any smooth surface was fair game for gang graffiti.

"What kind of trouble could I be in, Sgt. Cooney?"

I felt wearied. The sleep was saving me, I suppose, from boredom during the past three days of lockdown—or from too much thinking, but I couldn't clear the fog out of my head and concentrate for more than ten minutes at a time.

"Nathaniel, the guy who worked you over, the bouncer? He's turning state's evidence, so we've got him in protective custody over in Walpole. One of his crimeys told him something is going down in here really soon. Lotta bread changing hands, according to the grapevine."

"And?"

"And usually it means set-up time. Somebody buys a contract. Word is, you should be in protective custody. Pronto."

"Why?"

"Contract's out on you. The administration isn't moving on our recommendation, and that's a first. Haven't you noticed how vulnerable you are in here? Lifers, Aryans, Mexican Mafia, Latin Kings every kind of Crip and Blood going—shit, everybody who comes in here has to *claim* some affiliation so they know where to put him."

"Booth told me Lindell's keeping me safe from harm."

"Not what Nathaniel says. This lockdown is just an excuse to put the big factions together so they can agree on the split. No matter who does you, they all share. It's serious money."

"So I'll skip Thursday night's film from now on."

"Listen to me, motherfucker. You almost wrecked my investigation, so I don't care what you do or don't do in here. You broke the law just like these dirtbags. You didn't follow advice—"

A caterwauling siren erupted.

"What the fuck is going on, Haftmann?"

"Sirens go off in here. It's a fact of prison life."

"All right, fuck you. I've tried. Why do you think you're finishing your sentence up here instead of Ohio? The things run *concurrently*, don't they? Boston don't need you here."

I don't know what abyss it came out of, but I was weary of him. He wasn't a good enough cop to put a patch on Jack's ass—or mine, for that matter.

The wings of his nostrils whitened, and a tic along his jawline started to fidget.

"You shit-for-brains, private-eye moron," he said. "Fuck if I know what to make of you. You must have a real death wish."

"Thanks for the tip, Detective."

"Yeah, right. Good luck in there and don't drop the soap. I just called to tell you to watch your back. Slug a guard, get into SHU, but do something soon."

My antennae—or Micah's other way of describing my sudden hunches—were quivering. This wasn't the old Cooney from Boston I knew. Something had changed. How I knew it, I don't know, but I had clear image of him with his cell phone to his ear weaving back and forth across lanes like the prince of the city he thought he was. I imagined a big vein in his neck throbbing.

"Eat shit and die," I said.

"Cultivate that attitude, Haftmann. It just might keep you alive."

The laugh he sent back at me told me he didn't believe that for a second.

• • •

Two days later the routine of prison was restored as mysteriously as it was taken away. With it, I received my mail: one letter from Ingrid. I took it outside with me so that I could read it away from my cellmate, who fussed over me and tried to nurse me back to a better humor with little cakes purchased from the vending machines. Ingrid sent me two twenty dollar bills. The money wasn't inside the envelope but a note from administration said that $40.00 had been deposited in my account. She also sent me a picture of herself, as I had requested. She said she might try to visit after Labor Day holidays. For the first time in a long time, I began to feel a contentment. I found a tray of dainties set on my bunk when I got back from the exercise yard. I tried to get him to stop, but the effort was more trouble than eating the snacks.

"You have been looking peaked, Thomas. I'm glad you went for some sunshine and air."

"You shouldn't be spending your money on me," I said. He told me that Frank, his lover, sent him the proceeds from one of his black market operations; as a lifer, he had the shiv concession.

"Can Frank get me a blade?" I asked him.

"Of course, but it'll cost you thirty-five dollars cash. Not scrip. Can you afford it, honey?"

"Tell me again who brings cash into the place."

In his usual convoluted fashion, he told me how we could go about it, but it would cost me the equivalent of sixty dollars in scrip to get the thirty-five in cash I needed. One of the cons in C Block had an old lady who smuggled in cash in balloons inserted in her vagina on visiting days. I told Donald to get in touch with him.

"Thomas, I'm so glad. Do you know how strange you've been acting lately? Honestly, I've been afraid for my life. You know you actually sat up on your bunk the other day and wanted me to look at your watch because you said the hands were moving backwards! *My God,* I thought, *he's gone mad!* I didn't dare say a word for fear of my very life."

He wittered and lisped for another half hour, but I had stopped listening. I was thinking of Ingrid and wondering if two people like us, already mangled by life, might not be able to find a reason to be together. I didn't want to jinx it by thinking too seriously about it. Prison does have a way of concentrating the mind, however, and I found myself daydreaming thoughts about the two of us together in various domestic scenes.

Now and then, a sharp image of her naked flesh would sear my imagination, and it would catch me and put me into a cold sweat. I imagined what her breasts would look like outside that industrial sized bra and would see my hands kneading them, squeezing her nipples, and plunging my face between them. That, however, would entail a night's lack of sleep or, more often, precipitate my hand's releasing the tension. Donald was a light sleeper, and I did not want to give him another excuse for sliding his hand under the sheets and finding me there, swollen and ready to succumb. He once offered me his mouth, but I refused, half in fear of Frank, a confirmed psychopath who was given a wide berth by inmates and staff alike and partially because I did not want to give in to the pressure.

The days passed. My muscles grew slack from inactivity. I cultivated my slug-white prison pallor. No one who wasn't a member of one of the gangs was allowed to use the weights. One of the lifers, a tattooed hulk with the story of his life in indigo ink on his biceps and back, informed me I was trespassing in the weight room the first time I walked in there. I bought my knife from Frank. A sharpened piece of stainless steel made in shop which I kept taped inside my thigh. I stood next to the toilet, homemade jack-off curtains obscuring me, and practiced pulling it out. I fell back into my routine of sleeping twelve hours a day. I told Donald not to call me for chow in the morning.

More days passed, Ingrid sent no more letters.

Chapter 11

White worms tented up from the corners of his mouth; suture scars, I could see now. He had two rows of even white teeth. Dentures, I figured.

"Don't you find," he said to me one day during the first week of June, "that prison—no, confinement, real *confinement*, I should say, more than anything causes one to experience what Kierkegaard calls 'the despair of finitude?'"

Blue shirt, crisp collar points, ash grey silk tie with red splashes, black tasseled loafers. Impeccable. Small hands, folded neatly in front of him. He nodded his head as if confirming his own question. We were in the lawyer's conference room, a privileged place. He wasn't my lawyer, though.

I was looking into the brown eyes of Richard Galen Paracelsus Lindell.

"Please, Tom," he said in the practiced manner of a man used to relaxing his social inferiors, "call me Rich or Richard, if you prefer."

"You are fucking unbelievable," I said.

"Not at all," he replied. "I'm a man comfortable with himself and one who wants others to be comfortable around him." He stuck his thumb behind his upper front teeth and popped out the bridge.

"Look," he said, pleading with his brown eyes, "woulth a man who stanth on his thignithy do this? Show himselth to an enemy thuthly?" He winked.

Gooseflesh rippled up my back and shoulders.

"What do you want, Lindell?"

The bridge back in now, a little pop as it displaced air. "Just a chat. A talk between us to set the record straight. Nothing more nor less. I am not your enemy Thomas Haftmann." Another conspiratorial wink. I know you well," he said.

I broke my stare. "This is crazy," I said.

"Not at all, not at all. You have to allow for a kind of reasonable insanity in a lifetime. You're a gumshoe in that quaint jargon—forgive me—I should have said private eye. So you will have read Dashiell Hammett, if I'm not mistaken. Do you remember the passage in *Maltese Falcon*—"

"Never got around to reading it," I said.

"You've undoubtedly seen the film—"

"No, I haven't. I don't like movies and made-up shit. I like numbers."

"Why?"

"Simple," I said. "Because they're real."

He didn't know what to say to that, but he looked at me hard. I looked back. Not a muscle in his face twitched; he betrayed nothing. Very cool demeanor, a man difficult to ruffle.

He clasped his hands on the oak table again. "Let me put it this way," adopting a professorial manner. "There's an ordinary man walking to his office one day in downtown Seattle when a falling steel beam crashes next to him, an accident, but it scares him. He considers his life. He leaves his family, wife and kids, goes to Tacoma where he takes another job and marries a new woman and raises a second family. What's the moral, do you suppose?"

"I wouldn't know."

"He was nearly killed, you see. He had to adjust to a world where steel beams fell out of the sky and nearly obliterate him. Then he had to adjust to a world where steel beams don't fall out of the sky." He smiled.

"I don't get it."

"*Reasonable* insanity. You must adjust to life's beams falling out of the sky, but you must not judge. That's the secret."

"What about a world of women and girls—*girls*, you fuck—what kind of world do you adjust to?"

"A reasonable world. A very reasonable world, to be sure. I must ask you not to raise your voice, however. Don't worry. I've ensured us total privacy, but we ought not abuse the privilege, don't you agree? I'll answer all your questions. That's why I'm here."

Then he laughed as if hugely pleased with himself.

"Good Lord, what kind of cheer is this that I tediously set forth as if I had made discoveries? Every talk show host and politician has been belaboring this point for years. It is only that I am deeply moved by events as I seek, in my New England-derived Puritan way through my own failing civic duty to find solutions—"

Here, he paused and looked at me. "Do you know Herostratus,

Thomas?"

"Fuck you."

"Herostratus set flame to that wonder of the world, the temple and statue of Artemis of Ephesus so that, as he bragged after the deed, he would be remembered forever for the destruction he wrought, destroying the world's most beautiful thing."

"Her name, fucker, was Annaliese Marie O'Reilly. She was only twenty years old."

"Since you know something of my career, I feel hurt. Odd how one responds to calumny, the blow to narcissism perhaps but rationalized as the child's plea for justice, or the prophet's for vengeance."

"You don't hear well, do you? You *kill* children."

He shook his head vigorously in denial. "No," he said, "you're altogether wrong. You do not know what destruction is. Hope you are never in a position to be taught by me what destruction is."

The look he gave me was something he had pulled out of the abyss. I had never seen a look so malevolent on a human face. I remember the shrinks at Basic Sciences said that certain types, *devoids*, who were incapable of experiencing the normal range of emotion simulated them at an early age to blend into society. Sometimes their facial expressions were mockeries of the emotions they were intended to express. I was lost in thought when his mesmerizing voice brought me round: ". . . if you take our polity and its civilized riches as beauty, we see a myriad of killers, keen junk bond dealers, unscrupulous politicians—all memorializing their small and satisfied selves as agents of the destruction of this beauty which has been our land."

"I saw photos of the bodies."

"So you saw photos. It is the usual thing. Ah me, when my hangnail hurts, my brother's broken leg seems distant. Let me try to explain myself another way. I had this notion while growing up that I lived under a lucky star—a notion which should have faded by age six months—"

"Your mother should have strangled you then."

"—but somehow, as lunacy does, probably stuck with me through adolescence and then, because things did go quite well for many years, probably took on the status of doctrine."

"I don't want to know why you became what you are, Lindell. I don't suppose anyone will be able to look inside your mind."

He smiled at that: an ant trying to contemplate an angel, no good.

"I remember," he said, ignoring my comment, "a study a few years ago which said only depressed people had an accurate view of how others evaluated them. You see, the depressed knew others thought badly of them, whereas those 'normal' were consistent in thinking those who knew them well thought better of them than those people did, as measured by ratings or some such. In this world depression is realism, so is being paranoid."

Like Micah when she was pissed off. Indirect, oblique, answering a question with a question. Never met anything head-on. Even my friend Reg did this: lawyers.

"Why do you do it?"

"Not a simple answer, Thomas. There is no more paradox in this than in believing in God even if there is none. Delusions sustain us. Television merchandisers are not selling imagery, as the media parlance has it. They are selling the very stuff of *necessary* unreality."

"You want polemics, write on the bathroom wall. I'm not interested."

"But you should be! We're not much alike, of course. I don't find you interesting."

I looked around to signal a guard.

"I'd like to leave now, you sick fuck."

"Oh, I'm boring you."

"Fuck you."

"You overuse that expression. Your crude upbringing, I suppose, having been raised by a semi-literate woman from the old country. Do you know, I've decided to do a monograph on nausea and vomiting. The anatomists call it a reflex, but it turns out to be a ubiquitous human response which seems entirely maladaptive. It quite turns Darwin on his head."

I rose to go.

"How are you finding it in here?"

"Entertaining in a Hollywood, media-saturated sort of way," I said, standing.

He maintained composure, ignoring me, speaking on in that monotonous voice just at the edge of hearing, as if I were still sitting in the chair.

"There is not theory that entirely satisfies with reference to etiology. My reading includes neuroendocrinology and cognitive psychology. I have an advantage, you see. No complicated university permission to do human testing. I've seen them vomit with the most . . . abject of fears. Fascinating. Your little Annaliese, for instance, spewed forth projectile vomit as soon as I removed the tape—"

"Shut up," I said, "I'll kill you if you say another word."

Not daring to turn around to see if he were looking at me or the chair. My neck hairs jumped with electricity. I felt a pang of profound anguish, hopelessness, even fear.

"My own situation," he continued, "is one of reasonable steadiness. Has Donald performed fellatio on you? Odious creature—"

I was banging at the door now, my flesh crawling in waves.

He regarded me as if I were a specimen of some interest. He said to my back: "Not to worry. Just the bathos of a little honest prudery is all."

The door opened, the guard almost had to tackle me to stop me, but I heard his small, articulate voice echoing in the room: " . . . just an interim state where neither great adventure nor commitment is possible. Let desire and witches burn . . ."

I was gone, unable to hear another word, running down a corridor that looked strange to my eyes, although its walls were the same lime green and floors the same battleship grey I had mopped in another prison in a different state in another time.

● ● ●

After that visit, I had dreams of him. I left instructions with the guards that his name was to be removed from my visitor's list immediately. The captain of my cellblock wrote down my request disinterestedly and said he would forward my request to administration.

I went from sleeping all the time to insomnia. I couldn't buy sleep. The noise of clanging metal reverberated on all sides of me, and I was aware of each shocking intrusion. Donald wrung his hands in dismay and looked at me with a solemn pout that I grew to hate. Time nailed me to my cross and every screech of metal drove another spike in deeper. The cruelest of ironies was that, in my freedom, I thought of suicide; in the confinement of prison and wrapped in my own suffering, I couldn't bear the thought of ending my life.

The lack of sleep stunted that part of me that should have been alert. I grew reckless and indifferent to my safety. I failed to pay attention at times to my location inside the cellblock. Trespassing gets you killed in the joint. I watched a couple gangbangers flashing signs from the top tier one day while Frank came up behind me. "Baboons," he said. "Can't fucking spell their real names, but they can spell all this gang lingo at each other with their fingers."

He showed me a couple curled fists and smiled at his own humor. "You hear what those fuckin' coons did to the new fish? Got him over there inside one of their cribs on top and beat the shit out him. He had to suck off all those niggers before they let him go. He'll be wearing a dress before long."

I had heard that was more or less how Donald was turned and acquired via the prison bartering system. Frank probably never missed a night's sleep, but he fell upon some poor family on a picnic at a state park and killed them all. He talked about a heavyweight fight tomorrow night at Caesar's Palace in Las Vegas. Frank meant in the lifer's only rec room. "This guy's from Russia like that seven-foot giant. No heavyweight's worth a tinker's damn since Tyson."

When he left, he winked at me over his shoulder: "Anything happens to Donnie, I'm holding you responsible." Down the block, someone was playing rap.

That night I tried to write down everything I could remember from my conversation with Lindell. It was a language beyond time and space, an alien tongue in a calming, dispassionate voice. I could hear those precise inflections he gave some words, while others acquired the extra syllables of a Boston accent, but I could not remember how we began or what determined the flow of his thoughts. His voice was mesmerizing, easy to listen to, so much so that despite my own revulsion for him, I wanted to hear him speak again.

I got my wish. Despite my instruction to have his name removed, he returned on the first Tuesday of June. The previous night had left me more exhausted than usual. The papers said there was to be an annular eclipse today, and my mind focused upon that and worried it into fragments of worthless speculation.

Cause and effect, I kept thinking. *Cause and effect*, I would mumble to no one. I sat in the lawyer's conference room with one arm shackled to an eyebolt in the table and waited for him to be brought in.

I heard the guard's shoes coming down the hallway, and the first thing I saw of Lindell was his shoes: the same he wore when I cornered him in the Ritz-Carlton.

"Apologies. A little business with your warden delayed me somewhat."

"I don't want to see you any longer."

"Why?"

"You and I have no further business. We have nothing to discuss."

He said, "I think we do. I think it's important that we talk to each other."

"Lindell, leave me alone."

"That's not what you really want, though, is it?"

I looked at him. "What exactly is it that you think I want?"

"You look tired. Aren't you sleeping as much these days? I understand you were all but comatose earlier. I can get you a prescription—"

"Just tell me what the fuck you're doing here."

"All right, fine."

He drew a packet of photographs out of his blazer and tossed them at me. *Ingrid.* All of them. She had been snapped by a telephoto lens at work. Outside the Anchor Inn motel where she worked, pushing a cart, entering a room, sweeping a white-blonde lock of hair from her eyes. One caught her inside her room sitting at a table. She was in profile. The last showed her lying on a futon; her eyes were closed. A little surge of adrenalin hit me, but I shifted that photo behind the others and pushed the pack across the table.

"It's OK," he said. "She's only asleep."

I stared at him.

Shifting the photos to his inside pocket, he said, "Now you see."

"See what, fucker?"

"You see how easy it is for me to get to her. So either we talk like two civilized men or the next photos of her you see will remind you of her daughter. They were shot in a motel too. Like mother, like daughter. An affinity for cheap motels, it would appear—"

I was out of my seat before I remembered the chain; my free hand reached for him but all I clutched was the air in front of his face.

He ignored me and began talking, and he didn't stop for an hour. I remember watching the hand move around the face of the clock. Now, I was convinced they were doing things because the hands were moving ahead way too fast. His speech was just like the first time—slow, measured cadence in a voice of silk. I saw the scars I had given him white around his mouth. On occasion he would pass his hand across his hair in a boyish way that was unlike the primping manner of Booth it brought to mind. My throat was parched; it was as if I had done all the talking.

He told me about his life, where he grew up, what schools he attended (almost breaking a family tradition to go to Princeton), his friends and family, the names of his pets. At one point he was talking about California and his research, but he digressed from that to speak of a ranch house in the mountains. Although it soothed me with its hypnotic flow, I had to think of other thoughts, and I forced myself to imagine Annaliese's last moments in the room with Lindell. I fastened on something Reg used to say between shots during our games of pool at the Lake: *When crimes are plotted in hell, don't expect angels for witnesses.*

I tried to keep my mind blank while the words he spoke created a viscous film over the reality of a psychopathic murderer speaking to a captive audience of one miserable convict:

" . . . the rain would fall on my mountain. The redwood trees made sweeping boughs of windy delight, roses would bud even in the cool of December offering the rich and fragrant grace of great invention, theirs and not theirs in design and the bountiful gift, not so bad this green rich, rose yellow, rose red. A great horned owl would hoot hello to the cosmos of the nearby. How fine, Thomas. I used to think if we could talk to that owl, that rose and tree, like shamans in the golden time of which Eliades wrote so optimistically where humans beings can venture to the center of the earth, know the tree of life . . ."

"Lindell," I begged, insensate from listening to a voice that had become a whisper, "I don't want to understand you. I don't want to know what potty training you had that warped you into the way you are."

That stopped him for a moment. "Insane? I suppose. I am an optimist, Mister Haftmann. One does not ignore the hard practical work of the optimism of Pericles, Cicero, Boethius, Luther, Jefferson, and Lincoln. We owe an immense debt. I did not ask to respeak the message or be the old new dream enacted. I am one who, like others, has come forward at this time of crisis in our nation. My civil courage is undaunted but the range of my civilizing voice is but as a whisper, none I think to hear."

"You kill people. You don't create anything. You are the reason we have prisons."

He checked his wristwatch and stood up. "Ah well, fortunate enough are we to know you, Mister Haftmann. I shall visit you one more time, and then I shall tell you why I killed those women. I'll tell you why your little Annaliese had to die."

He arose and with a Harvard ring tapped on the glass reinforced with chicken wire. The guard left me chained to the table so long that I fell asleep and when I awoke, I discovered that I had wet myself. They escorted me back and I could feel dozens of pairs of eyes witnessing my shame.

• • •

His third visit came three days afterward. I was called out of my cell at eight o'clock at night, so I didn't expect a visit from anyone. When I was bolted to the table, I knew it must be Lindell. This time, my free hand was cuffed to the chair.

He came in wearing a tuxedo under his trench coat. His gold cufflinks contained diamond inserts in the shape of his initials. He sat right down, and as if we were resuming a conversation in which there had been no hiatus, completed the story of his life where he had left off. He had, it seems, experienced a midlife crisis or a nervous breakdown at the very zenith of his success, a glimpse into the abyss:

". . . so many books one recalls one has written yet no echo of an audience fossilized as proof any word or idea left an imprint. Such petty offices as might have been held, or political engagements fought, or entered on calendars . . . even a grain of sand in a sirocco-whipped desert seems more readily placed and counted. That public voice of mine is only softly heard in its structured place. St. Paul's dark and enigmatic Prince of this World as Iatros of sorts teaching within institutionalized medicine. Tiny steps to continue the Enlightenment. I believed that knowledge will relieve pain. I could make women well, and that thought itself, as scientific imagination, is itself beauty. . . . One marks Thucydides in exile, Origen writing the greatest theology before his torture and death, Servetus at the stake, Anne Frank trusting in her attic, all those wise innocents who insist upon the anthropic dream, that humankind has a place in the cosmos, and that both might reciprocally benefit, if only . . ."

I broke in. "You were going to tell me why you killed those women."

He laughed. "Haftmann, you should read the classics. Prison affords such time. I commend Boethius to you, the last good man of the classical world. He explains the richness of classical civilization as only lately having left the savagery of Emperor Theodoric and the despicably decadent, ever so modern in the politics of cunning—"

"Lindell, tell me."

"Sheer good fun. Why else?"

I must have been screaming but I don't remember. I heard the clacking of the guards' shoes in the hallway. Some scuffling at the lock on the door before it opened and then I remember being held down and somebody was wrapping one of those old-time straightjackets we used to call Kansas City vests around me. Then I found myself in a lit room with a bulb in the ceiling behind a grill mesh. Isolation. I slept and dreamed lurid dreams of angelic figures pirouetting and cutting. Blood spatter all over the walls, a regular season of blood.

• • •

I don't remember how long I was kept in solitary. I kept hearing voices and had imaginary, intense conversations. I remember, very clearly, hearing Lindell's words in that soporific voice of his talking about Annaliese and about Annaliese's mother. Try as hard as I could to recall it, I no longer knew what he had said to me in the lawyer's conference room and what, in my delusional state, I had made up. I remember trying to convince him not to go after her. I made every appeal and threat I could, but he refused to promise me he would not harm her. At times, I thought he was in this cramped cell with me. I shivered in the bunk at night and gagged on the smell because someone before me had left feces in the toilet, and large flaking brown turds swam about as if we were shipboard and the room had a list. The Judas window opened and closed a few times in the midst of my babbling, and I remember trays of food being set into the room and withdrawn, but the hand that brought them and took them out must have come while I slept. After an interval of time, I was returned to my cell, allowed to clean up under an escort of guards, and restored to the daily routine of prison life. I recalled what Lindell had said during his first visit about the "finitude of despair."

I was summoned on a Tuesday or a Wednesday from my assigned job as toilet cleaner by no less a personage than the assistant warden. "Let's go, Haftmann. You have a homicide detective here to see you."

Detective Cooney had a twisted smile on his face when I sat down behind the plexiglass. He brought me the photos.

"They just faxed them from Ohio," he said, "so the quality's not good but you can see well enough."

"Yes," I said, "I can see."

He held them up against the scarred plexiglass like a kindergarten teacher showing flashcards to a dull child. One at a time, each one a knife in the guts.

He said, "The manager thought she was ill, sleeping in or something, so he didn't knock until about ten o'clock." He opened it with a master and there she was."

There she was.

Her hands were tied to ropes that were stretched taut and tied off somewhere out of the range of the photographs. Maybe the table and the futon if they were solid enough. She thrashed around a lot from the looks of the blood.

"Autopsy will tell us whether she was doped. But it doesn't look like a struggle. Looks like she expected it. He had her there all night, apparently. Columbus CID is on this one, so we'll get all the paperwork, the photos, and the ME's report as soon as possible. Your man Booth has pulled some more strings, right to the governor. I'm hoping there's no jurisdictional hassle on this. FBI's liaising—so far. They haven't taken over the investigation, but I figure that's just a matter of time."

I wasn't saying anything. I didn't have the words.

Cooney said, "I'm sorry, if it means anything."

"Did she—" I groaned.

"I know she meant something to you."

"Did she have anything under her nails?"

"Word right now is no. FBI's sending a hair and fiber team in, assuming your yokel cops from that two-bit resort town of yours didn't fuck it up completely."

"How, how bad was it?"

"How bad does it look to you? He gave her a mastectomy among other things. What are you, a glutton for punishment? The woman died horribly. She suffered like hell while that maniac cut on her—"

I was trying to control the sobs in my throat from bubbling out.

"No witnesses, naturally. A resort motel in summer has people coming and going all night. Nobody noticed anything. When is your release date?"

"End of the month."

"Use your FBI juice to get out of general population. Stay out of trouble is all."

"I'm going to kill him this time."

"Haftmann, you can't say that to a cop."

I must have had a weird look on my face.

"What the fuck's so funny?"

"*Reasonable*. He said you have to adjust to a world where steel beams fall out of the sky and a world where steel beams don't fall out of the sky."

"I heard you came this close to getting transferred to the state's rubber room. Your FBI man must be arm-sore from pulling strings to keep you here."

"It wasn't Booth."

"Huh?"

"It was Lindell," I said, rubbing my face as if I could rub all the exhaustion and pain out.

He asked me how I could know that.

"It's a reasonable assumption," I said.

Realism is paranoia. I thought: *I'm thinking like him now.*

Despite the fact that my brain was frazzled by too little sleep and troubled by darkish nightmares that came with an hour's sleep at dawn, I knew that Lindell was still orchestrating events from afar like a dark omniscient anti-God in his private universe.

● ● ●

The routine of my day before my release date was identical to the thirteen months before it. If they were going to get me, I'd be an easy target. I was aware of clusters of men everywhere I went, and as much as I could, tried to change my route to and from my cell. I thought of staying inside, but I figured that would force their hand; they'd just come for me there. I had more options if I stayed mobile as long as I could.

At lockdown I went back to my cell from the cafeteria, and I found Donald inside weeping. He had had another fight with Frank that day. As I lay on my bunk, I tried to imagine the minutes dropping one at a time into a bucket like prisoners playing dominoes, slamming them onto the metal tables. At ten o'clock in the morning they were going to set me free. I knew I was afraid of dying, and that's when I realized I wasn't free in my head. The sounds of the tier finally shut down, the coughs and grunts of men rose above the faint hum of the generator, and the lights went down. Donald sobbed into his pillow for another hour and then I heard the rhythmic breathing of his sleeping.

I thought of Annaliese, then her mother. Two lives chewed up by the savagery of men. All of life's horror comes down to brutalized flesh. I was sickened by my own kind, every variation of it, every human face I saw. Life's bounty and variety came down to nothing more than a jumble of genetic equations in search of an answer over millions of years. *No answer was ever going to be found*, I thought, *as long as human beings populate the planet.* Lindell obsessed me, frightened me to the very marrow of my being, and made me sick at the cringing desperation of the cells comprising me to preserve themselves. For what? What? Lindell's face and soothing voice intruded so often into my reflections that I didn't know whether I was awake or dreaming with my eyes open. I wanted to write down something in the dark before I forgot it—something about Lindell's view of God as a violent force, visible in history. Donald was nattering on about the "crucial" difference between two shades of Maybelline. I was a split-second from tuning him out. I felt a clammy sweat all over. That's when I knew Donald was my designated killer.

I had just moved my arm over my face to fetch the pen and notebook I kept under the pillow when my forearm connected with the downward thrust of his arm.

I deflected his aim just enough to see the shiv in his fist plunge through the pillow, sheet, and mattress. He tried to jerk it out, but I locked my arm around his wrist and held it so that it stayed embedded. He tried to whipsaw it out of my grasp, neither of us uttering a word, except to expel breath in the struggle. Then he lowered his face over our clutching hands and bit me hard at the base of my thumb. He was leaning over me from behind and pinning me as much by my exertion as by his force. I felt the blood flow warm over our locked hands and then I heard his teeth snap on bone as he tried to get a deeper purchase on the flesh of my hand. He was too small a man to hold me long. I measured the distance and drew back my left hand and sent it toward his face. My awkward position kept the blows from being more than jabs, grunting with each, but not losing his hold. The pain was numbing my arm by now, but I was so twisted that I couldn't change position for better leverage. I began striking him in series of three and then resting. This ludicrous struggle in the darkened cell went on a long time but I couldn't tell how long we stayed like that—him panting for air, bubbling the saliva and blood that flowed over our joined fists, a ratcheting pain up my arm as he twisted his teeth around the bone of my thumb. Neither of us spoke a word throughout the struggle.

I was afraid the numbness was going to make the difference, so I gave myself a long moment to imagine how I should do it first and then stopped struggling. That was all the signal he needed because he let go with his teeth, snapped his head out of the way, and joined both hands around the shiv. I felt the air of it passing my face as he prepared to strike once more, both arms upraised with one to guide it downward. In that moment of hesitation, I struck first: one shot to the center of his face, just an oval blur in the dark, but I had shoulder behind it. I missed his nose but caught the upper bridge of his mouth and felt teeth break. He just went backward and struck the toilet and lay there motionless.

When I could sit upright without fainting, I crawled over to him and felt the pulse along his neck. Weak—but alive.

That's how they found him in the morning.

I was interrogated and put back in isolation during the investigation.

No charges were filed because the shiv was seen by a rookie guard who wrote it into his report. The fix was in on all the other guards on the shift except one; apparently, he didn't have the stomach for it, and the man's cousin was put on this crew at the last minute by the shift captain. If it weren't for that, I might have faced trumped up charges that would have kept me inside.

The prison grapevine reached me easily in the infirmary where I went for tetanus shots and twenty-seven stitches to close the wound in my hand. My whole hand was infected, and while I recuperated, I learned that Frank was organizing the lifers for a second shot at me. One of the hospital trusties had an Aryan connection close to the lifers, and he told me that his source said that Donald was supposed to let the real killers inside our cell—the entire block of cells was to be racked open at once—where I was to be beaten unconscious and taken down to the shower room. The job was to be done with a sharpened piece of wire. My eye first. Then I was to be revived and certain other things were to be done throughout the rest of the night. But Donald wanted to impress his lover and muffed it. I was to leave prison on the day of my release all right—except it would be the back way with a tag on my toe.

Instead, three days after my date of release, I was escorted down the corridor to administration to sign forms for my clothes and valuables, including the last of my money. They informed me that my Plymouth was in a South Boston impound lot. At five minutes after eleven o'clock in the morning of an August day, I found myself a free man on a street corner in Boston waiting for a bus.

I took a bus downtown to get a room. I wanted to shave and bathe away the prison stink and refine the details of my plan to get Lindell. I realized with a sharp pang of clarity I had finally become a free man, totally free in my head. Nothing mattered, nothing meant anything now. No rules.

Haftmann has no more rules.

I was going into battle without fear because they can't hurt you if you're already dead. My laughter caused the bus driver to stare at me in the rearview mirror. I knew what he was thinking: another nutjob on a ride to no place special.

Chapter 12

The front desk man at the Ritz-Carlton eyeballed me with as much disdain as one can put into a look without being called outside to a duel. Maybe the paper sack with the articles I took out of prison, stuff I couldn't cram into my pockets, or the two-day beard stubble put him off.

His eyes bulged and he looked pale when I said I was paying cash, but took my $192.96. That left me with less than three hundred and no great confidence that this was going to go as planned.

I asked for a room high up and that drew another pained look of surprise. For the first time since that day, I noticed the vast mural behind him while he punched up numbers on his computer; it covered the entire curved wall. I had seen the Diego Rivera murals in the Detroit Art Institute once while tailing a man on a case. I liked their vivid colors and energy. This one was a little too neoclassical for my taste—youths in toga-clad dalliance prancing about a garden. A fat-faced cherub voyeuristically hovered above one further along in courtship than the other pairs. Swingers' websites facilitate such wango tango now; even college kids create them in their dorms to facilitate stress relief caused by exams.

My staring must have provoked the clerk's comment because, without looking up, he said, "Rococo, eighteenth-century."

Surprised that he spoke, I asked him what he had just said. He ignored me and handed me the room card. "You do know how this works?"

At that point, I realized I was back in the real world again, with liveried monkeys like him all about me. I said, "Yes, I think so," and went into a crotch-grabbing, stumblebum routine I hadn't done since my street days with Jack.

As I made for the elevator, I watched his faced twist with concern as if he had just let a wolf into his fine establishment. I straightened up immediately and gave him a thumbs-up sign. I had business to attend to, not much time or money for play.

After the bath, I called the One-Five and asked for Detective Sgt. Cooney. They transferred me around a bit, and said he was unavailable—I heard a voice shouting his name around the room—would I like to speak to another detective in Crimes Against Persons? Somebody else came on the line and said he wasn't there, could he take a message?

"Tell him Lindell called and would like to see him at his earliest convenience," I replied. I gave my hotel and room number.

• • •

Cooney's eyes bulged like the Ritz-Carlton desk man's.

He started to talk out there in the hallway, and I said for him to save it.

"Are you out of you fucking mind?"

"My ex-wife's a lawyer," I said. "If she were here, she'd advise me not to answer that question on advice of counsel."

Inside, he asked me, "How did you know?"

"That you're on his payroll? It figured," I said. "He knows everything, everybody's movements, the progress of the investigation, my plans and thoughts while I was inside, everybody's whereabouts all the time. Somebody had to tell him. It had to be an inside source. You were the only one who could have done it. You were in the right position every step of the way."

He was more relaxed now, as if a weight had been dropped from his shoulders. I knew what he was thinking before he said it.

"Knowing ain't proving, Haftmann. You should know that."

He crossed his legs and took out a pack of Marlboros.

"You were the liaison between those shitbags and Lindell," I said, "You were his eyes."

He stood up and began moving about the room, opening closet doors and looking under the bed. "Let's say, hypothetically speaking, you're right. Where does it get you?"

"It got me this far."

"Oh?" He came up to me, patted me lightly on the chest and reached around to the small of my back. "Wired?"

"No," I said.

"I don't believe you. I think you got too many goofy ideas from jail. Maybe you took it up the ass too many times from your fudgepacker cellie, huh?"

Looking at the gauze wrapping of my hand. "He really fucked you up. Those homos like to bite, ever notice? Messiest homicides are blowboys falling out. They do like their knives."

Cooney was smaller by twenty-five pounds and three inches. But he was younger, and I wasn't so sure he was all swagger. I was in the worst shape of my life. I had aged years for months.

"How much did you make from Lindell?" I asked him.

He gave me another light frisk down my legs, and said, "Strip. I wanna see down there. Dickie check."

"I'm not wired."

"Do it, asshole. Just like we do the gangbangers."

He reached inside my briefs and gave me a feel. "Lucky for you, Haftmann. If you'd been lying to me now—"

"How much for selling out, Cooney?"

"None of your business, shitass. I will tell you this much. There's never going to be a case on Lindell. The chain of evidence is all screwed up. Seems he bought the evidence room boys too. Hair and fiber stuff got lost, boo-hoo."

I threw a punch that caught him flush on the chin, and he staggered backwards and fell on the bed. I had my knee on his chest before he could move and my bad hand gripped tightly on his scrotum sac. He knew it too and lay very still.

"Now, you listen good, fucker, or I'll pop your testicles," I growled above him. "I don't give a fuck about you or any other grifter at the precinct. You tell Lindell I've got all the evidence I need back in Ohio. Just give him the message."

I eased off on the pressure so that he could talk. "C-crazy sonofabitch . . . my nuts."

"You going to do what I say?"

"You coulda told him that yourself on the fucking phone," he groaned.

"He'll believe it from you. I've got the evidence in Ohio."

"You know what he can do to you?"

I said, "You knew about this Phineas Priesthood all along, didn't you?"

As I withdrew my hand, he struggled, grimacing, to a sitting position. Without looking at me, he said, "You dumb shit. Fuck you, him, and the Phineas Priesthood."

"Lawrence Gallatine, Cooney. Tell me how he comes into this?"

"Lindell's got a hundred Gallatines all over the country. He finds these people. I don't know how. He throws money at them and they all come running to serve him."

"That's how he got you," I said.

"Fuck you and the horse you rode in on, motherfucker."

He tried to spit on me, but I sapped him before he finished another sentence. I used a melon-sized, silver-plated decorative apple from the bookshelf above the bed. Maybe it was Rococo too. I wanted to hit him to get the rage out of my system for being so goddamned blind. I might have saved one from the maw of that psychopath.

I took the page out of my notepad that I had copied from a prison bible, folded it in half, and secured it with a rubber band to Cooney's index finger. He twitched and his eyelids fluttered a moment before he fell back into unconsciousness. I slipped his Sig Sauer out of his shoulder holster and found an ankle gun and tucked them into my pants.

● ● ●

I left Boston on a Trailways bus that afternoon. I had just enough cash to get me back home. As I settled into my seat, I heard a black male's voice saying, "Better cease that shit, woman," and heard the smack of a hand on flesh.

Nothing ever changes, I thought. I felt the sleep coming on, kicking in again—my protective coloring against the world: *Look, everybody, this one-eyed, ineffectual cretin is asleep even when he's awake. Nothing to fear when Haftmann's on the job . . .*

Chapter 13

The ride home was a miserable twenty-two hour affair with stops every fifty miles except for the Dewey Thruway. I made it most of the way home from the Ashtabula depot by hitching a ride on the back of a pickup truck filled with concrete blocks and stacked lumber. I walked the remaining two miles to my house and discovered that I had never locked it the last time I walked out the door. It seemed like years ago.

I showered and slept another eighteen hours straight. As Mike Tyson said famously after his demise from boxing: "I guess I'm going to fade into Bolivian." No dreams, no grotesquerie or mocking faces from a misspent life. Just a prevision of my afterlife: nothingness.

When I awoke, I took the quarter-mile walk to the Strip and found my office closed with that chalky soap smeared across the windows. The phone and the office furniture was gone, but my file cabinets were still in place. My key didn't fit the new lock. Someone had stolen or removed the sign with my name on it.

I walked to Tico's and found him washing glasses behind the bar. He brought me a chilled glass of tomato juice and the local news since I'd been away. Business was good. The bikers were expected to ride through over the Labor Day holidays. Gossip about a rumble between the Santa Monica Pagans and the Cleveland chapter of the Hell's Angels over a patch with CALIFORNIA on it—a big no-no among these cretins, a dissing of Angels everywhere. The tattoo parlor busted by the state cops for fronting drugs. The usual trivia of resort-town low life in high summer. Millimaki closed the case on O'Reilly: autoerotic asphyxiation.

Tico asked me what I was going to do now that I was no longer a private eye? "Opera," I said.

"Tomás, why'nt you settle down for a bit? Take things easy. You don' look so good, man, and you been hit on the head more times than a foosball."

"Football. I'm fine."

"You remember that migrant worker from that one summer? Came in here babbling about Jesus. Hay-suss told him to kill his bebé?"

"Yeah, so?"

"Yeah, well. You got the same look. You better go real slow for a few weeks."

• • •

That night I had a fever dream. I left my penicillin pills in the drawer of the Ritz-Carlton back in Boston and my hand reinfected; it was swollen and painful. That was all I needed: the NRSA virus to eat away my flesh. After some hesitation about falling off the wagon, I had drunk some Jack Daniels for the pain and consoled myself for the latest failure. What right, I thought, did this cesspit of a society have to hold me to any standards?

I went out less often, stopped shaving. My bad eye was red and my good eye bloodshot. I looked like a walking vampire. I thought about calling someone but there was no one to speak to. I did call Doc Harris and asked him how he could have signed off on O'Reilly's death certificate like some first-year med student. I accused him of taking money and he slammed the phone in my ear.

I fell asleep on my faded red velour couch and watched the dust motes bounce and float around my head in the middle of a steaming afternoon. I had not worn a shirt in two days because the air was so heavy with humidity that you could wring the sweat out of your clothes by standing still. I drank some more. During my lucid hours I tried to think of my plan to get Lindell, but I wearied of following one harebrained scheme after another down some cul-de-sac.

Gallatine was the key but how to get to him?

I was running out of cash even on my liquid diet. One check left from the last bank credit card that still did business with me. Worse, I was running out of time before Lindell called my bluff.

Jesus, Hay-suss. Everything's fucked up beyond all belief.

• • •

Hydra, the Serpent constellation, was declining in the West; its three-starred tail upright. Just another indecipherable omen. Time to go. I loaded up the backseat of Tico's son's car, which I had pried loose from Tico on the strength of a vow on my mother's grave to bring it back in the same condition it was given. I wondered, briefly, where my mother's grave could be. It occurred to me that I always imagined her dead, although it was conceivable she was still alive somewhere; whether she was happy in the life she chose after abandoning a child to her own mother or declining into old age, senility, and a lonely death, I did not know. I never tried to find her.

The night sky alternated moonglow with pitch blackness as a cold front crossed Lake Erie that ended a ten-day drought in a torrential downpour that afternoon. Crowds of tourists fled the low-hanging scud that precipitated another bout of rain. I sat under the awning in Freddie's Grill eating hot dogs and drinking coffee. My hand was giving me such pain that I couldn't sleep. I could barely make a fist. All day I lay around fearful of a blood infection. I turned on the television hoping to hear the world was ending; instead some vapid tabloid show with an anorectic blonde was talking earnestly about why Charlie Sheen's "Torpedo of Truth Tour" ended prematurely.

When I could stand my own company no more, I made my decision. I got in my car and drove. I cut off I45 and made the last mile down Route 307 as slow as possible. I saw no cars since leaving the Lake where the last of the biker bars would be pouring their clientele out the doors. The grungiest of them all, the Far Side, came to mind; that's where the Jack-in-the-Box serial killer had found his last job as a bouncer right in the midst of all the state's criminal investigators and FBI men on his trail—hiding in plain sight.

I could use some of that luck, I thought.

About a hundred yards east of the house, I pulled over. There was a flattened area of cattails on what used to be marsh. I took a chance that the downpour hadn't affected the baked earth too much and pulled the car into the middle. The cattails rattled like sticks on a tin roof. I slewed it around as the dampened earth gave under the tires, but it looked solid enough. I grabbed the equipment from the backseat. The moonlight came back just enough to help my bearings.

I circled the house and worked my way to the back where some trees stood. I picked my spot and dropped onto the ground; the air smelled of rotten cabbage. I trained my Zeiss glasses on an upstairs light. The rest of the house was in darkness except for a light over the kitchen window.

At dawn Gallatine appeared in the living room window. No wife or kids anywhere. I retraced my steps back to the car and drove home.

The next night I followed the same pattern except that I arrived around nine o'clock. I kept my vigil until dawn when Gallatine appeared in the same window. I stank of mosquito repellant and body odor. No wife or kids about the house. On my first night I had stumbled through beaten-down grass where someone had made a path for off-road three-wheelers. I tried to find this again, but it was a darker night, and I was shredding my clothes in briars; figuring that I was opposite the house I took a chance and made my way close to the road's edge. I saw no cars in the driveway and wondered if Gallatine's wife had left him.

My fifth night of surveillance paid off. I was raw from mosquito bites, and chiggers had penetrated my thick socks and eaten red speckled rings around my ankles. My resolve was failing badly, so I brought a pint of bourbon to keep me warm and provide whatever liquid courage I needed to get through another night. Cooney's gun was jammed uncomfortably behind me. The hours passed and the night sounds grew louder with insect trilling. Swallows overhead were replaced by bats feeding on bugs. The small animal noises kept me awake as before but this time it rained about three o'clock in the morning. The booze I had rationed to pass time was gone, and the bottle lay at my elbow, empty and accusing. The noise of grackles awoke me this time, and it was well past the false dawn I had used to cover my escape. I was worrying about how to make my exit when I heard the scrunching of gravel in front of the house.

Somebody coming. . .

I heard a door slam but could see no activity in any of the windows. A figure loomed at the kitchen momentarily, Gallatine, and then he was gone. The sun put a glare on the windows that made it increasingly difficult to see, so I moved to a better position behind a clump of Rose of Sharon bushes.

Two men, then a third, passed in front of the window. Two of the men were similar in size, so I couldn't tell if there were three men in the house or two. I decided to get closer.

The back of the garage offered the best security but it was too far from the windows to see or hear anything. I broke at a run for the kitchen window; flat against the house, I'd be open to exposure, but someone would have to walk out of the house to see me. I worked my way west of the house with the trees as cover and crossed the open expanse between the farthest gate of the pool. Made it. My back to the wall of the den, I sidled along the surface of the house, ducking under windows or belly-crawling past the patio doors. I made it to the kitchen area, and as I approached I heard two voices speaking loudly.

Gallatine's voice was the higher, plaintive, urging, but the words would not come. Then the other, its nasal Boston accent all too familiar. It shouldn't have surprised me that Cooney was here, but what I didn't know was whether he was Lindell's advance guard or sent at his command. Do a little strongarming act on Gallatine to keep him quiet. I moved closer until I was directly beneath the kitchen windows; someone had cracked them for ventilation.

Cooney's voice was now soothing, reassuring Gallatine. I heard my own name once or twice, and then Gallatine, the equal in size of the Boston cop, took his usual arrogant tone. Cooney spoke little thereafter. I heard *tonight* and *settle this thing*—and then silence.

A door slammed, then a car door, and an engine caught. Gravel sounds. I bolted back for the cover of the woods and then made my way by the same route to my car hidden in the cattails. Tonight I would bring some equipment I had stored at my house. A little electronic eavesdropping gadgetry purchased from my earliest days in the private detective business; most of it testified to my gullibility in thinking I would need this stuff, but I had taped enough adulterous spouses to justify its expense. From my hiding spot, the directional mic, at least, would pick up conversations from the glass. Somewhere from the abyss of my darkest self, I felt the thrill of imminent combat.

Oh yeah, Lindell himself was coming for a visit.

I drove home and paced the house for an hour. I had Cooney's gun in my fist the entire time, but I was acting out scenes in my head, dialogue, what I was going to say, what he would say. I drank a little to ease down. The sweat was pouring off me and my entire system was working overtime. I walked and drank. I thought of eating something, but I didn't. I had broken all my Haftmann rules so often by now, I didn't know who I was anymore. I had revenge for food. Nothing else would do. I lay on my couch for a little shut-eye at five and set the alarm for six thirty. The heat was stifling, so I downed a couple shots in quick order to help myself relax. I felt the exhaustion begin pressing me down into the couch, flattening me like bricks on top of my chest and then, mercifully, I slept.

Saturated with booze as I was, oblivious to my own degeneration,

I was given the most startling of psychic warnings in the dream sequence that began as soon as I fell into sleep. I was in a cave echoing with sound; someone was trilling an operatic air, then piano music: *Claire De Lune*. Dripping sounds accompanied by intermittent hissing. That weird little psychiatrist from Cleveland, Matrooshian, was in my dream, nodding and beckoning from a far corner of the cave; his spherical moon face glowing at me. He pointed me toward another room in the cave. I went in. *Ah fuck.* An autopsy room, two bloodied sheets covering two female forms. I knew without seeing their faces that it was Ingrid and Annaliese, mother and daughter on the slabs awaiting dissection. Old Doc Harris, nattily dressed in his bow tie, came in wearing olive green surgeon's garb and went to work on them, flung the sheets aside and began cutting. I watched him make the Y-incisions on each bloodied torso. The mother's sagging breasts blue with veins. The scalpel passed across the bloodied torsos of mother and daughter and then I heard the buzz of a saw and noticed that Harris had an assistant; he was masked and intent on his work as he cut the caps off the backs of their heads to remove the brains. I turned away and put my face in my hands and sobbed like a child. When I looked again, Harris was gone, the room was a blood-spattered chaos, their gutted bodies were hanging upside down from the ceilings, blue intestines trailing down to the floor.

Fiendish laughter from the corner; then a naked, blood-smeared Lindell charges at me with a knife too large for any surgeon and hisses as he thrusts it into my stomach . . .

I rolled off the couch. Awake, panting in terror. I actually patted myself. Just sweat, the booze was coming through my pores and had soaked through the couch. I was wet down to my underwear. I remembered the smell of the skin coming off the Jack-in-the-Box killer when he hoisted me aloft. A burning stench like leaves and old socks. Booth told me once that serial killers had an excess of cadmium or something that gave them a rank odor.

I looked at the window for a long moment before I realized that it was dark, well past sundown. I grabbed the alarm clock from the floor: 8:17. I threw it against the wall and raced upstairs to the hall closet to retrieve the equipment I needed, threw it all into the backseat, and hit the gas pedal and careened down my driveway in third gear. I did eighty-, eighty-five miles an hour all the way down 531 and hit

Route 307 in eleven minutes flat.

Goddamn, my self-loathing was at an all-time high: a drunk, a failure, a derelict, a fool. Every species of subhuman I had bagged in years as a homicide officer came roaring in my ears. *Shame, shame.*

I had let them die because I wasn't good enough, strong enough, sober enough . . . I choked back self-hatred and cursed, my good eye wet with tears: *tunnel vision,* I told myself, *concentrate, do it right.*

I slowed down but almost drove past my hiding spot, missing the cattails, and bucking the car onto softer ground that sucked the front end right up to the fenders. I grabbed the equipment and realized it with an icy shock:

No gun, I left the fucking gun underneath the seat with Henry Lee, my wrench.

I clambered and stumbled, careless of the route and took chances on being spotted from the front of the house. *Stupid, stupid,* I thought. I was dripping wet, wheezing, and my khakis were nearly shredded from the brambles I had stumbled through. I moved up to the edge of the trees as close to the open as I dared and set up the mike. The house was dark, completely blackened. No windows or night lights. No sound evident from any room as I beamed the mike at all windows in rotation. The house was outlined clearly beneath the moonlit sky.

Then a light.

I saw Gallatine, bound and gagged in his own living room, sitting on a chair. Gray duct tape was wrapped across his mouth and he was pointed right at me. All the curtains were drawn back. No other furniture in the room. Just Gallatine, naked and tied to a chair, looking right at me.

Lindell. His doing. They know . . .

At this, the moment of my worst epiphany, I felt the gun barrel jammed hard into the nape of my neck. Cooney spoke, "Get up slowly. Don't move or I'll drill you."

I did what he said.

He cuffed me, patted me down. "Where are my guns, asshole?"

I told him I wasn't carrying. He grunted something and then pointed me toward the house. We went in the back, Cooney flipping lights in each room while I stood in the dark. Gallatine's eyes looked at me in pure animal terror. I knew the blow was coming before I felt it because I saw it happening in Gallatine's eyes as they drifted from my face to a point over my shoulder.

Payback time . . .

When I snapped to, I was tied down with ropes in a dining room chair; ropes were crossed in front of me and cinched around my thighs and then pulled taut and tied off somewhere beyond my vision. I couldn't move anything except my fingers and my head from side to side.

Cooney tore off a strip of duct tape for my mouth. I heard a voice behind him say, "No, Sean. Leave it."

Lindell, of course. How much more fucked could I be?

Cooney argued a moment and then Lindell said in that mesmerizing voice, "There's no one for Mister Haftmann to alert. We're in the country. Let him scream. I rather hope so."

I turned my head but I still couldn't see him. I saw the rest of the room's furniture piled haphazardly in the next room, toppled chairs and table, settee; china dishes lay scattered on the floor. I looked at Gallatine again, but his widened eyes were holding the same expression.

The scalpel creased my skin a couple times on the back and shoulders but the remnants of my shirt came away in a gentle tug. The ropes held the fragment of the rest of my shirt to my skin. Cooney pulled off my shoes and then my pants were sliced away the same as my shirt except for what was held in place by the ropes. He pulled at my clothing after each movement of the scalpel. I felt warm blood trickling down to my ankle. Cooney threw my shredded clothing into the room with the furniture.

"Comfy?" asked Lindell. Cooney laughed.

Then the voice began, a drone, that moved closer to my ears and then he stood in front of me. If it were a color it would be flat grey: "You are hopeless, Haftmann. Detective Cooney tells me your little campsite in the woods out back would have been spotted by a trainee fresh out of school. Fortunately, he has some experience in detection, like you. What took you so long?"

I knew that speaking or not speaking was all the same. It was a game too sophisticated for me, and I remembered how I had leaped for him when I couldn't take it any longer. This was not a Boston prison. I was not going to be escorted back to a cell. I clenched my jaws to keep my teeth from chattering.

Gallatine began making muffled noises behind his gag. Lindell glanced at him, then to Cooney. "Not too hard. Just stun him a little." Cooney stepped over to him and hit him across the temple with the edge of his hand. Lindell said, "Manners, Larry. We don't interrupt our betters when they're speaking."

He returned to his position in front of me. His hands behind his back, rocking slightly on the balls of his feet. Cooney had moved off to the doorway and crossed his arms across his chest as he leaned against the wall. The gun, a cobalt blue .45 dangled from his hand.

"You see, I'm not disappointed to have to be here. Things should be tidy and you were becoming an annoyance."

He removed a wadded up piece of paper and read it to me: 'Breach for breach, eye for eye, tooth for tooth.' *Leviticus*, Chapter 24, verse 19. I know *Leviticus* also. Perhaps you're familiar with these. Same chapter, verses one and seventeen. 'And the Lord spake unto Moses, saying, And he that killeth any man shall surely be put to death. And if any man cause a blemish in his neighbor; as he hath done, so shall it be done to him.'

Then his face butted mine, his nose touching my own. "You're a killer, aren't you, Mister Haftmann? Don't you deserve justice too? I know all about you. I know you better than you know yourself. You're a sad, wretched failure of a man. Yours is a wasted life. I've spent thousands gathering all the facts of your life. None of it adds up to a life worthy of respect. But I believe one should not underestimate an enemy. One should know one's adversaries strengths as well as weaknesses."

I thought of sharks who roll their eyes back in their heads behind a thick layer of cartilage to keep the prey clamped in their jaws from getting to their eyes. If he brought his face near mine again, I would try to catch his flesh in my teeth, pull him downwards, bite my way to his eyes . . .

"Haftmann, don't you realize that I have gone beyond your puny ability to fathom? I am going to be someone who will be remembered centuries from now for what will happen in this country soon. Did I tell you, Haftmann, I was once a Marxist? The Hegelian dialectic, the inevitability of the proletariat's overthrow. I bought it all, as they say, lock, stock, and barrel. I was a young man then, eager for belief in a

system. Of course, like any intellectual worth his salt, I was contemp-
tuous of Christianity. As Marx said, the opiate of the masses. *Panes et
circenses*. Bread and circuses"

He laughed and began pacing in front of me. "It delights me even
now to think of it.

"Haftmann, those girls, all this bother about fourteen worthless
lives? Don't you understand there is no significance to them? They
were my little piglets. I had to resist the little touches of artistry I am
so capable of. No embellishments such as will occur tonight, I assure
you. With the detective's able assistance, I kept them varied in style.
They were chosen, you might say, like you. Like Lawrence here."

He walked over to Gallatine and stroked his head.

"I took care of his little wench as a personal favor. The Visigoths
are at the gate, Haftmann. Thousands streaming across the borders,
boatloads of human filth washing ashore . . . a fifth column of the
black race so entrenched in crime, poverty, and welfare that the system
is cracking at the seams. Sad but true. The United States of America
is dying. Another is being reborn in these momentous times, slouch-
ing toward Bethlehem, inevitable, cruel, cleansing, glorious to behold."
He clapped his hands and rubbed them as he looked from Gallatine
to me.

"You two are at the epicenter of the revolution."

He embraced Gallatine's shoulders and leaned his mouth in to kiss
the imprint of Gallatine's lips.

"You used me for revenge. You betrayed my affection and for
what? Did she jig, and amble and lisp like a woman? What our friend
Haftmann might call cooze, a little half-breed pussy. It's really your
fault, Larry. Haftmann here is merely an *üntermensch*, but you call yourself an intellectual." He unconsciously traced the white line of scar I
had put there.

He patted Gallatine under the jaw and said gently: "It's all right. Be
strong."

Gallatine was hyperventilating and the tape covering his mouth
puffed out like a frog in courtship.

He stepped in front of me. "Since you like to quote so much,
Haftmann, listen to this: 'Anyone who wants to cure this era, which is
inwardly sick and rotten, must first summon up the courage to make
clear the causes of this disease.' *Mein Kampf*. Like Hitler, I too am going

to give the order to burn down to the raw flesh the ulcers of this poisoning of the wells."

Cooney came up behind me and threw a cloth around my eyes. The last thing I saw was the tape puffing in and out over Gallatine's mouth and his eyes moistening with fear and terror.

Noises, footsteps, the scraping of a chair.

Lindell spoke to me as he moved about the room: "Did you know I once worked in Mexico on a federal grant? A DEA thing, actually. Mexico and drugs. Mix two thousand years of Aztec cruelty and the Conquistadors and the result should not surprise one. But I had most interesting discussions—there, that should do it—with a profound and silly priest. The man was inspired by the late Father Camillo Torrés of *La Revolucion*. I myself prefer Subcomandante Marcos, a believer in technology and the machine gun. But I did him no harm in the capacity in which I myself was traveling. As I said, we had strong discussions where I sought to persuade that radical Catholic that his own Christianity should disallow his embrace of violence as solution. You see, Haftmann, I had not yet come round to his point of view."

I felt myself tipped backwards in the chair and then dragged in a semicircle. The wrapping around my head was removed and I was sitting directly across from Gallatine, separated by about a yard of space. There was black tubing snaked out of his mouth; it was wrapped with the same gray duct tape to a green garden hose that twisted behind his chair and trailed out of the room toward the kitchen.

"*Ecce homo*, Haftmann. Behold the man. I want you to watch."

As he spoke Cooney began looping a cord several times around my forehead so that I couldn't move my neck.

Lindell put his face close to mine but I was unable to budge a muscle from the position.

"This man," he said, jabbing a finger in the direction of Gallatine, "has earned the enmity of the Priesthood because he betrayed me. He is going to pay for his little obsession with your nigger wench, and you will witness his punishment. I wouldn't have had to come to this backwater, but when I read in your little hick papers that a certain item was missing from a certain crime scene, I knew what was afoot."

"I was invited to the hacienda of a drug lord in Chihuahua. Unbelievable poverty side by side with ostentatious wealth. The village square had pregnant girls who could not have been more than ten years old scrabbling in the dirt beside a doorway. Eating undigested kernels of corn right out of cattle feces. Unbelievable unless you see it with your own eyes. Squalor and hunger and filth as bad as Africa. You might say I had my own conversion right there in that village square. Something had to be done."

He continued speaking as he paced the room, and this time he spoke softly into the face of Gallatine. "It was right at our doorstep, Larry. How many more generations do you think it would take before we are Mexico? The icons of our age are all Hollywood fools or criminal financiers like Bernie Madoff."

Gallatine's eyes were as big and round as cue balls. "This man Haftmann is just a sad clown, a thug—but you, Larry. You betrayed *me*. Hitler dragged his friend Otto from the bed of his boy-lover and shot him."

Gallatine tried to make eye contact with him; he gargled behind the tape.

"What is it, Larry?"

Lindell, emerging from his own rhetoric like a man awakening from a pleasant dream, turned to me. "Save your breath, Haftmann. I pay the detective more in a week than he can make cleaning the scum from the Boston streets in a year."

He rubbed his hands and spoke to Cooney: "Almost ready? Good."

To me, he said, "The man who provided me with such a memorable experience was guilty of some picayune transgression against the drug lord. These bloated slugs have a medieval concept of themselves as complex as a baronial fiefdom. It pays to humor them, so the agents who brought me to his ranch didn't interfere with the *padrone*'s primitive justice. It wouldn't have done any good. *Mordida* would only have insulted him. We were in no small danger ourselves because this was a risky kind of field investigation. The little *campesino* was doomed for some transgression, I forget what. They brought his wife and daughter to the shed. They were raped and killed in front of him. Then they took him to a shed Garcia had built for carrying out extreme sentences like this."

Fear throbbed in my throat.

He ignored me, continued to move about beyond the range of my peripheral vision. "They tied him to a chair and inserted a hose exactly as you see—down the throat. I have added a refinement or two. I greased the tubing for Gallatine. The urethra is tied off. The water turned on, and *voilà*, a human water balloon materializes before your eyes. "

My fear throbbed in my throat despite my effort not to betray it.

I broke down blubbering, spewing obscenities.

Lindell continued uninterrupted. "The pain is exquisite and horrible to contemplate."

He grabbed me under the chin. "And you *will* contemplate it, Haftmann. You will see it in his eyes. You will see his body distort until this yard of space separating you is taken up with the baggage of this human balloon, and be assured, I have calculated the flow of water into the vessel, and timed the amount of absorption into a body his size, with absolute precision. I know to the minute when the saturation point is reached. He will explode. You will be covered with human gore." My mouth was too dry to spit. I couldn't think of anything   to say. I could feel the onset of shock; my mind was trying to find a way out of the labyrinth. His words etched themselves into my brain, but it was as if his voice had become disembodied and hovered in the air.

"Your mind is telling you right now that this isn't happening or that it isn't possible. Let me tell you that it quite definitely will happen as I say. That is what medicine is all about—fooling nature, defeating the body's systemic reactions."

He held a syringe in front of my eyes. Then he stuck it in my right nipple. "Relax. I could have put it in your lingual nerve behind the tongue. A little injection to thwart those histamine blockers from gathering in your own system."

He took a long needle from a small case inside his blazer pocket.

"Don't move, Haftmann, or I'll blind you," he said as he stooped to look me in the face. I felt the needle go through my right eyelid it and then through a fold of skin he pinched over my eyebrow. With quick fingers he sutured my other eyelid to my eyebrow. "There. A little salve around the corners to work in some moisture later on. There won't be anything but pink gore on the walls when I return. Believe me, we stood behind a glass partition when the *peon* exploded and the entire shed was sodden with such human filth that it took a steam pressure hose to clean it afterwards. Not even enough to give Chapo's pigs a good feed."

He touched my face gently and said, "I'll return at dawn to give you the *coup d'grâce* myself. But first I shall cut all the skin away from your face with a scalpel—"

He etched my hairline and traced the contours of my face. "Then I'll gently peel it back, slowly, slowly, ever so slowly. You'll beg me to kill you, Haftmann. You will beg me to die just as she did when I inserted an extra-large dildo in her anus. It triggered a vagal nerve reaction. When that happens, the heart stops, you see. I tried to bring her around, alas."

I heard the hiss of the kitchen tap being turned on, footsteps, then the front door shutting. The car started and drove down the driveway.

Gallatine tried to rock himself free, but the ropes were too tight. I could see what looked like a cat's cradle extending from the legs of his chair in opposite directions, and I knew that he could never free himself that way. My own must be the same, although I could see nothing except the grotesque apparition of a man tied to a chair in front of me, the black tubing lolling obscenely out of his mouth.

Gallatine struggled. The tube dangling from his mouth pulsed like a king snake with a rodent in its belly. He was trying to make himself vomit. I attempted to nod my head to him, but even that was impossible.

How many hours to daybreak?

Time split into a thousand fractured pieces, and each piece fragmented itself as many times. I began talking just to talk. I must have told Gallatine the whole story of my life. I don't know why. I was babbling. My skin sweat rivulets and then dried and burned to the touch. The merest draft from the kitchen windows gave me excruciating sensations; my skin felt as if it had been turned inside out.

Gallatine's eyes blinked back the tears that streamed down his face. My exposed eyeball was drying out and itching so badly that I wanted to smash my face against something to stop it. My mind contracted and expanded with images and flashbacks so often that I hoped I was going insane. I remember lucidity coming and going like the systaltic beatings of a heart; in these interludes of insanity and clarity, I would laugh hysterically, gibber whatever came out of my mouth—words, sounds, animal noises—I couldn't recall. I was reduced to a level of feeling that I did not know human beings could experience. Like finding yourself in a deep pit, babbling in a foreign tongue and wondering how you got there. As terrifying as the descent into madness was, it was nonetheless a brief interlude of escape from the present scene, a small respite from hell.

The hours passed, but I could not tell from the blackness of the windows. Five minutes meant no more to me then than five hours would have.

I was aware of the changes in Gallatine. He was condemned to an ongoing living horror that my mind could not conceive of. I felt the shock of feeling his stomach touch my knees and involuntarily tried to jerk backwards. His eyes were still bright with fear at that point, but the terrible strain had begun to show: red-rimmed, bloodshot—eventually a glazing waxed over them. My own vision was clouding despite the grease Lindell had dabbed around my eye.

Time continued to split and fracture. The periods of lucidity grew further apart. My jaw grew slack. At one point I recall a pushing sensation from Gallatine's bulging flesh that irritated me. I could not comprehend what it was. There was a sour smell of Roquefort cheese gone bad in the room. I was having trouble gathering air into my chest at one point.

Then someone else was screaming, a sound that echoes my own from far off. I shook myself back to consciousness and realized there was a vast, gelatinous lump smothering me. I could still hear the faint hiss of water moving through the hose, but I could barely see anything in front of me. *Where had Gallatine gone?* I thought that Cooney must have returned and cut him loose, taken him away, but left me here for some reason.

It was light out. The first beginnings of dawn. There was a woman standing outside and she was screaming. I saw papers fluttering from her hand. She stood there screaming.

Christ, Gallatine's wife had come home.

The next thing I knew she was inside the house because a wailing sound such as I never heard was trailing behind her like a stream of flying ants. I heard footsteps running from room to room—a phone. Lindell must have cut the lines—she was in the room, although I could not see her clearly.

"You're *that* man," she said at me. "What in God's name? Where is my husband?"

She doesn't recognize him.

"Help me," I said, but my lips were cracked and my throat was so raw that the sound came out differently. I tried again, "Help me. Cut . . . ropes."

"No, no!" she screamed, and ran out of the room. I heard the front door slam, and I thought, *now I am going to die.* I willed myself to lose consciousness, to blank out. But my instincts fought my will, and every agonizing pain I had endured during the night flooded over me.

Then a sound. Footsteps returning. One pair. *She was back.* She stood in front of me, but this time I could see she was holding a .22 rifle in her hands.

"Help me," I said. "Please, please."

I kept repeating the word. It's one of two words that every murder victim has on his lips before dying; the other word is *No.*

I heard her set the gun down.

"Shut . . . water . . . off," I managed to squeak between my lips. She ran back to the kitchen and turned the tap.

With a butcher's knife she began working at my ropes.

"No, no!" I gagged out in what passed for a scream. "Call police, police!"

"I can't," she sobbed. "The phones don't work. Where's my husband? What is going on in my house? What have they done?"

I was so numb that I couldn't tell whether her hacking at the ropes was working. I could see more light coming through the window.

". . . hurry," I gasped. "Coming back. Men who did this—"

I heard the knife clatter to the floor.

"It's too hard to cut!" she wailed.

My voice returned, "Try or we'll all die."

She went back to fretting at the ropes, and this time I could feel the loosening effect as my feet were able to move for the first time all night. She stopped sawing and put her face in front of me. "What— who is this?"

"Don't look," I pleaded. "Just cut."

Another wrench and my feet were completely free; she went to work with both hands on the ropes binding my thighs.

"No," I screamed. "Cut the ropes from the chair first!"

She sliced them through and that enabled me to stand free of Gallatine's bloated stomach. "My hands," I urged her. "Hurry . . . hurry."

"I can't get through these ropes," she said. "The knife won't cut them. Oh God, I'm afraid. Where's my husband?"

"Get in your car. Now! Drive around to the back of the house! Then bring me the key. Do it!"

She left, and for long, terrified moments I was afraid that she was going to leave me. I heard the sound of gravel crunching, and the door opened again. I nearly vomited from fear.

She came back into that room of horror stumbling like a drunk into traffic, her face so pasty-white I was afraid she was going to drop to the floor right there.

Some reserve of strength made her grab for the knife and go to work at the ropes binding my hands. The light coming through the windows was reddened now. Full daybreak. No more time. She had one hand, then my left arm loose. I snapped it back and forth to get sensation into it, but it was like shaking a ragdoll. I couldn't make a fist.

"Hurry," I said. "They'll be here any second!"

She sobbed, dropped to the floor on her haunches, hunkered there exhausted, so I took the knife from her and went to work on the cords, but I kept dropping it.

I heard the sound of gravel. She looked at me in panic.

"Give me the rifle," I said.

She handed it to me by the barrel. I worked the bolt action by jamming it against the palms of my hands and the edge of the chair; then I cradled the stock in my midriff and rested the barrel over the chair's arm; it might look convincing.

The front door opened and my stomach nearly heaved as I recognized Cooney's voice calling my name. They hadn't seen the car and didn't know. *If I could squeeze off one shot,* I thought, *that might hold them off until I can get free.* I signaled Mrs. Gallatine to keep silent and leveled the gun at the doorway. Cooney was first.

He stopped cold when he saw me. I had a face that I hoped looked as bizarre as it felt. He kept his eyes on me and inched his hand inside his jacket. "Don't do it, Cooney," I said. "I can't miss you from here. I'll put three in your belly before you get off a shot."

To Gallatine's wife, I said, "Cut the ropes now."

She whimpered but did as I said.

"Where is he, Cooney?" I asked him without letting my eye drift

213

from his face. I could feel the barrel slipping downwards because I hadn't the strength to hold it steady at him. "He's in the car waiting for me."

"Just stay where you are and I might let you live."

For the first time I felt hope surge through me. I could see fear in Cooney's eyes, see him calculate the odds now. It gave me power. The ropes around my legs binding me to the chair were free, but I didn't trust myself to try to stand up yet.

"Now my head," I said to her.

Her face was a mask of fear but she responded. Cooney watched her. The wrapping of nylon cord fell away. I felt tingling in my fingers and my eyes burned as if someone had jabbed their thumbs into them. I wanted to rip the sutures from my eyelids, but I didn't dare take my eyes off Cooney. I was going to kill him as soon as I could get the pressure to do it, but I had to keep him distracted, so I began talking about his chances of getting out of this, turning state's evidence, tried to keep him off balance.

"It's Lindell they'll want," I said. "You're just a flunkie. They'll see that. You can go into the witness program, testify against him, start over somewhere. You can put him away, Cooney. You're the only one with credibility."

Cooney's eyes darted from my face to hers and cut to the window. His hands twitched. *Going to make his move soon.*

"Cooney, listen to me. He's a lunatic. He's got to be stopped."

"Fuck you, Haftmann," Cooney muttered, dazed with fear.

"I'll kill you if you move again."

"It's too late, it's way too late," he said. His stare switched from me to Gallatine and a twisted smirk crossed his expression. "He's going to blow any second."

Gallatine's wife ceased whimpering and looked at the sodden hulk that was her husband. She would have recognized him only in the eyes. When I last looked, he was still conscious.

She whispered, "Oh no," and then said, Oh God," and a long, high scream tore itself from her throat.

"He'll come in for me any second, Haftmann. The man keeps a timetable like a Swiss watch. I'm going to walk out. You enjoy the party because alla you assholes are fucking dead!"

"Cooney, don't," I said.

I felt the tingling more acutely, but I still didn't know if I could apply enough pressure.

He took a step backwards and then another. I kept squeezing the trigger, willing the necessary pressure to be there. Cooney wasn't going back outside to tell Lindell he had failed. He took another step, pivoted around so that his back was to me.

Any second now.

Cooney's right hand was already on his shoulder holster.

Now, now, I begged.

Cooney planted himself like a wide receiver making a cut and spun as he came around in a two-handed shooting stance.

The rifle cracked twice to Cooney's single shot. A deafening roar inside the small, empty room. I felt the bullet pass my cheek and a slight moan behind me.

When I focused my gaze, Cooney was standing in the same position except that there was a red dot in the center of his forehead beginning to bead with blood. Still clutching the gun, he dropped on his face. I looked behind me and saw Gallatine's wife slumped on the floor with half her face missing.

I heard a car start up. *Lindell, fleeing the scene.*

He must have understood the significance of the gunfire and was playing the smarter odds. I couldn't let him escape.

I hesitated a moment between my desire to stumble toward the driveway and empty the rifle in his direction or do something for Gallatine. I looked at him. His eyes were cast in the direction of his wife's body.

I went over to him and instinctively pulled the hose out of his mouth. His massive, elongated form was a caricature of a human shape. His head whipped back and forth above a massive stomach distorted by the rope's pressure. He made a loud, whooshing sound like air escaping a balloon. A frothy pink spume of vomit ejected itself in geyser-like ribbons and splashed the walls and ceiling.

Without realizing it, I had backed up to escape being sprayed by the foul-smelling liquid. My legs did not work well enough to run, and I fell over Cooney's body. I rolled off him and reached for the gun. Every muscle in my body was quivering, but I was able to crawl out of the room on all fours.

That's how I left the house. I crawled out the front door in time to see a white Oldsmobile roar down 307. I managed a crabwalk to Mrs. Gallatine's Cherokee behind the garage out back and clambered woozily into the driver's seat.

I don't think I could have gone back inside. My stomach was tossing around enough bile and acid to dissolve ten yards of railroad track. I turned the key, the engine caught on the first crank, and I was shooting gravel out the long driveway, bouncing crazily from one side of the road to the other as I missed the narrow culverts at the road's edge. The Cherokee gave me eighty m.p.h. in a matter of seconds.

Lindell didn't know these county roads; one error and he'd wind up on a dirt road to nowhere. My only hope.

I caught sight of him at the outskirts of the township. He was traveling at sixty miles per hour, not yet panicked, but too fast for some of these dips and curves. The .45 automatic bounced on the passenger's seat. My mind held one thought and it was sweet: *Revenge*.

With one hand on the wheel, I plucked at the sutures until I found the knotted ends. I pulled one end through my eyelid, not much blood, but I had to keep wiping my eye to see.

We were the only two vehicles traveling the same direction at a high rate of speed. Lindell knew I was behind him. I could see him decelerate as he came to intersections, indecisive.

Soon, you fuck.

At the end of Countyline Road, he made a left and hit the gas hard. I closed the distance. In a mile or so he'd have to make a choice: the eastern fork meanders through farmland on a narrow road where, as locals say, there is nothing to be seen between Ohio and the North pole but a barbed wire fence and a lobo wolf. Lindell could gun the Oldsmobile right to the Pennsylvania state line and there would be nothing to link him to Gallatine.

He braked at the fork and took the western road. *Perfect*. Right through Amish country parallel to the Grand River. *No place to run*: the road narrows and then peters out until you're looking up some Amish farmer's dirt driveway.

I stepped on the gas until I had the Cherokee's fender touching the Oldsmobile. Lindell was running out of road and I swung the Cherokee at 90 m.p.h. right up against his side. He turned his head and showed me no fear. I rammed him, and he nearly lost control, took the shoulder and then, unable to right the car from the slide, smashed through a barb wire fence and pummeled through a corn field.

I skidded to a halt as he churned the car through the corn stalks in all directions, blindly seeking a way out. As I put the Cherokee into the field I saw him blast through just ahead of me and jump the culvert that sent blue sparks from the chassis; his tires grabbed the road once more and he was off with the Cherokee burning rubber in pursuit.

I was gaining on him once more when I saw Amish buggies in the distance. I knew what he was going to do right at the moment I saw him sideswipe one of the buggies, causing the driver to tangle himself in the reins and pitch headfirst onto the road while the horse bucked and reared in panic. As I roared past on the opposite side of the road, I saw two children in dark clothes tumble out of the buggy just before it careened onto its side.

Up ahead, I saw the lights of the Oldsmobile fishtail once again. This time, as I blew past at ninety, I saw the buggy overturned and an Amish woman sprawled on her back in the road. The man was being dragged in the traces down the side of the road by his horse at full gallop, and I could see a face that looked like red jelly as I passed him.

I hit the gas and gained a little. Lindell suddenly swerved to the center of the road and floored the Oldsmobile. From a quarter-mile I saw cars, pick-ups, buggies drive off the road at the last possible second to avoid collision.

Not much road left, I knew now. Lindell, as if following some internal compass of his own, jerked the car across an open field next to a field of soy beans and cut a diagonal toward the Grand River. There was nothing out there but scrub and clusters of oak and pine standing since the Iroquois roamed this patch of the Western Reserve. I stuck the Cherokee's nose right after him and gained fast. The Cherokee took Lindell's makeshift track in a glide that was nothing compared to what he must be feeling ahead; the Oldsmobile sashayed and fought and bounced and seemed unable to keep a direct course.

I was twenty yards behind his offside fender, and I maintained the distance and pace with ease. Lindell must have seen my face in his rearview mirror. I waved the gun so he could see that too.

At the trees, instead of hesitating, Lindell roared full speed ahead into their midst, barely missing head-on collisions. I kept the distance but my lack of vision kept me from gaining on him or anticipating his next move. We drove like this in a figure-eight pattern, smashing the cars against saplings and swerving for the big trees. There was light above getting through this small forest, so I knew the trees were thinning out near the river. The Oldsmobile kept the lead and broke through the trees at seventy miles an hour.

Lindell saw it at the same time I did—a small humpbacked bridge over the narrowest stretch of river. He'd be on it in seconds unless I cut him off. I floored the Cherokee again and aimed it at the bridge.

He beat me to it, and I just caught the Oldsmobile's rear enough to send him flying over the bridge and land upside-down in the middle of the Grand River. Unable to right the wheels in time, the Cherokee jumped a ditch and plunged down the riverbank into the water.

My right calf was gashed open, but a blinding pain in my left knee pinned me while the water rolled up and over the hood, submerging the vehicle in its muddy waters. My left kneecap was shoved halfway up my thigh. I could feel it with my hand, but I fainted when I tried to push it back down my leg.

The water flooded into my mouth and choked me. That was when I recovered enough to roll down the window and wait until the roof of the car was flooded before sliding into the black water. The current pulled me immediately, but the drought we had probably saved my life; I was too weak to fight a rain-swollen river. I made it to shore and lay gasping on the rocks like a fish.

That's where they found me, and when I awoke this time, I was handcuffed to the hospital bed, and state troopers were positioned inside the room and in the hallway.

I had a thin tube in my nose that ran down my throat. Something inserted up my cock. *Jesus Shit Fuck, not that.* I tried to jerk out the hose in my nostril, but something stopped my hand from pulling it free. My first thought was pure terror: Lindell had me tied down again and I was going to get Gallatine's fate—but it was only the nurse's hand. The hand around my wrist held me in an iron grip. I wondered why the nurse was squeezing like a man. When my vision cleared and I shook off the narcotic effects of the drugs, I saw that it was a man's hand.

218

I felt hot, syrupy breath on my face, and then a voice I knew said, "You've got more lives than a cat, Haftmann."

Fuckola. Special Agent Booth.

I lay my aching head back and slept like that dead man everyone speaks of.

CHAPTER 14

From my hospital bed I watched the spectacle of yet another country in the Middle East agitate for democratic reform. This time it was Libya and the rebels against Ghaddafi were getting the worst of it despite NATO's no-fly zone.

I knew there were powerful and divisive forces burrowing like ants from beneath the soil of every country on earth, some good ants like those in Egypt and Tunisia, some bad like those that wanted to destroy the American democracy and make the oligarchy of the wealthy official. By 2050, the majority would be the minority; my own life had begun at one end of the scale and it was about in the middle with a long slide toward a new America, one of Hispanics, African-Americans, Asians, Muslims. No more East and West or Midwest. One country, I thought, and whoever, like the white supremacists or the fanatical Muslims, got their message out there at the right time, could take this nation deep into a labyrinth from which we might not find our way back. Then I remembered that nobody elected me to anything or pretty much cared what I thought, *so fuck them too—all but six . . .*

I spent two days being prodded and poked and was turned loose as soon as the hospital realized the odds of my paying for their services were about the same as my being the next James Bond. I had long, brooding thoughts about Annaliese and her mother but not much else, least of all a future. Good existentialists, I told myself, live in the present. And I intended to do that very thing as soon as the loose ends of my abortive career in private investigation were tied off.

The Get Well card from Booth on the table next to me said that he would be flying in to Cleveland for two days; there was a number to call. I called and got the Sheraton near the airport—not one of the deluxe suites he was used to, and because Booth could pad expense accounts with the best of them so I figured he was back in the doghouse with his superiors. When I reached him, he told me that the bodies of Ingrid and John O'Reilly had been released for burial. He said he'd be in town the next day to drive me out to Greenlawn for the internment. We could talk then. He ended the conversation the way he had every other one I had with him via the phone: he simply hung up on me.

I was waiting for him in the hospital lobby when he met me for the drive to Greenlawn. It was a cloudless, muggy day and a haze hung over everything; the sweat popped out on my skin inside the car. One of Booth's theories was that air-conditioning shortened your lifespan. *Enough to make the cat sob,* my grandmother would say.

Booth said little, wasn't in a mood to answer the questions I had. The two local papers, the *Jefferson Gazette* and the *Star Beacon,* had zippo on the case. I checked several days' worth to be sure. Same with the Cleveland *Plain Dealer.* Not a word about that wild ride down County-line Road, except for three Amish killed, five wounded—and then it was "an unidentified hit-and-run driver being sought by police." I was never mentioned. The crash in the Grand River never happened, as far as local authorities were concerned. I'd seen the FBI muzzle local law enforcement many times. I'd seen it in Cleveland homicide too, for that matter. But something was wrong. If I were given to paranoia, and I am, I'd be inclined to think somebody was muzzling the FBI on this one. In his own good time, I knew Booth would give me some information; until then, he was as cooperative and reclusive as a badger.

● ● ●

The cemetery was baking under the sun, but all the tenants were stiff and cold underground. Booth made six calls from a cellular phone on route, one of which was to a sexton who was to lead us to the gravesite. I had called O'Reilly's father in Boston from my hospital bed and told him that I wanted Ingrid to be buried with her husband. He was worried that I was asking for money, so I told him I was good for the money because I was selling my house. My office had sealed up, the windows soaped over to keep the passing crowds on the Strip from staring in at whatever furniture hadn't been carted off by my creditors before I went to jail. My voice mail was nothing but robocalls asking for money. I was getting out of town as soon as I could. The old man grunted and said he had no objections. I wanted them to reserve a space near the parents for Annaliese. It was pigheaded of me, but I once told both parents I would bring their daughter home.

I remembered the locale from the memorial service earlier. The earth had been dug already and the three men were using a hydraulic rig to lower the casket. When the hole was shoveled in, the sexton asked me if I wanted to say a prayer, and I snarled at him.

Booth looked at me with that look I had come to loathe.

"What is there left to pray for? There's no excuse for God, no excuse at all."

The sexton scurried off. Booth shook his head in disgust.

I waited a moment to calm myself and said, "You dragged the fucking river, right?"

Booth interrupted me. "Of course, we did. We had divers from Youngstown and Warren flown in within hours. Nothing. No body. The car was submerged and had moved about a hundred feet in three hours. That's a heavy car too. The current was very strong."

I looked at him this time. "So he's loose."

"We just haven't recovered the body yet."

"Maybe he washed ashore and an animal dragged him into the woods and ate him."

"No, I doubt it. There's nothing big enough around there to drag a man."

I said, "I was being sarcastic, Booth."

"Oh," he replied. "Pardon me, Mister Coffee Nerves."

"Booth, a manhunt would ascertain his whereabouts, don't you think? I assume even Washington by now is willing to call him a fugitive escapee."

"The Hoover Building has its reasons," he said smugly. "Besides, if he is alive, we'll catch him. How far do you think a man can go under those circumstances?"

I turned to look him full in the face. "Booth, do you recall us having a similar conversation some years back about a man the whole *country was looking for and yet he managed to elude every cop in the state including your own fucking FBI?*"

"I'll thank you not to shout at me, Haftmann. You're lucky you aren't being indicted for those dead Amish. Several witnesses identified Gallatine's car and a few got a good look at your face. This sect of Amish will testify in case you're thinking—"

This time I got close enough to his face to smell his aftershave.

"Booth, what are you telling me? What kind of shit are you giving me here?"

"Relax, Haftmann. There's no coverup. I said we'll get him and we'll get him. No thanks to you, by the way. We've got some evidence to indict for a couple of those girls he murdered in Boston. Some DNA testing matches up."

"Only a couple? He killed fourteen."

"Don't ask me to explain it. Something called band shifting occurred on the other samples. They ran it through the gel. There were problems with the semen" Booth said.

It sounded thin even to him. We said nothing for a while. I thought of the day Annaliese's father had come into my office and dropped that clipping in front of me and sobbed as I read it.

Lies, all lies. Everybody lies all the time.

Without a word, he had turned and started walking back to the car.

I followed. "I thought your labs were the best in the world," I said to his back.

"They are, damn it. But this is technology right at its limits. You can't have everything. It's enough, believe me. Two or twenty-two. He'll go down hard and never come up if we put an airtight case together. Too many local agencies can screw things up. You know how that is. You were a cop once."

I also knew that FBI never hesitated to use its muscle to take over a case. They never cared whose jurisdiction they were in. Booth wasn't coming clean on this, but I didn't know the right questions to ask.

We drove back in silence.

I asked him to drop me off at Tico's. The season was over; the bars would go back to the locals again for. He stopped in front of the bar. I saw one of Tico's boys, Enrique, washing glasses. I thought of his brother's car I had abandoned in the weeds and hoped that Tico had forgiven me. He just said OK when I gave him directions to find it from the hospital. He didn't sound disappointed but he didn't sound pleased either. It was that tone you take when you deal with somebody you knew all along was going to screw up and then did screw up. It gave me a sick feeling to know that one of the few men I admired on the planet considered me a fuck-up.

Booth waited for me to get out; then he said, "I don't suppose we'll be seeing each other again. I got my transfer."

I wasn't sorry, but I said I was.

Then he gave me a brief smile and patted his silver hair. "No, not another reservation. New York. I'm heading up counterintelligence."

No happy coincidence there, I thought.

I held the door open. "You don't want the locals to bag him because you fucking want him for what he can tell you about white supremacy in the US, right? He's too valuable. You're going to let him get away with killing all those people. How could you agree to this, Booth?"

"I don't know what you mean. They think I'll do a better job in New York."

I could have puked. "You didn't see O'Reilly," I said, my teeth gritted. "You don't know what he did to Gallatine. You didn't sit across from him for hours at a time while he filled up with water like you'd fill a sack with shit and explode it on Halloween. His own wife couldn't recognize him. What about those Amish he ran down just to put a little debris in my way? Christ, Booth, what about those fourteen women in Boston. I turned green just looking at the police photos of what he did to them. Annaliese, what about Annaliese and her mother—" I broke down, almost sobbing, out of control.

Booth reached across from me and pulled the door handle, but I got a foot in it before he could close it.

"All right," he said, "get a grip." He tossed me his own linen handkerchief. "You must have a Christ complex or something. You think you can save the world, but all you've ever done is get obsessed and then fall on your ass. Come down off your cross, idiot, and live in the real world for once!"

"I hope not," I managed to say, recovered. "Well, it comes down to this, Haftmann. Washington wants him. Not just us. Those studies I told you about? That wasn't just academic pinhead stuff. That was the NSA. The world's changing faster than you can imagine. Things are volatile in this country. We can move forward or we can fall behind very rapidly. Genetic cloning, artificial intelligence. Do you realize that whoever owns that technology has just discovered Eldorado and the Fountain of Youth at the same time? Nothing is inconceivable now. The technology is already in place. But no society at war with itself is going to get there first. This country is going to solve its problems in the next decade or we're going to wind up in second place. And, Haftmann, that's not acceptable."

"You know who you sound like, Booth? Like Lindell. Your dream, his dream. Nobody gives a fuck. Nothing means anything to you people. Human beings are scrap."

"You have to see the big picture. He can expose the whole network of white supremacists. Names, places, addresses, phone numbers, plans. Isn't that significant enough to justify—"

"—a few lousy murders?"

"Grow up, Haftmann."

"And you say I've got the Messiah complex?"

"I can't waste any more time with you."

"You just came here to pick my brains, see if I knew where Lindell might go next."

"I've done a lot for you. I've kept you out of serious jail time. I've watched your back in more ways than you'll ever know."

"I don't owe you shit, Booth. I figured something else out too. You knew all along Cooney was a dirty cop. That's why, every time I turn around, you're trying to stick him up my ass. That day in the park, you weren't watching me. You were tailing Cooney so he would lead you to Lindell. Lindell was your target all the time. You watched Cooney killed Marcus Gordon, and you figured that would put him in your pocket. He was greedy and wanted to play both ends against the middle—"

The tires squealed and he was gone.

I stood looking at Tico's sign, wondering if going inside was the right thing to do.

What the hell, I thought. You fall off the wagon, it gives a person something to strive for. Failure, after all, was my familiar demon.

• • •

"Keep setting them up, laddie buck, and I'll keep knocking them over."

"Sure, Tómas."

"One for that lovely woman at the end of the bar too, whatever she's drinking."

He set another Jack Daniels and water in front of me and moved off to make a Sidecar for the blonde who had come in an hour ago. She was voluptuous in that way slender women are. She stretched on the bar stool with feline grace, and I noticed her can and her cheekbones were both high. She looked at me and raised the drink I bought her in my direction. Elegant dress, blue eyes, hair in a French braid.

Those spendthrift Vikings, I thought; they could make a mutt like Millimaki but a beauty like her too.

I must have overdone it and missed my chance because the next thing I knew, Enrique was nudging me on my elbow. I had fallen asleep at the bar.

Christ, pissing my pants next. I got up to leave.

"My bill, barkeep."

"That's OK, Mister Haftmann. My dad says you got a tab anytime you want it."

"Listen, about the car, Enrique, I'm sorry."

"*De nada.* Just a little mud. No problem. We got it out back all cleaned up."

"Good, that's good. I'll be coming into some cash real soon. Tell your father thanks for me and I'll catch him tomorrow. I think I left something under the seat—"

"Got it right here, Mister Haftmann. Don't go smoking any bad guys tonight, OK?" He handed me the gun in a folded newspaper.

"Thanks, I won't."

I stumbled out the door, the gun tucked into my belt in back. My vision was all cocked up. My lust dissipated by the onset of a migraine about to move in as soon as the alcohol cleared off. There was a full moon like my birth moon. A full moon in Cancer. The night air had the chill of a season in change. I was the only thing in the entire landscape that didn't change. I put one foot in front of the other and began hoofing it the quarter mile to my house.

As I passed the car, I thought I should check to see if my pipe wrench was left under the seat where I had placed it beside the gun. There it was.

"C'mon, Henry Lee," I said, "time to go home."

I managed the walk but not without a few blasts of passing car horns to keep me on my side of the road. I slipped once and hit the pavement, the bar ringing on the road. As I got up, I could see that I had torn up the skin on the palms of my hands. I had those maudlin, stupid thoughts of a drunkard trying to console himself for too many failures.

I made it home and did a little jig on the front porch just to make noise and urinated into the tall grass of my front lawn. Maybe I was trying to scare away hobgoblins, but the walk had sobered me enough

226

to make me understand they were all inside.

I tossed Henry aside on the porch, found the key under the welcome mat, and let myself in. I stripped off my shirt and headed right for the velour sofa where I collapsed in a heap. I scraped my shoes off with minimal effort and in getting comfortable, dug the hammer of the gun into my back.

Somehow I knew I was on my way to a bad dream. Too much inside for the booze to handle or maybe drinking only lubricated the wound channels. I just knew that I started to drift into familiar scenes and patterns of horror. I was traveling a road, much as ever, seeing multitudes of walking cadavers. Men with guns and men on horseback shouted and fired random shots at us. Some were hit and dropped in their tracks. I saw limbs and heads explode in red mist. People kept walking despite their wounds. I wept as I traveled among children holding their guts in their hands. Mothers and babies lying beside the road. The babies dead or crying for their mother's warm flesh. Sometimes the mothers' dresses were hiked up to their thighs. I passed alongside a skinny boy in a black uniform raping a woman. His white horse flashed its teeth at me, and I could see a machine pistol tied to the saddle's pommel, but I was afraid to reach for it. Meanwhile, the boy continued thrusting into the woman as if he knew I did not dare to interfere. The woman looked up at me as I attempted to walk past. She seemed embarrassed. Her exposed backside and pelvis quivered from the rocking action; her heavy breasts swayed from side to side. The boy's trousers were bunched around his knees. A lock of white-blonde hair fell across her eyes: Ingrid. I passed on, unable to stop it or too afraid to interfere. The horses pranced among the crowd; the men would club the heads of anyone within reach—old men, children—it made no difference.

At one point the dream returned to its pattern: the walkers, mostly those who survived the savagery were walking uphill. It was the dreaded revelation at the top of the hill, a place of horror I knew was coming, but I could not stop myself from going on nor could I turn back. There was no escape.

As usually happened as I approached the top of the hill, I felt as if I were surrendering my will, in some crucial way. This time, however, the dream did not take me to the crest of the hill. Something was different. I turned back and ran through the crowds of people, oblivious of the uniformed men shouting at me, and with an agility I had never known in life, I ducked under their rifle butts. I even pulled several off their horses and stopped long enough to kick one in the head until he lay there, dead or unconscious. I had a mission. In my dream I had to get back to the woman being raped, and as I made my way back to the spot where they had been, I found them. He had finished with her and was drawing out a sidearm, a .45, to finish her off.

I charged him and knocked him backwards to the earth. I drove my fist time and time again into his face. Rights, lefts, roundhouses, hooks—everything. I cracked bones in his jaw. Felt the cartilage of his nose splinter. My assault was so frenzied that I heard the bone of his skull crack and split open like a melon. Finally, I was sated. My fists two bloody, raw stumps. I grabbed him by the collar and began dragging him backward toward the river. I saw the water of the river wasn't deep enough to get him into the current, so I walked him out into the water's edge until he began to float. The water was up to my chest, and the current's tug was beginning to pull at my legs. I turned around stiffly the way you do in deep water and as the corpse drifted past me, I could see he was alive. He winked at me going past. Lindell. *He's alive.*

Then, without anything in the house being different, without a sound to alert me to any change. I knew as I lay sprawled on my face inside my dream that he was inside the house. I could feel him there in the dark. My good eye snapped open, but I dared not make a sudden move unless he too could feel the infinitesimal difference in the way that one senses another's body. The very air in the room was different, as if in having to flow around another body changed the current. I awoke from my dream, and reached my hand—slowly, slowly—from my side to the floor and felt the gun with my fingers. I flicked the safety. Adrenalin was pumping through me in waves. Every muscle in my body stirred to act, and I could feel the neck hairs standing up.

Seconds passed . . .

I was not alone.

He must have gone upstairs to wait for me in the bedroom. Ever since hearing me flop on the couch, he had been working his way down the stairs. Knowing the house to be old, he must have moved with the patience he alone possessed, careful not to give away by the merest groan of old floorboards the terrible surprise of himself. He would want me to see him, to know that he was going to kill me. I waited for him to move again, not sure how far that first sound had been. I fought my quickening body and by an act of will stilled it to silence. In every move, I had been the novice; he the teacher. He had played with me the way a cat plays with a mouse, tortures it before killing it. He watched me squirm in prison while he tormented me with his voice and knowledge. And when I failed to react interestingly enough to his sadistic game, a little swat from one of his paws would send me into some response that, like a maggot, he could feast upon and savor.

The next noise was about ten feet off and directly behind me. I waited. Another twenty minutes passed before I heard the next sound: a floorboard his step miscalculated, but it was barely a sound indistinguishable from the house settling at night. My eyelid itched and I was afraid I was going to give it away too soon. I remembered how he withstood the brutal beating in the Ritz-Carlton. Fearless like those berserk Norse warriors in battle.

Be like him, I commanded myself. *Be dead.*

My blood pulsed in my veins, and I had a terrible microsecond of panic. Maybe he was not where I thought. Maybe I would miss him.

I stilled myself for the next sound. My life depended on it. If it were no more than the rush of air impelled by his body moving forward, I knew I would pick it up. This time, he had underestimated me. Heard me come rolling in drunk, pissing off the porch, a hopeless stumblebum ripe for the slaughter. He must be savoring every moment as he listened in the dark to my boozy yawps and snores. His mind so vastly unlike the ordinary human being's that he could content himself with those images of terror and violence he created. I was not even a challenge. My own death would change nothing, I knew. Booth could not care less that he added one more victim to the heap as long as he got what he wanted.

The next sound took fifteen minutes. It was just above my head. I expelled my breath in a long sigh as if my drunken sleep were taken down a notch deeper. I released the tension of my gun hand just enough to keep my hand from cramping. I had the move calculated in my head. I knew the arc of the swing. I wanted one more sound, a last bearing.

It wasn't where it was supposed to be. Something in the dark had moved by my feet.

Oh Jesus Shit Fuck. Where was he? I had two targets in my head and not more than seconds to decide, if he were inching toward me at the rate I had calculated between sounds. *Now!* I heard myself think, *He's going to make his move—Now! Do it!*

Tensed, still prone on my face, I whipped the gun off the floor and fired behind my head where I expected him to be. Three shots in a straight line: head, heart, stomach.

The muzzle explosions told him right where my hands should be. I heard a whispery movement from the other end of the couch and then felt a displacement of air next to my head. The numbing shock that went through me began at my arms and tore through me so fast that I thought, irrationally, that I had been hit with a live transmission wire. By the time I recovered my senses, another lightning bolt hit me—this time, I thought my spine had been severed.

A baseball bat.

He had my aluminum softball bat from a closet upstairs. I nearly passed out from the pain. I tried pulling the trigger on the gun but there was no longer a gun in my hands; it had been knocked loose from my hands with the first blow and I never felt it.

Got to move or die . . .

I was beyond thought after that. It was just animal instinct. Instead of scrambling away from the pain, however, I threw myself in the direction that blows had come from. That probably saved my life. The next swing put the meat end of the bat at an angle where my head had been a second before. Lindell wasn't going for a KO with plans to revive me for a night of torture. He was going to kill me and be done with it. By now, I was in a crouch position too close for leverage for a killing swing.

He must have figured that and taken a measure because I heard his feet shuffle. I had my feet under me well enough to spring toward the noise, and using my fist like a bowsprit, I connected with a solid form. He grunted with surprise. That gave me all the incentive I needed. I swung my left arm at him and clutched his clothing. The bat came down again—on my shoulder—but not hard enough to break my grip on his clothing. I had him measured now and I sent an overhand right into what I hoped was his face. I missed, grazed his head, and he wrenched free. My arms and hands were still too numb to be effective.

I heard him panting some yards away. It was black in the room, not enough light for either of us to see.

"Haftmann," he whispered from somewhere by the wall, "I'm going to beat your brains to pulp."

I thought of trying to find the gun on the floor behind me, but I gave that up as useless. I heard him laughing. "Your luck is ended."

Then somewhere else, a corner by the wall. Moving around, speaking softly in that hypnotic voice, calmly. "Over here, Haftmann. I'm going to kill you. I'm going to dismember you into a dozen pieces."

Over there now.

" . . . tiny little chunks. I may even serve you up. A rotisserie of Haftmann morsels. Invite your neighbors.

Reversing his direction, trying to get behind me now.

The only sound in the room was my labored breathing.

Something stabbed me in the ribs. I swing my fists and connected with nothing but air. I could hear the sound of my own drops of sweat hitting the floor. Slick as an eel, soaked in nightsweats.

"I'm going to kill you, make you pay for Annaliese."

"A nigger once said that it ain't bragging if you back it up. Can you back it up, Haftmann? I think not."

"You're going to die for what you do to her, her mother, all those people," I said into the dark, turning every which way to catch a sound. He kept moving on silent feet. I couldn't place him.

Then, he whispered, "That poke you felt? You'll be in twilight sleep very soon. Know what that is, Haftmann? A caudal block. To ease the pain of childbirth. A little morphine and scopolamine. I nearly drowned in that river. Fortunately, I didn't lose my trusty syringe kit in my pocket. You're in pain now. That should speed things up nicely. Soon you'll find it hard to concentrate—"

"I'll kill you first," I said.

"We'll see, won't we?" His voice . . . so lulling.

I lunged toward his voice but slammed into a table and went down hard.

I heard Lindell laughing from a corner of the room. "Missed me."

I was dizzy and panic was surging inside with every breath. The blackness was the worst. I started to shake—first my hands and then my legs.

"Did you enjoy Gallatine, Haftmann? Too bad I didn't get a video

231

of it."

He seemed far away. Near the staircase. "You'll be dead on your feet in a moment. Maybe I'll take my time with you . . ."

The drug was a rivulet inside me taking away all my senses.

He took me from behind. The bat struck me over my right ear and slammed into my shoulder. My knees buckled and I went down.

Fuck this, too much pain. I heard the bat thunk into the floor all around my head as he tried to measure me lying there. Instead of crippling me with body blows, he made the only mistake he ever made. The third blow landed a hair's width from my forehead and cracked the floorboard.

I stuck my hand out and held the bat in place with a deathgrip.

He put all his might into dislodging it. His foot flailed and caught me in the neck and stomach, but he didn't have enough force for fear of surrendering the bat to the enemy. I counted the moment between blows and then jerked myself from the floor with the bat as a pivot and swung my body directly into him. We both went down, and he scrambled out of my grasp once more. This time I didn't let him slip away; our momentum sent us reeling into the next room and into the wall. He clawed and grunted and spittle flecked my face. But I had him firmly—both fists clutched into the fabric of his clothing under his neck. This time I knew from the feel of the wall and the banging rattle of the front door in the door frame. Nothing was square or plumb. He dug frantically, wildly for my eyes.

Locked together like furious lovers, Lindell and I waltzed and smashed our way from the living room into the front room.

I smashed his hard, wiry body into the wall, gaining a little momentum but slipping each instant into the drug-induced torpor of twilight sleep. Once more: we hit door, wall, and—hoping I had the distance—I flung him with the last of my fading strength right where the window should be.

The force carried us both through it. Wood and glass splintered, exploded. I had thrust him into it back first, and I found myself still gripping him hard. He writhed and churned beneath me on the porch. There was enough light for me to see the outline of his shape. I took my hands from his shirt front and pushed them over his face and let my thumbs find his eyes. I felt the hollows and then the eyeballs and dug my thumbs in as hard as I could. My body had him pinned, so all he could do was postpone the inevitable. I used my fingers to squeeze the sides of his head still and dug harder into him. I felt him slip a little, but his squirming and flopping was now useless; his mouth opened for air, and I could see that his bridgework had come loose in the struggle. He was losing strength fast in the effort to throw me off.

I took a deep breath and then I gouged out both of his eyes at the same time. The scream was worse than anything I had ever heard, but I kept digging until there was jelly, and then there was not even that. After some minutes, he stopped twitching and then I got off him.

• • •

The next part's a little fuzzy, and I have had to reconstruct what happened by talking to some people, so I'm not one-hundred percent certain of things at this point. I do remember coming to, struggling to walk back inside, and seeming to take an hour to do it. I remembered thinking I ought to call the police. Then I remember not being able to find the phone.

I sat on the sofa and nodded off, as the drug ceased roller-coastering through my body and just surged with enough force to make me aware of what had happened before I succumbed to the next surge. It was like being hit on the head at intervals by someone with a rubber mallet. I couldn't think or focus. The ripsawing pain in my arms distracted me from any coherent thought longer than three seconds. I vomited between my knees.

I must have sat there like that until daylight illuminated everything and finally broke through the nausea and pain. I was suddenly aware of a cacophony of starlings and grackles outside. I had never greeted a dawn like that before or since.

I stumbled and groped around the kitchen, opening cupboard doors at random, but I don't remember doing it. The next thing I know, there are sirens and flashing lights all over the yard. A truck with Mexicans en route to pick grapes at the wineries drove past my house and saw a body lying on my porch. Our local cops aren't much, but that was sufficient cause and effect to send Code 11 or a DBF (Dead Body Found).

I heard crunching of broken glass, and then I turned to confront a deputy sighting on my midsection with a Magnum. The deputy was staring at me. I didn't realize how badly I must have looked. Both forearms were fractured, my collarbone broken, and my right ear was pulped to a mass of swelling at the side of my head like a crusted cauliflower ear. I was trailing blood everywhere from a slice along my left leg that would take forty-six stitches to close.

As I said, I don't recall much of any of this, but I met the deputy who held the gun on me at my hearing some weeks afterward, and he said that I told him I was looking around for bird seed.

"The sparrows need to be fed," he claims I said.

Frankly, I don't know what I said. I know that for the first time since Micah left me I stopped dreaming.

EPILOGUE

I don't live in Ohio now. It's been a couple years since I left. I used the money from selling my house to take me out of there. I followed the lakeshore and wound up in a flophouse off Woodward in Detroit. Then I stayed a few months in Eastpointe, better digs, but not doing much of anything, nor finding substantial work.

One afternoon in the middle of winter, I was sitting in a Greek restaurant on Gratiot Avenue. There was a giant decorative torch in front of the place. I drank coffee and read the paper's classifieds; something drew my eye to the horoscope column, so I read these and found the one for my birth month. It said that the wolf moon augured well for me. I should break with the past and start over.

I left town that day. Found a ride with a logger driving back to Upper Michigan. When we crossed the Five Mile Bridge, I felt better about my decision.

I live in a little town, more a village, near the lakeshore. I don't feel right unless I'm near the water. I go down to the lakeshore to sit and watch the water. Sometimes I think about buying some fishing gear and going after the steelhead and pike. The yellow perch isn't as good as Lake Erie's. At dusk the bats come out for the flies and midges and the sun sets. It's very peaceful.

I found a little work to do as a caretaker. Mostly I'm left alone in my cabin and that's how I want it. I send a postcard to Tico every three months. Nothing comes back because I haven't put a return address on any of the cards. It's better this way.

But something strange happened to me yesterday when I was down by the breakwall. I saw something spray-painted on the rocks that I had not noticed before; at least, I'm sure it wasn't there the last time I came down to review my existentialist rulebook. I couldn't see it very well, my vision being what it is, so I moved closer.

WE DON'T DIE WE MULTIPLY.

I thought of my conversation with Agent Booth back in Tico's Place when he was first introducing me to this mad conspiracy of haters and killers. Bureaucrats, gangbangers—these will be the final inheritors of post-apocalyptic America.

Something vaguely familiar about the writing bothered me. The

235

block letters reminded me of something I'd seen before; all the letters were in capitals except the *e*'s. They were lower cases but shaped like the schwa, a broken arrow tipped upward.

Just my imagination, I suppose, but I felt like a rabbit imprisoned in its hop.

Maybe it's time I got another gun.

AUTHOR BIO

Robert White grew up in Ashtabula, Ohio. He has published several Thomas Haftmann tales in various print magazines and webzines. Like his private eye, he is a full-time lapsed Catholic and part-time existentialist. He has worked in grocery and department stores, sailed as a deckhand on ore boats around the Great Lakes, worked as a mold puller in a plastics factory, and on the clean-up crew at Mexican Original, a taco factory in Fayetteville, Arkansas. He writes book reviews and does interviews for *Boxing World*. Although he once spent two extraordinary weeks in China about ten years ago, it's now clear that Ashtabula is the hill he's chosen to die on and that's fine by him.

CPSIA information can be obtained at www.ICGtesting.com
Printed in the USA
BVOW031752091011

273067BV00002B/1/P